WHO IS THE TIGERMAN?

A HARRY BLACK THRILLER

GORDON WARDEN

Copyright © 2021 by Gordon Warden

All rights reserved.

No part of this book may be reproduced in any form or by any electronic or mechanical means, including information storage and retrieval systems, without written permission from the author, except for the use of brief quotations in a book review.

ACKNOWLEDGMENTS

My thanks to my editor Ceri Savage and as always, my wonderful family and friends.

1

The man in the cream suit walked across the lobby of The Grand Hotel, conscious of the interested looks of two women. One was wearing an alluring, black dress; the other had on a smart, beige trouser suit.

He went into the cloakroom to freshen up. The humidity of Kuala Lumpur was at its seasonal worst. When he returned to the lobby, the lady in the black dress had gone. The other was leaning against one of the pillars, examining her nails. She pulled a clip from the back of her head allowing her hair to fall to her shoulders. The movement drew his attention.

Their eyes locked, and she beckoned for him to follow her. They walked in silence through the marbled corridors. She led the way through an exit door. The intensity of the sun was like the hot waft of a baking oven being opened.

Outside was a newly concreted area containing various construction vehicles that were resting for the weekend. The other woman stood waiting for them, her black dress fluttering in the warm breeze.

He eyed them both with curiosity. 'Can I be of help?' he enquired politely.

He was used to unusual approaches; it went with his line of work.

But he was disappointed when the one wearing the trouser suit undid a couple of buttons on her blouse. 'Perhaps you'd like to spend some time with us? One of us or both, you have the choice.'

The man looked around. Everything was Sunday-quiet, and no windows overlooked them from the hotel.

'You don't have to worry,' Black Dress said. 'Just tell us your room number and we'll come and relax you.' She spoke with a soft Spanish accent.

'There's been a mistake,' said the man politely. 'I actually thought you were, well, someone else. I'm sorry for wasting your time.'

As he turned to go, instinct made him glance at Trouser-Suit, and too late, he saw the flash of metal lunge towards him. Feeling the full force of the knife sink into his leg, he grunted with pain as the metal tip hit his thigh bone.

As she released the knife, he grabbed her hand and twisted it hard, whilst smashing his elbow into Black Dress's face. She staggered back, clutching her nose, blood spurting. He twisted Trouser-Suit's hand even more. He could feel bones break. Amid her screams, he applied further pressure.

'What do you want with me, who sent you?' he demanded.

Black Dress was fumbling in her handbag. She produced a gun and levelled it at him, her expression one of professional indifference.

He yanked Trouser-Suit in front of him while pulling out the Glock from the shoulder holster under his jacket, and fired. The force of the bullet blasted Black-Dress against the wall of the hotel. She slid down slowly, already dead, the blood from the wound in her forehead merging with that from her nose, making her face look like a grotesque mask.

Trouser-Suit's screams intensified, as she stared with horror at her colleague.

'I'll ask once more, who sent you?'

Minutes later, the man in the cream suit was again crossing the hotel lobby, this time casually holding his jacket by his side, covering the widening patch of blood that was spreading down his leg.

2

The leader of the opposition was clapped to his feet. Charles Brandon was a formidable character and a popular figure within his own party.

He hooked a thumb into the pocket of his waistcoat and made a theatrical gesture toward the Prime Minister. 'You are a disgrace to your position and are not fit to run your party, let alone the country.'

The Speaker of the House half-stood from his throne-like seat. 'I'm sure that the honourable gentleman is aware, but may I remind him he cannot address the Prime Minister directly.'

'I'm sorry, Mr Speaker. I only meant to say that the Prime Minister is a disgrace to his position, and a liability to this country and an embarrassment to his own family.'

From his position on the Tory back benches, Peter Finch, the MP for Middlington, stared at the leader of the opposition with a grin of appreciation, his hand rubbing at a missed piece of unshaved bristle on his chin. Prime Minister's Questions was his favourite part of the week.

A few hours later at the Garrick Club, Covent Garden,

Finch lounged in a leather chair regarding the man opposite. 'I have to say that you did an admirable job today. Our leader would certainly have felt those stinging attacks of yours. It's a great pity you're not on our side.'

Charles Brandon took a gulp of brandy and set the crystal glass on the polished table next to him. 'Thank you, Peter, but I sometimes wonder whether I give him too hard a time.'

'Why wouldn't you? It's your job.'

'True, but these days, politically, there is negligible difference between the two parties. The Tories have always favoured the capitalists, but now they also champion the workers and poorly paid, which was always Labour policy. But the voters don't seem to care either way, these days. Politics has become all about populism.'

Finch grinned. 'God, Charles, you're talking like a Tory. If the PM heard you speaking like this, he'd be pulling you over to our side of the Commons and offering you a job in the Cabinet.'

'Not a chance. I enjoy the charade too much. Anyway, what about you? Isn't it time that the PM offered you a position, instead of you hiding in safety on the back benches?'

Finch shook his head. 'Not me. I'm just happy to serve my constituency.'

Brandon held up his glass, marvelling at how the crystal caught the light, reflecting tiny, blue and white beams. He cleared his throat. 'Peter, I need to say something to you.'

Finch waited, as Brandon seemed to ponder on what to say next.

'Despite being on opposite sides of the house, we've been close friends a long time, and what I am about to say to you, must not be repeated.' He looked hard at Finch. 'To anyone. Agreed?'

Finch nodded and sat forward, his expression curious.

Brandon took another gulp of brandy and cleared his throat. 'I'm being blackmailed.'

'You're what!'

'You heard.'

'Do you mean metaphorically, as in the political sense?'

'No. Someone is actually trying to blackmail me, and I'm not sure what to do next.'

Finch looked searchingly at Brandon's face. 'You're actually being serious. So what is it they've got on you? Have you been a naughty boy? Have you been watching porn, cheating on your wife, fiddling your expenses... What?'

'I'm probably guilty of at least one of those things, Peter, but it's not me that has strayed from the straight and narrow. It's my wife.'

'Petra? What's she been up to?'

'She has been having an affair,' Brandon said. 'Or to be more precise, affairs.'

'Are you certain about that?'

'Look, Peter, I'm sixty-four. Petra is still in her forties. When we married, I was so proud of the fact I had such a young, attractive wife and...'

'She's still attractive,' Finch said.

'Exactly. The problem is...well...' He paused and fiddled with his watch. 'The problem is that I can't keep her happy in every sense, if you see what I mean.'

Finch nodded. 'I understand, but that's no reason for her to be cheating on you.'

'Peter, I really don't care. When we're together, she makes me laugh, and she's great to look at. I see other men tripping over themselves to ingratiate themselves to her. When we go out to dinner or parties, she turns heads. If that makes her happy, then I'm happy.'

'So how does this blackmail situation involve her?'

'I'm about to come to that. Before we met, Petra worked as an escort girl.'

'What, like a prostitute?'

'No, no... I mean, she was a proper escort. Men would book her through an agency, and then take her to dinner, functions, that sort of thing.'

'And then sleep with her?'

'Well, I suppose...'

Finch looked amazed. He leaned forward, 'So tell me exactly how you are being blackmailed.'

Charles Brandon pulled out an envelope from his inside pocket and passed it across.

Finch turned it over. 'It's House of Commons stationery. How did you receive it?'

'It was in my post tray. To be honest, anyone could have put it there.'

Finch took the letter from the envelope and paused. The potential enormity of the situation seemed to hit him. 'Charles, shouldn't you be going to the police with this?'

'I can't, and I won't. There's too much at stake. Read it.'

Finch pulled out the letter and unfolded it. At the top of the letter was the House of Commons crowned portcullis, above which was printed "Charles Brandon."

'They've used your own letterhead.'

'Yes, I know. Cheeky bastards.'

The printed message read, "FAO Charles Brandon. You are to step down as Leader of the Labour Party, otherwise the world will discover that your wife hasn't always been the perfect lady."

Finch handed the sheet back and put his fingertips together. He looked at Brandon. 'This could be a shitstorm. Who would do this to you?'

Brandon shrugged. 'I don't know. I haven't any enemies apart from most of the Tory party.' He smiled humourlessly.

'This person obviously knows your wife was an escort. Or maybe they're an ex-lover. What are you going to do?'

'I'm afraid I'm going to have to think about stepping down. I don't see that I have much choice. I don't want our children to know about their mother's past, and I certainly don't want it all over the front pages of our beloved national press.'

'And you definitely don't want the police involved?'

'Absolutely not. Apart from anything else, the Home Secretary would inevitably find out, and that would defeat the object. I don't see that I have any alternative other than to resign my position.'

'It seems a shame,' Finch said, signalling to a passing server for a refill. 'This could just be someone chancing their arm, with no proof, hoping that you'll be stupid enough to believe their threat.'

'No such luck,' Brandon said, slipping a hand into his other inside pocket. He pulled out a small bundle of photographs. 'These were in the same envelope.'

He placed them on the coffee table between them and pointed to the one on the top. It was an older photo of Petra, half naked on top of a man, facing back towards the camera, smiling.

'Oh my God, Charles. This must be awful for you.'

Brandon gave a thin smile. 'It gets worse, carry on.'

Finch put the photo face-down next to the pile and picked up the next, which looked as though someone had cut it from a magazine. It was of Petra posing with another man. She was wearing a maid's outfit and had a stockinged leg outstretched across his lap.

Finch picked up the next. Petra was wearing a short, black dress and was with a fellow MP, Gavin Smart. The photo showed them leaving a hotel in Knightsbridge hand in hand, clearly enjoying each other's company, and oblivious to the photographer.

'These are just photos of your wife from years ago. They could have been snapped at a fancy-dress party or even a themed charity event. The one with Gavin Smart might raise a few eyebrows, but it's no big deal to hold someone's hand.'

'Look at the next one,' Brandon said.

The next photo was far more explicit. Someone had clearly pushed the lens of the camera through curtains to get a picture of Petra naked on her knees, getting rear attention from another of their colleagues, Nigel Kendall.

'Good grief, I thought he was gay,' remarked Finch.

Brandon smiled. 'It just shows you can't judge anyone.'

The server appeared, and Finch quickly concealed the photos as the drinks were placed on the table.

'You'll find the final picture interesting,' Brandon said as the server left.

As Finch turned it over, his stomach did a somersault and his face whitened. 'Oh God, Charles. I am so sorry, I...'

Charles Brandon sat back in his chair. 'There's not a great deal that you can say, is there, Peter? That is you with my wife, isn't it?'

3

Resting the rifle against the scaffolding, he waited. He was unconcerned about being observed by any of the tourists or locals. As far as they were concerned, he was just another construction worker doing his job. Besides, he was far too high up for them to notice him.

Thick, plastic weather drapes protected the construction site, through which protruded the ends of the scaffolding. One more metal tube poking out was unlikely to be spotted, he thought.

Holding the scope to his eye, he squinted through the lens, adjusting to the sudden vividness of the imagery, and moved the device slowly along Garrick Street until he could see the entrance to the club.

He had it on good authority that his target would leave shortly after eight. He glanced at his watch. Ten minutes to go.

Putting the scope down, he took another careful look around the construction site, listening intently for anything untoward. Although the workers had long gone for the day, he felt a sense of unease. He'd been experiencing this feeling since the attack by the two women in Kuala Lumpur a few days ago.

Involuntarily, he put his hand down to the side of his leg and winced. He still felt the pain where the blade had hit bone.

The attack made him wonder who would want him dead, and how they'd traced him. Very few knew his true identity, let alone his movements, and yet the two women at the hotel had known he was going to be there.

He breathed in slowly and deeply, and then focused his whole attention on the entrance of the Garrick Club.

INSIDE THE CLUB, Peter Finch was sitting open-mouthed as he studied what seemed to be a damning photograph of him sitting next to Petra Brandon with his arm around her shoulders.

'Charles, I can assure you that this is not what it seems. I was just comforting her, for Christ's sake. There's no way that she and I would...'

'What's this, what's this?' a deep voice interrupted. 'The leader of the Labour Party in cahoots with a Tory back bencher? I can't wait to put this on my front page!'

Charles Brandon leapt to his feet and opened his arms.

'Giles Cranberry, you old bastard! Good to see you.'

The men embraced warmly, Cranberry pounding Brandon on the back.

'You must know Peter,' Brandon said, indicating Finch. 'He's a good friend of mine. His only problem is that he sits on the wrong side of the Commons.'

Finch stood up and shook the big man's hand; Brandon was plump, but Cranberry dwarfed him.

'I've heard of you,' Finch said. 'You're the newspaper owner.'

'That's me in a nutshell,' Cranberry said, heaving his opulent frame into one of the leather chairs.

'So, what brings you here?' Brandon asked, looking around for a drinks server.

'Are you going daft in your old age? You invited me, or rather your secretary did. She said the table had been booked for Bel Canto for eight thirty and to meet you here at eight for drinks.'

Brandon looked puzzled. 'Did she?'

'Oh, Charles, don't tell me I've come all the way across London and I'm not going to get fed.'

Brandon's face broke into a smile. 'Yes, of course we're having dinner together. I had obviously got the wrong date in my head,' he said. 'What will you have to drink? A large gin and tonic, I presume?'

'Thank God, the man's remembered,' Cranberry said. 'That would go down rather well, thank you.'

They sat gossiping about political opponents until Cranberry announced he was going to "The little boy's room." As soon as he'd gone, Finch leaned forward. 'Charles, you've got to believe me when I say nothing happened.'

'Don't worry, I do believe you, Peter. My wife has had lunch with many men. It makes her happy. Given what she's been up to, even if something had happened between you, it wouldn't really make much of a difference, would it?'

Finch sat back, obvious relief on his face. 'I understand, but I need you to know that I would never do anything to jeopardise our friendship.'

Brandon stood up and squeezed Finch's shoulder. 'Don't worry. Everything is fine.'

Cranberry arrived back from the toilet dabbing at the front of his grey trousers with a tissue. 'Damn taps splashed water all over my crotch.'

Brandon winked at Finch and smiled. 'Of course it was the taps, Giles!'

'Anyway,' Cranberry said, ineffectually trying to pull his jacket over the damp patch, 'I've been told our car is here.'

'Peter, would you like to join us?' Brandon said. 'There's normally decent scoff, accompanied by melodic serving staff.'

Finch looked pleased to be invited, then shook his head reluctantly. 'Thank you, but I can't. I've got a prior engagement.'

The men walked down the steps of the Garrick Club and stopped on the pavement.

'It was nice meeting you,' Cranberry said, grabbing Finch's hand with his oversized paw.

'You too,' Finch said. 'I hope you both have an enjoyable evening and...'

Suddenly, Giles Cranberry was sinking to the pavement, his eyes widening with the shock of the bullet that had thudded into his heart.

There had been no warning, no sound. The first sign of the shooting was the blood that was being soaked up by Cranberry's white shirt like blotting paper.

Despite the soundless assassination, fear spread within seconds. A woman screamed and ran into a doorway. Some people instinctively ducked down.

Finch knelt over Cranberry and felt for signs of life. He looked up at Brandon and shook his head, then stood up and pulled out his phone. Suddenly, the phone was flying in the air, as Finch clutched his shoulder and crashed to the ground, his face contorted with pain. He lay motionless for a moment, and then his eyes opened. He looked up at Brandon with a frightened stare.

'Get an ambulance quickly. I've been hit.'

FROM HIS POSITION high on the construction site, the assassin watched with a mixture of interest and bewilderment. His mission had been to eliminate one man, Giles Cranberry. So why were there two bodies lying on the ground?

He held the scope to his eyes. The second person appeared to be wounded and was being tended to by a portly man with fair hair, who he recognised as a well-known politician.

He put the scope down thoughtfully. He had fulfilled his contract. No problem there. But who the hell was the other shooter? And why was their contract taking place at exactly the same time as his own? Coincidence? No chance.

After spending a couple of minutes taking in the scene below, the sight of flashing blue lights galvanised him into action.

Early that day, he had donned a hi-vis jacket and hat and had blended himself into the bustling background of the construction team that were working on the site. He had used the opportunity to make a trough in the concrete flooring. Now he laid his rifle into the hollow and shovelled shingle over it, knowing that first thing in the morning, it would be probably be buried under a layer of concrete.

He wasn't concerned if they found the gun, as long as he was long gone from the area.

Taking another glance over the parapet, he noticed Garrick Street had now been closed off with police vehicles, and even without the magnification of the scope, he could see police everywhere.

It did not surprise him at the quick response time, given

who the victim was. Giles Cranberry was the owner of Cranberry Press and had introduced a political satire magazine called House of Comics, which poked fun at politicians and the institution.

He idly wondered what dark depths Cranberry had plumbed to become a target, but, as always, it was none of his business.

More sirens were joining the cacophony down below, which made him decide to speed up his exit. He quickly made his way down the ladders and along the wooden platforms, balancing across the more thinly boarded areas until he arrived at the security gate that led out onto the street.

His yellow, high-visibility jacket and helmet meant that no-one gave him a second glance. He was just another construction worker going about his business.

His rehearsed route took him past boarded-up shops to a railway crossing, where he ducked under a barrier and walked along the side of a railway line. Now his yellow outfit made him look like a railway worker.

After a few hundred yards, he squeezed through a hedge and walked into a dense, wooded area that led to a communal garden, where there was a large, rusty iron gate leading to the street.

He frowned. There was a substantial padlock on the gate that hadn't been there when he'd rehearsed the route. Looking around for another means of escape, he noticed a gap in the bushes, which revealed the back of some properties beyond.

He climbed onto a brick wall and jumped down into the back garden of a red brick house.

He paused and listened. There were no shouts or exclamations. Now he had to hope that there was a way out to the street.

There was a patio at the rear of the house which hosted an assortment of child's playthings. He stepped over a plastic truck and tried the handle of one of the French doors. It was unlocked. Sliding it open softly, he stepped onto the living room carpet, quietly closing the door behind him.

He padded across the room, almost holding his breath, and stepped into the hallway. Just as he was about to open the front door, a voice spoke behind him.

'Stick your hands up, mister!'

He froze. He turned slowly and faced a small boy who was pointing a toy gun at him.

'Hello,' he said with a big smile, putting his hands up. 'What's your name?'

The boy giggled. 'I'm Michael. Bang-bang, you're dead!'

The man clutched his chest theatrically as if he had been shot, and then opened the front door with his free hand.

Michael discarded the gun and showed the man a colouring book. He pointed to a page. 'Look, this is my zoo with all the animals. This one's got a yellow coat just like yours, but it has big teeth and eats people.'

The boy made a growling sound and clawed at the air with his hand. He looked around for approval, but the man had disappeared.

There was the sound of the bathroom door being opened, and then his mother was coming down the stairs. 'Who are you talking to, Michael?' The look on her face changed to horror at the sight of her four-year-old son standing by an open front door.

'Michael! How did you reach up to unlock it?' she demanded.

'I didn't,' little Michael said, looking worried. 'It was a man with a yellow coat.'

She looked at the trail of muddy footprints on her carpet leading from her French doors.

'What man?' she asked, a different concern clouding her face.

Michael pointed to the yellow animal character in his book.

'It was the Tigerman.'

4

Harry Black rubbed hard at the short, frizzy growth on his head, and looked down at his mother's final resting place. Rain drummed down onto the coffin lid, the droplets bouncing away. He looked up at the sky in frustration. Why bad weather today of all days? The polished wood was going to tarnish. He immediately felt stupid at the thought.

His tears hadn't arrived yet. There was anger that she'd been taken, accompanied by relief that she was no longer suffering. There was grief, sorrow, and self-recrimination at not seeing her often enough, and plenty else. But no tears – at least, not yet.

Harry heard a sob beside him and felt instant guilt. He wasn't the only one who'd lost their mother. He reached out and rubbed his sister's arm awkwardly, not knowing what else to do.

The vicar cleared his throat. 'Mr Black, did you want to say a few words?'

Harry shook his head. He had already said everything he was going to say to her in his head.

Instead, he trudged back towards the church carpark, the muddy ground of the cemetery sucking at his shoes. His sister, Helen, ran to keep up with him and linked her arm through his.

'Harry, I'm worried about you being on your own, why don't you take some time off and stay with us? You'll love Queenstown. The scenery in New Zealand is amazing. You could tour from one beauty spot to another. It would do you good.'

'No, thank you. I'm fine. I have things to do.'

Helen looked at him doubtfully. 'What things?'

He stopped and looked at her. Her long, dark, curly locks reminded him of how his own hair once looked. 'Work, of course.'

'I'm sure that the police force can do without one of its finest for a few weeks,' she said. 'Your boss will understand.'

She was right. Everyone back at Farrow Road police station had been so kind.

'Helen, I want to go back to normality.'

'All right, don't say I didn't try,' she said with a touch of petulance. 'But please tell me you'll take some time off at least.'

There weren't many in attendance, just Harry, Helen, the vicar, and a couple of nurses from the home where Harry's mother had been staying. They all went back to Harry's small but functional flat and sat politely as Helen passed around sandwiches and prepared hot drinks. Harry's brown leather three-piece-suite and some dining chairs had been pulled out to form a semi-circle. The vicar sat in the middle, holding his teacup daintily.

'This rain will be so good for the crops. It's been so warm for the time of year,' he commented.

The nurses smiled indulgently and murmured agreement.

'Has it really?' Harry said, with a trace of sarcasm. He stared down at the remnants at the bottom of his cup and went to the kitchen to give the vessel a cursory wash. After rummaging in the cupboard, he produced a bottle of single malt. Half-filling his cup with the golden liquid, he knocked it back and poured another. He went back into the lounge, holding the bottle aloft.

'Something stronger than tea, anyone?'

The women shook their heads, but the vicar gave a little cough and held out his cup. Harry gave him a generous measure.

'The weather will much improve after that, vicar.'

The two men raised their cups to each other.

'God bless you, son,' the vicar said with a smile.

5

The newspapers were full of it.

"Who is the Tigerman?" was emblazoned across the front pages in bold, black print. It was an editor's dream, the murder of a well-known figure and a suspect with a superhero nickname.

He smiled at his unintentional wit. Nickname. His birth name was Nick Marshall, although he was continually using different aliases.

Folding the paper carefully, he placed it on top of the others. This was bad news. His success depended on him being virtually invisible. No face on record, nothing. His reputation was exemplary – a one-hundred-percent success rate and no-one with a sniff of a clue about him. Until now.

Marshall felt as though something was unravelling outside of his control, and he didn't like it. Someone else must have known about this job, someone aside from whoever who had ordered the kill. Unless it was some kind of double-cross. Those two women back in Kuala Lumpur hadn't been an accident. He'd got a name from one of them, but nothing more.

'Jefe.' He'd recognised it as Spanish for "boss." She had spat it at him just before she died. 'El jefe will kill you.'

He had no choice but to kill her. The woman wearing the trouser suit had reached into her hair and produced a long pin, which she had stabbed in his direction. He had assumed the tip was poisonous and was proven correct when he'd twisted her arm so that the tip of the pin jabbed into her own neck. Seconds later, she was dead.

Marshall knew that the word would have somehow got back to whoever had sent them, and that they would try harder to... What? Kill him? Usurp him somehow? The more he thought about it, the less sense it made. That attempt to kill him in Kuala Lumpur had been clumsy, amateurish even.

He stared unseeingly at the off-white wall of the rented cottage, the images of recent events playing out in front of him like a cinema projection.

It was as if someone was toying with him, manipulating events around him. Pulling the strings. He shrugged away the thought as being ridiculous. He'd be jumping at shadows next. He rubbed at his face and took in his surroundings. The place was stark, the only character being provided by framed prints that were screwed, rather than hung, on the walls. The owner of the rental property clearly wasn't the trusting sort.

When he had first started in the business, he'd stayed in hotels as he moved from one contract to another. He'd liked the convenience and the culture of anonymity where uninterested staff knew you as either sir or madam.

But Marshall had reconsidered the idea after he'd been trapped in his hotel room after gang members had gained entry by blowing the door off its hinges. Luckily, the room was on the first floor, so it had been easy for him to escape through the window. But the thought of what might have happened if he'd been on a higher floor had stayed with him. Since then, he'd only rented places where there were easy avenues of escape. Such as this cottage in the middle of nowhere.

The thoughts fed his increasing paranoia. He got up and stood, his body angled away from the window, and scanned the fields outside.

If they could find him in Malaysia, then they could certainly find him here.

He went to the window on the opposite side of the room and studied the tranquil landscape. No sign of anything untoward – why would there be?

But the unnerving feeling wouldn't go away. It was the same sensation that had helped to keep him alive on so many occasions.

The hit on Cranberry had been a polished success. However, that someone else had been shot at the same time couldn't be coincidence.

They'd known he was at The Grand Hotel in Kuala Lumpur a few days ago, even though he hadn't stayed there before, and the fact he rarely used a hotel these days made it even more incredible.

Marshall was sure he hadn't been followed, as he'd switched transport modes several times. So obviously, he must have been tracked somehow.

He cursed himself for his own stupidity. Of course, someone must have somehow slipped a device into his belongings.

He pulled out the luggage items he'd had with him in Kuala Lumpur. There was just a travel case and a computer bag. Taking a knife, he pulled the case towards him and sliced into the stitching that held the leather around the handle. After a quick examination, he set to work with the panels and, before long, there was a pile of materials in front of him. But no sign of any tracking device.

He did the same with the computer carrier, again cutting

open the straps before demolishing the bag itself. Nothing. He stared at the laptop, unable to see how anyone could secrete something in a sealed unit.

A thought struck him. He unscrewed the plug of the power supply and immediately found a device. The fuse in the plug had been replaced with what looked like a microchip.

'So that's how you've been a step ahead of me,' he said to himself.

Knowing his location was exposed, it was time to leave. He didn't know the agenda of the people tracking him, but they'd tried to kill him in Kuala Lumpur, and that was enough.

Marshall gathered his possessions in readiness to leave. He looked in the wardrobe and found a battered suitcase to replace the one that he had just demolished. He packed and was pressing down on the lid when he stopped. Something was wrong.

His ears pricked up; his body switched onto full alert. The bird's shrill chorus outside had suddenly halted.

He went up the stairs and looked out of the window. A slight breeze was ruffling the trees beyond, and darkening clouds heralded a change in the weather. But there was no sign of anyone. However, his senses were racing. His instincts were shouting, "Leave now!"

He waited, barely breathing, so he wouldn't miss a sound, but there was just a dull silence.

Perhaps a stray animal, he thought, and let out a deep breath.

For goodness' sake Nick, pull yourself together.

He took a last look across the countryside and turned on his heel to go back downstairs.

A stair creaked.

He was too late. He'd been found.

Marshall stiffened, ears straining toward the sound, and pulled the lounge door so he could peer through the crack.

The back of a man's head was coming into view at the top of the stairs. He looked professional, methodically taking one stair at a time, and pausing after each step.

He held a semi-automatic shotgun which looked like army issue.

Marshall pulled out his Glock and went into a state of icy calm. This was going to be difficult. His Glock against the semi-automatic was going to be like David against Goliath.

Another creak announced a second intruder. This one wasn't as professional as the first or he would have avoided the creaky stair.

So, they had sent two or more for him. The cottage was of the upside-down style, where the bedrooms were downstairs and the living area upstairs, which afforded wonderful views of the countryside. Right now, that was a curse. He was trapped upstairs. Yes, he had the advantage of surprise, but shooting one of these men would enable another to take his place, their machine guns against his Glock.

Marshall leapt into action. He shot out the glass in the window with the Glock and then hurled himself through the frame, crashing onto the slippery grass below. He grunted as searing pain from his recent stab wound shot through his leg as he tried to shield himself from the floating fragments of glass that splintered towards him.

The momentum had thrown him onto his back, which had winded him, but had also given him the perfect position. He lay still and waited, both hands pointing his gun towards the shattered window above.

Seconds later, a man's head bobbed out and looked down at him. Marshall squeezed the trigger. An explosion of blood erupted from the back of the man's head as he was blasted back into the room. There were shouts from inside the house and then silence.

He waited a few seconds, hoping that someone else would make the same mistake, and then got to his feet. He ran to the front of the building, ducking under the windows. As he approached the door, a man came running out pointing his weapon at Marshall.

Marshall quickly shot him twice – a bullet in the wrist, and then one in the knee. The man let out a bellow and fell to the ground, writhing.

Marshall kicked his gun clear. 'What do you want with me?'

The man seemed in no mood for conversation. 'Go fuck yourself.'

A noise from inside the house prompted him to abandon the man. 'We'll chat later,' he said. 'Or rather, you will.'

The man glared at him and spat in his direction.

Marshall retraced his steps to the rear of the cottage, wondering how many others there were. He slid himself through the back door and waited.

He could hear movement ahead of him and followed the sound. As he turned the corner of the hallway, there was a burst of gunfire that spattered the walls with bullets.

Marshall ducked into a bedroom doorway. When there was a pause in the gunfire, he blindly aimed his gun around the corner and let off a few shots. He edged back into the hallway, expecting a further hail of fire, but all seemed quiet.

Then from outside, he heard a man's voice. It sounded as though he was pleading. Then there was a single shot.

He yanked the door open and nearly stumbled over the man he'd shot in the knee and wrist a couple of minutes ago. Thoughts of interrogating him vanished when he saw the man was lying still with a bullet hole in his forehead. They had taken his life to prevent him from talking.

Marshall looked around for signs of the man's executer. In the distance, he saw a figure dressed in khaki appear from shrubbery. He gave chase, following the man into an adjoining field.

His quarry was about a hundred yards ahead but was gaining ground.

The pain in Marshall's leg was slowing him down, and he started to worry that he might lose the chase.

The man seemed to speed up and headed into the woodland. Marshall followed him, vaguely remembering that on the other side of the forest was a road. Perhaps the man had a vehicle waiting?

Marshall ducked under branches and ran through brambles and bushes, spurred on by the thrashing sound ahead of him.

Suddenly, he slipped on the wet leaves and crashed to the ground, his sore hip taking the brunt. He grunted in agony and rolled over onto his chest.

Ahead of him, the thrashing stopped. It was as if his quarry had sensed Marshall's problems and was waiting for his next move.

The thrashing started again, but now it sounded as though it was coming towards him. He realised he was the one in danger of becoming the quarry.

He stood up, his adrenaline racing, which somehow helped to ease his pain. Seeing daylight beyond the dense bush, he ran towards it, ignoring the brambles that tore at his skin, and he threw himself through the opening.

He landed on soft grass in a clearing and was immediately back on his feet. Hurling himself over a five-bar gate, he ran through a field, stopping when he arrived at a hedge that ran along its perimeter.

Marshall listened quietly, resisting the urge to draw long lungfuls of air.

He could still hear the thrashing sound but now it was slightly ahead of him. His quarry seemed to know where he was going, which strengthened Marshall's view that there must be a vehicle waiting ahead. He bent low behind the hedge and tried to keep pace with the sound from the woodland.

Another gate led into a lane. The firmer ground allowed Marshall to move faster, but he paused every so often to make sure his quarry was within earshot. He got the feeling that the man was eager to escape and didn't seem to care how much noise he was making.

Marshall saw an empty Jeep at the side of the road and hid in some shrubbery and waited. He could hear the thrashing sound get louder. Finally, the bushes broke open, and the man appeared. He held a pistol by his side and appeared nervous.

Marshall stepped out from the shrubbery. 'Don't make a move!'

The man spun around and fired at Marshall, the bullet lodging itself into the trunk of a tree right next to where he had been standing.

Marshall threw himself to the ground, simultaneously firing back.

The man staggered but stayed on his feet. Marshall moved quickly towards him, ready to fire again, but the man laid his weapon on the ground and stepped away from it, his hands high. 'Please don't kill me,' he said.

'Why not?' Marshall replied. 'You want to harm me.'

The man looked down at his bloody wound in disbelief. 'One shot and you got me. How lucky can you get?'

Marshall gave a slight grin. 'No luck. It's sort of my job. Why are you trying to kill me, and who sent you?'

The man didn't answer but sat down on the ground, his face screwed up with pain, his hands holding his midriff.

Marshall raised his gun. 'I won't bother asking again.'

'I don't know,' the man said in a defeated tone.

'What do you mean?'

'I don't know who sent us. We get told what to do by our boss, who gets his instructions from someone in Spain. I don't know his name. We just do as we are told.'

'Bollocks,' Marshall said. 'I think you're the boss. You shot one of your own crew back at the house just to stop him from talking.'

'That wasn't me. I didn't, I swear!'

Marshall looked at him. He was starting to get a cold feeling. 'It must have been. If it wasn't you—'

A shot rang out from behind and Marshall felt a hot, searing pain in his side. He fell to the ground, his gun dropping beside him. He lay still, the shock of the bullet screaming through his body.

He opened his eyes and could see a man in the distance, his rifle raised, taking aim to shoot again. Marshall couldn't move. He closed his eyes and waited for the inevitable.

The second shot sounded louder than the first, but Marshall felt nothing.

After a few moments, he opened his eyes again. He could feel the strength returning to his body.

The man with the rifle had gone. He looked round at the man he'd been interrogating and saw he was lying very still, his head a bloody mess.

They wanted us both dead, he thought. *Christ, these people are savages.*

Marshall pulled himself onto his elbows, trying to assess how badly he was wounded. He was lucky; the bullet had cut straight through him, but there was a lot of blood.

He ripped off his shirt and scrunched in into a ball. He

used his trouser belt to compress the material next to his wound, which helped stem the flow of blood.

Marshall reasoned there must have been three men sent to kill him, plus a backup, known as a sweeper.

He walked back to the still figure on the ground. A bullet in the head from a long-distance shot. He nodded with grudging respect. Pretty good. However, if the shooter was that good, then how was Marshall still alive?

Searching through the dead man's pockets, he found nothing of any relevance apart from the keys to the Jeep.

In the glove compartment of the vehicle, there was a rolled-up map and a blown-up Google image of the area around the cottage.

Marshall hefted the man's body into the open boot of the Jeep and drove back to the cottage.

He stitched and bandaged himself, thankful that the cottage had a first-aid kit, and then examined the human carnage around the cottage. He could easily have been one of the still bodies that were lying on the ground.

Rummaging through the cupboards, he found a roll of dustbin liners, which he sliced into squares and laid on the floor. After methodically searching through all the pockets, he dragged the bodies onto the plastic.

The noise of the gunfire seemed to have attracted no interest, but he knew it was time to move on.

He pulled out his phone and dialled a number.

'Takeaway service. How may we help?' the monotone voice said.

'The usual, please,' Marshall said.

'For how many people?'

'Three.'

'Would you confirm the location please?'

Marshall told them and ended the call. Within a short

space of time, the cottage's recent history would be wiped out, the bodies removed, and everything would be back to normal.

Ten minutes later, Marshall had left the cottage.

6

Harry woke up bathed in sweat. He kicked off the sticky sheets and lay, trying to focus.

He had been told not to come back to work until he felt better. Better? What did that mean? He wasn't ill.

Come on, Harry, they are only trying to be supportive and you're being difficult. As usual.

He swung his legs onto the floor and wiped at his forehead with his arm. The perspiration was the downside of drinking too much. Tentacles of pain were stabbing somewhere behind his eyes. Why had he drunk so much?

He idly wondered if the vicar had got home okay. When he'd left, Harry remembered seeing him urinate in the neighbour's garden, before sprawling onto some geraniums. The thought brought a brief spark of humour to his eyes. He went into the kitchen and surveyed the mass of dirty crockery, the empty whisky bottle, and the half-dozen squished beer cans.

He made tea and padded through to the lounge. His guests had offered to clear up, but Harry had declined, wanting everyone to just go, apart from the vicar and the rest of the single malt.

Slumping onto the settee, he munched a dried-up sandwich. His mum's funeral the previous day now felt surreal, like a bad dream from which he would soon wake up.

He looked at his phone. A missed call from his sister. Shit. She probably phoned to say farewell before flying home to New Zealand. He pressed the button to return the call and waited. Eventually, there was a single tone followed by an announcement. He was too late. He put the phone down, making a mental promise to contact her soon.

Harry sat back and looked around. His home felt emptier than normal. People had told him it was a typical bachelor pad, which was understandable, given the big, brown, leather furniture and extra-large stereo loudspeakers that commandeered the room. His home was small, the kitchen tiny, and there was just the one bedroom. Still, it was a nice area – Kings Langley had a bit of everything, including a couple of pubs. His flat sat around the corner from one of his favourite haunts, the Fred and Ginger coffee shop, where he'd spend many an hour mulling over a crime that needed his attention. Or just mulling.

At his age, he knew he ought to make more of an effort, but now wasn't the time. Even his sister had dropped big hints about having a woman in his life. 'What happened to that nice Alex?' she had asked.

'I don't know,' he'd replied. 'What happened to Maria and all the others?'

She had looked at his face and then shut up.

When Helen arrived from New Zealand, she had said she'd be fine on Harry's settee, but he was having none of it. He'd put her into one of the rooms at the local Holiday Inn, and paid upfront for her stay. He hadn't wanted anyone staying with him; he didn't want the interruption to his thoughts.

So God and the powers that controlled his life couldn't win. He didn't want company, but the flat felt empty.

Harry sat up. It wasn't the flat. It was his own life that suddenly felt empty. He hadn't seen his mum as much as he should have in recent times and had thought she'd be around forever. Now she was dead, he was already feeling a sense of loneliness – and a heap of guilt.

He stood, wanting to be somewhere – anywhere. Just not here.

Throwing on some clothes, he walked towards the front door, catching sight of his image in the hallway mirror.

Harry looked a state. His eyes reflected alcoholic over-indulgence. His pale skin was exacerbated by a couple of days of facial growth.

He wanted a drink on his own, but with people around. He needed a pub where he was unknown. He didn't want sympathy. He wanted peace.

When his taxi arrived, the driver queried his destination. 'The Angel? Are you sure that's where you want to go?'

'Positive.'

Driving through the town centre, he watched people going about their business – women with prams, old men sat on benches, staring ahead. People with normal lives.

As he climbed out of the cab, Harry pulled out an old, cloth cap from his pocket and stuffed it onto his head. He was wary of being recognised; he knew coppers weren't much appreciated in this area.

He walked into the pub, his feet sticking to the filthy carpet. He paused and looked around, allowing his eyes to adjust to the gloom, and then sat on a bar stool. There was a smell of stale beer in the air.

'Yes, mate?' The barman looked at him with bored eyes that had seen plenty.

Looking at the top shelf, Harry reckoned it would be

pointless to ask for a decent single malt. 'Large whisky please.'

'House or Teachers?'

'The best you've got.'

The barman shrugged and poured from one of the cheaper optics.

'Anything else?'

'Pint of strong lager.'

The barman placed the drink in front of Harry and carried on looking at the muted television.

Harry sipped the beer and stared into space, losing himself in memories.

He picked up the whisky and downed it in a single gulp, hoping that it would deaden the pain. He knew these feelings about his mum were pointless now, but he couldn't help but wallow in the cloud of guilt.

Harry was slightly surprised at himself. He was normally clear-eyed about emotional matters, particularly his own, but this was different.

'Please,' he pushed the whisky tumbler towards the barman. 'Another large one.'

He sat for around an hour, hardly moving. He was vaguely aware of people coming and going like shapes swirling around him, but he remained lost in his own thoughts.

'Hey, mate, do you want this?' a voice asked.

'What?' He looked up. A man who'd been sitting next to him had stood up to leave and was offering Harry his discarded newspaper. 'Thanks.' He took it and settled down to read. He stared at the front page. "Who is the Tigerman?" the dramatic headline asked.

He read the story before turning to the sports pages at the back, then ordered another drink and went to the toilet.

Harry looked at his reflection in the mirror. The alcohol

had made him feel better, and his face seemed to have lost some of its sallowness.

Taking off his cap, he rubbed at the sparse growth where luxuriant, curly hair once was. He grimaced. He found it difficult to accept that his hair would probably never be the same after the fire. The burning building had nearly killed him and the lady he'd saved.

He put the cap back on firmly, as if putting a lid on an unpleasant memory.

Then Harry made his way back to the bar, where he found a thick-set man on the barstool where he'd been sitting. He reached around him.

'What the bleeding hell do you think you are doing?' the man asked aggressively.

'Just getting my drink and paper,' Harry answered calmly.

The man swung round on the stool, an aggravated expression on his face. 'Oh, it was your paper, was it? So you brought it in with you, did you?'

'Look, mate, just keep it.' Harry took his drink and moved further down the bar to sit on another stool.

It had been obvious that the man had been spoiling for a fight, and if the truth be known, Harry was tempted. Perhaps a good dust-up would sort out the demons in his head.

Common sense cut in. The very last thing he wanted was to attract attention to himself, but it seemed it was too late.

'You're the filth, aren't you, mate?' The voice belonged to a youngish man with close-cropped blond hair. Suddenly the pub had gone uncomfortably quiet.

As Harry was wondering how this guy could know that he was a police officer, he noticed a balding man staring at him from across the bar. He recognised him as a villain who he'd help put away a couple of years ago, Jimmy McNeal.

McNeal raised his glass and smiled. Harry was sure that

the smile must have been sarcastic, as it couldn't surely be friendly.

I can't believe they've released him already, Harry thought.

He looked around the bar area. The young, cropped-blond guy was still giving him an unpleasant stare. 'Well, are you?' he asked.

'Am I what?' Harry turned on his stool to face him square on.

'The filth.'

'What if I am?'

The young man seemed uncertain what to say next and looked at his mates for support.

'If you're the filth, you can fuck off,' one of them said. Several of the others sniggered.

'Yes, that seems a good idea.' Harry stood up and swallowed his drink. He made towards the door. It felt that the entire pub knew who he was, probably thanks to Jimmy McNeal, and whilst Harry was in the right mood for a scrap, he knew it wasn't the best of ideas.

He walked out of the pub, squinting against the sudden glare of the daylight. He felt relieved to be out of there; the atmosphere had suddenly turned sour.

As he contemplated whether to carry on his drinking session, he was aware of quick footsteps behind him.

He spun round expecting trouble; Jimmy McNeal was running towards him.

'Mr Black... Harry... Hold on a minute.' Jimmy caught up and stopped to catch his breath. 'Sorry I couldn't talk in there, but I had to keep up appearances in front of the lads.'

'You told them who I was, though. Thanks for ruining my drink.'

'There's no harm done. Don't take any notice of that young lad. He's my son. A wet sock would knock him over.'

'What do you want, Jimmy?'

McNeal looked around guardedly. 'Let's go into the next pub. It might soil your reputation to be seen with me.'

Harry paused. 'I'm not sure that's a good idea.'

'Come on, please. I'll buy the beers.'

Against his better judgment, Harry allowed himself to follow McNeal into The Swan, which only had a slightly better reputation that the pub they'd just left.

Minutes later, Harry was setting down his pint and appraising the man opposite. 'Prison seems to have done you little harm. You look healthier than I've ever seen you.'

McNeal gave a hollow laugh. 'It was no picnic, that's for sure, and no thanks to you.'

'Then why are we drinking together?'

Jimmy gave him a look. 'I was really pissed off with you at first, but then later realised you were one of the better coppers out of a bad bunch.'

'Thanks,' Harry said. 'I think.'

'When my wife visited me, she told me how kind you'd been to her, and how you'd pointed her toward various support services who really helped her while I was inside. I'm really grateful for that. So I think I can help you and help myself at the same time.'

'Okay, I'm really touched, but get to the point,' Harry said, curious, despite his manner.

'When I was first inside, I was bullied. This bloke called Paul Martin was transferred to us from Wormwood. He saw off the toe rag who was bullying me, and as a result we became good mates. He said he'd been done for handling stolen weapons, but also told me he'd taken the rap for someone else on the understanding that his wife would receive a lot of money when he was put away, and a large lump sum would set him up for life when he was released. But no payment to his wife was ever made. As a result, he tried to tell the prison governor what had taken place, and when the governor did nothing, he told others. Shortly afterwards, he had an accident in his cell and was found dead. He supposedly slipped on a wet floor and banged his head.'

Harry said nothing but waited while Jimmy took a sip of his pint and wiped the froth from his mouth with his sleeve.

'Anyway, before all that, he knew I'd be out well before him, and he made me promise that I would tell someone what had happened.'

'And I suppose I'm the someone,' Harry said, resignedly. 'All right, so what happened then?'

'This bloke he took the rap for is a Frenchman who makes a fortune transporting illegal weapons from England into Europe via France. He looks and acts like a gent but apparently he's a nasty bastard who happily drops people in the shit.' Jimmy paused for dramatic effect. 'A man who is a well-known person in the French government.'

There was silence while Harry took a sip of his drink and set the glass down.

'This sounds like a load of bollocks,' he replied. 'I think that you saw me in your local pub, and thought you'd feed me some cock and bull story about some corrupt politician, so you can have a laugh with the lads later.'

'Harry, I swear on my life this is true. I've kept this information to myself up to now – well, except for the missus, but I didn't know what to do with it. When I saw you, of all people, come into the pub, I took it as a sign. Harry, this is big. This man needs taking down.'

'Okay, what's the Frenchman's name?'

When Jimmy told him, Harry pushed his chair back and looked at him with complete disbelief. 'Gerard Tournier? But isn't he a top-level French politician?'

Jimmy nodded. 'That's right. That's what I'm saying.'

'But even if this was true,' Harry said, 'there's absolutely zilch I can do about it. Surely, it's France's business, not ours.

And anyway, it would need someone about sixteen pay grades above mine to start that sort of high-level investigation.'

Jimmy shrugged. 'You may be right, but I've passed the information onto you. So I've kept my promise. It's up to you what happens next.'

After Jimmy had gone, Harry sat with a fresh beer in front of him. Despite the alcohol he'd consumed, his brain was now startlingly sober. The interaction with Jimmy McNeal had completely taken his mind off his own issues and made him realise he needed to get back to work, and quickly.

7

Harry's return was met with sympathetic nods and murmurings of support.

He'd told his superior, Superintendent Mainwaring, that he was fine and would return to work. She had asked him if he was sure, and that he could have more time off if he wanted, but Harry wanted life to get back to normal.

He was catching up with what seemed like thousands of emails when his office door opened, and a blond head appeared.

'Thought I heard someone in here. Welcome back, guv. I'm really sorry about your mother.'

DS Adam "Sandy" Sanders was one of Harry's key team members.

'Thank you,' Harry said. 'I appreciate that. Have a seat and tell me who you think this is.' He swung the laptop round so that Sandy could see the image.

'He looks slightly familiar.'

'His name is Gerard Tournier. He is the French defence minister and is responsible for buying arms on behalf of the French government.'

Sanders looked puzzled. 'Okay, guv. What's this got to do with us?'

'At the moment, nothing. However...' Harry told Sanders about his recent interaction with Jimmy McNeal.

'He could be feeding you a load of tripe,' Sanders said.

'He could be,' acknowledged Harry. 'But why? What could he gain from lying about this? Anyway, it would do no harm to have a quick look into it.'

'Good luck getting it past the super, guv.'

'Good luck? Why?'

'Superintendent Mainwaring has instructed that all of our efforts should be concentrated on the Giles Cranberry assassination.'

'Okay, so we multitask.' Harry looked at his watch. 'I have a meeting with her later this morning, so I'll know more after that.'

Meetings with Liz Mainwaring were far more pleasant these days. When Mainwaring originally took over as Harry's boss, she had made his life difficult. Eventually, events had convinced her that he was an excellent detective and now they had a good relationship.

'How are you enjoying being superintendent?' Harry asked, looking around her new office.

'Obviously I'm delighted with the promotion, but between you and me, I was shit-scared at first. But I'm determined to do the best I can.'

She'd transformed a drab room into a technophile's dream. There was a bench that ran the length of her office, on which were various monitors and equipment that would facilitate research, while keeping her up to date with the latest developments around the world. The other side of the office was much softer and homely. Potted plants and family photos nestled between various career awards.

She looked at him over the top of her spectacles. Her red

hair was drawn behind her ears and the accompanying fringe gave the appearance of her being permanently cross, unless she smiled.

There was a kind smile on her face now. 'Now, Harry, are you sure you're ready to come back to work? After all, you've only just lost–'

'Now then, Liz,' Harry said. 'I'm sure you have genuine concern for my welfare, but I know we are short-handed at the moment. Anyway, I want to return to work.'

Mainwaring laughed and pushed her glasses to the top of her forehead. 'You're right, of course. I can't say that I'm not pleased at your return, especially with the recent shootings. How much do you already know about the events surrounding the assassination of Giles Cranberry?'

'Not much,' Harry admitted. 'I had a quick look at a newspaper which had a version of the story, so I probably know as much as Joe Public.'

'We don't know much more, I'm afraid,' Mainwaring said. She put her glasses back on the bridge of her nose and opened the file in front of her.

'It's a strange one. The two men were shot almost simultaneously. Giles Cranberry, who died at the scene, and an MP called Peter Finch. Have you heard of either?'

'Not until I read about it,' Harry said. 'What's the condition of this man, Finch?'

'He's in hospital but apparently his condition is okay and he's able to talk.'

'I'll go and have a chat with him. Do we have any further information on the assassin, this so-called Tigerman? According to the papers, a little boy actually spoke to him.'

'That's correct. We know nothing else yet, other than he's in the frame for the shootings,' Mainwaring said. 'The papers have as much as we do.'

'Yes, about that,' Harry said. 'How did the press get to

know about the Tigerman in the first place? And how was the connection established between the so-called Tigerman and the shooting of Cranberry?'

'Good questions,' Mainwaring said. 'A witness saw a man wearing a hi-vis jacket and safety helmet exiting the construction site at a time when everyone else had knocked off. The witness was an ex-employee of the site, and knew that there had to be a minimum of two people after normal hours for security reasons. We found images from CCTV that backed up his claim. We then found further footage that showed the suspect entering the railway area. Then British rail kindly furnished us with their images, enabling us to track him close to the property where the boy lives. We then told the press what we knew, hoping that when the images were published, other witnesses would come forward.'

'And did they?' Harry asked.

'Not as yet. So that makes the link obvious. The shot that killed Cranberry came from the construction site.'

'So we're putting two and two together and making a circumstantial guess?' Harry said.

'It's all we've got,' Mainwaring said, taking off her glasses and running her hand through her hair. Harry idly wondered if she dyed it red or it was her natural colour.

'It's a start, I suppose,' he said. 'What about the shot that wounded Finch?'

'It came from the opposite direction,' she said. 'That's all we know at the moment.'

Harry frowned. 'That makes little sense. Why would someone employ two assassins at extra cost, when one hitman could have done both? It's double the risk.'

'I agree. At least it makes it seem like a planned killing and not some random nutcase taking pot shots.'

Mainwaring put her spectacles back on and looked at Harry.

'On a personal note.' Her tone was soft. 'I've been meaning to ask, why didn't you put yourself forward for the DCI position? You know I'd have endorsed it.'

'That's very kind, but I'm fine as I am, for the moment.'

'Harry, if you stay in your current role, members of your own team could eventually leapfrog you and possibly become your superior. How would that feel? That's apart from the fact that the Met likes its officers to show evidence of ambition.'

'Okay, maybe I'll give it some thought,' Harry said resignedly.

'You do that. In the meantime, you'll continue to report directly to me, until the vacancy of DCI has been filled. That's all, thanks, Harry. Unless you have anything else?'

'There was something, ma'am.'

Harry gave her a slightly edited version of the conversation with Jimmy McNeal, leaving out the amount of alcohol consumed.

When he'd finished, she was staring at him long and hard. 'Harry, with respect, you are a talented, seasoned inspector, not a graduate. The information fed to you by your source was, by your own definition, second-hand and therefore hearsay. Also, the source itself was questionable, and even if this information had any credibility, would you honestly be prepared to put your career at risk investigating something that could blow up in your face?'

'Ma'am?'

She got up from behind her desk and went to a monitor. ' always keep recordings of the BBC news. This is fr yesterday morning.'

Harry watched the screen as a tall, suited, midd' man shook hands with the British Prime Minister.

'That's your Gerard Tournier,' she said, turr monitor. 'He met the PM to discuss buying ext from the UK to strengthen the European involvement in Libya.' She sat back down. 'That's who you are thinking of involving yourself with. A very respected French official. Are you bonkers?'

'Ma'am, with respect, any rookie police officer, even if they are fresh out of the academy, will tell you they joined the force to make a difference. I can't say any different as an inspector. How the hell can you make a difference if you don't stick your head over the parapet now and again? I agree it sounds almost unbelievable, a French defence minister who is also an arms dealer. But what if there's any truth in it?'

Mainwaring took off her glasses and rubbed her eyes. 'Look, Harry, you know I can't give you an official sanction on this. If you can come back to me with something more credible than a pub conversation with an ex-con, then maybe we can take it further.'

Harry smiled. 'Thank you. Don't worry. I'll tread carefully.'

'In the meantime, please let's keep our focus on the Cranberry shooting.'

'Absolutely, ma'am.' Harry stood up straight and gave her a mock salute. 'I'm off to see our wounded MP right now.'

'You're a cheeky sod,' she said. 'But it's good to have you back.'

~

FINCH WAS SITTING up in his hospital bed reading a newspaper when Harry arrived.

'Thank you for seeing me,' Harry said.

'My pleasure, Inspector, how can I be of help?' Finch said, folding the paper neatly and placing it on the bedside table.

Harry pulled over a plastic chair and sat facing the MP. 'How are you feeling?' he asked.

'Not great. It's just a flesh wound to the shoulder, but it hurts like hell and I'm apparently going to rest for a while.'

Harry smiled. 'I'm sure that your boss will understand, considering the situation.'

Finch picked up a box of expensive Belgian chocolates from the bedside table and offered them to Harry.

'Not for me, thanks.' Harry patted his waistline. 'I've been eating and drinking all the wrong things recently.'

'Pity, these were a gift from the PM. Don't like chocolate myself but didn't want to see them go to waste.'

'I'm sure they won't. There are plenty of lovely nurses around who'd enjoy them, I reckon.'

'You're not wrong there,' Finch said with a grin, pulling himself further up the bed. 'Okay, fire away.'

'Thank you, Mr Finch. I'm aware my colleagues have already questioned you, so if you have to repeat anything, I apologise.'

'Don't worry, Inspector. I understand how it works.'

'Mr Finch, is there anyone you know who'd want to kill you?'

'Apart from some of the MPs on the opposite benches in the Commons, do you mean?' He laughed and then winced as he inadvertently moved his bad arm. 'No, seriously, I can't think of anyone.'

'All right, what about Giles Cranberry? Did he have any enemies, as far as you know?'

'Inspector, I didn't really know Giles Cranberry. In fact, the night of the shooting was the first time I'd properly met him. But as a newspaper boss, he'd probably have enemies out there, I'd guess. The press is normally upsetting someone.'

The tea trolley squeaked its way in their direction. 'Tea or coffee, Mr Finch?'

Harry looked up. The lady pushing the trolley was tall

and dark, with startlingly blue eyes which were fixed on the MP.

Finch smiled up at the lady, clearly enjoying the effect he was having on her. 'Coffee, please.'

Her eyes flickered to Harry. 'Drink, sir?'

'Tea, thank you.'

As she poured liquid into the plastic beakers, Harry idly wondered why power was so attractive to others. The lady was clearly quite taken with Finch. Or was he being unfair? After all, Peter Finch had a full head of grey and brown hair, making him look handsome and distinguished.

I wasn't bad looking once, or so I was told, he thought, running his hand over his hair, feeling the tiny bits of curly fluff amid the scarred skin.

He waited until the tea trolley had squeaked away. 'Mr Finch, you and Charles Brandon meet up at the Garrick Club regularly.'

'That's correct, always on a Wednesday, soon after Prime Minister's questions.'

'Can I ask why, bearing in mind that you are on opposite sides of the house? I always assumed that the Tories and Labour were rivals.'

Finch laughed. 'True. Politically we might be disenfranchised, but some of us socialise with people from other political parties.'

'Tell me the events of that evening, as you recall them.'

Finch looked into the far distance. 'We were at the Garrick Club. Charles and I were sitting, having a drink and a chat. Then Giles Cranberry joined us. He and Charles had arranged to go for a meal, so we all left the Garrick Club, walked down the steps and then bang, bang, and that was that.'

'And when you and Charles had your weekly meetings at the Garrick Club, did you usually go for a meal afterwards?'

'Just occasionally,' Finch replied. 'More often than not, we'd gossip about other MPs and get reasonably merry.'

'And before Cranberry arrived, were Charles Brandon and yourself due to go for a meal on the night of the shootings?'

'No, I couldn't make it that night. I had things to do. It was Giles who instigated the meal. Hold on. No, it wasn't,' Finch said, almost excitedly. He winced as he pulled himself further up the bed again. 'Giles Cranberry said Brandon's secretary had phoned to invite him to dinner on behalf of Charles, but Charles seemed like he'd forgotten all about it.'

'Then the only people who knew in advance that the meal was taking place, and at what time, was Charles Brandon's secretary, and Giles Cranberry himself.'

'Giles could have told someone beforehand that he was meeting Charles,' Finch observed.

'He could,' Harry said, 'or the secretary could have let slip to someone that the dinner was taking place. Or it's possible someone else had access to Charles Brandon's diary.'

Finch looked impressed. 'Your brain seems to work in very straight lines.'

'Thank you,' Harry said. 'That's one of the more unusual compliments I've ever received.'

The tea woman returned without the trolley. 'Just wanted to know if you two gentlemen need anything else.'

'I've been stuck in hospital a few times, but I've never known such excellent service!' Harry said with a grin. 'I'll leave you to it. I'm off to see Charles Brandon.'

'Give him my very best,' Finch said.

As Harry walked through the ward, he glanced back and saw the woman's delighted smile as she accepted Finch's chocolates.

Harry left the hospital and stood by the exit doors. Many years ago, when he was a smoker, this would be the time when he would want to light up. It gave an excuse to stand in one place and just ponder.

With a hum, the exit doors automatically opened, and people poured out. Most of them wore blank expressions, but a few were looking upset. Perhaps their worlds had been altered by the illness or even death of a loved one. For a second, Harry connected with them. Then the connection broke. His mum had been fortunate enough to enjoy a long and fulfilling life, and he'd been very lucky to have had his mum around for so long. It was about time he grew up.

He flicked an imaginary cigarette onto the hospital steps and walked to his car.

Harry didn't go to see Brandon straight away, but instead made his way to the Labour Party headquarters in Westminster.

Yvonne Martin was middle-aged and bespectacled, with greying hair pulled into a bun. As he introduced himself, she welcomed him with a tight smile, which switched off almost as soon as it appeared.

'You're Charles Brandon's secretary?' Harry said.

'Personal assistant,' she replied, a frown appearing over the top of her glasses.

'And you handle Mr Brandon's diary?'

'You are quite correct, Inspector. Now what can I do for you?' Her tone was impatient.

'Mrs Martin–'

'Miss.'

Harry ignored the correction. 'On the day of the shooting, you spoke to Giles Cranberry and invited him to dinner on behalf of Charles Brandon.'

'You are correct again, Inspector.'

'When did Mr Brandon ask you to put that date in the diary?'

Yvonne Martin's face suddenly seemed to lose some of its

unflappability. 'I didn't write it in, Inspector. I suppose I assumed he did.'

It was Harry's turn to look surprised. 'Is this something that Mr Brandon did often? Writing his own entries into the diary?'

'Now I think about it, no,' she replied. 'Mr Brandon almost never touches the diary. He normally just lets me know, and I update accordingly. A big part of my job is to keep the diary as efficiently as possible. That means juggling events so they don't collide with each other.'

'I understand, but on this occasion, Mr Brandon may have created his own entry. Is it in his handwriting?'

'That's hard to say,' she replied, studying the page in the diary. 'It's been printed in capital letters.'

'Does Mr Brandon have a habit of using capital letters whenever he leaves you a message?'

She thought for a moment. 'No, he doesn't. I know this because he once wrote something on a pad, and I remember joking that his scrawl was worse than a doctor's.'

Harry couldn't imagine her joking for an instant. 'Who else has got access to these offices?'

'Mr Brandon's office is kept locked when he isn't here. I'm the only other person with a key. However, lots of people have access to my office. Cleaners, maintenance staff, etc.'

'So almost anyone could have got into the office and created that entry into the diary.'

'I suppose so,' she said, looking a little abashed. 'It's an old-fashioned system. I can't wait until everything has finished being computerised.'

'That'll bring its own problems,' Harry said, walking towards the door. 'Thank you for your time.'

He left Westminster with more to think about than when he arrived.

8

Harry stood outside Charles Brandon's house, marvelling at the ornate, wrought-iron gates that heralded the grandness within. He pressed a button and spoke into a little, black box on the pillar. 'Inspector Black for Mr Brandon.'

A female voice crackled back, 'Please enter, sir.'

The gates automatically opened, and he drove round the sweeping driveway, coming to a halt outside a sprawling, grey stone mansion.

The front door was already open, and a young maid appeared, wearing a black dress and a white apron. Her hands were folded in front of her.

Harry felt as though he'd been swept back in time as he followed her into a magnificent hallway with oil paintings on either side and a sweeping, marble staircase ahead.

The maid showed him into the drawing room, and excused herself, saying that Mr Brandon would be with him shortly.

Harry sat down tentatively in a huge, leather armchair

that threatened to engulf him, and looked around in wonder. He estimated he could probably squeeze most of his flat into this one room.

Blue-finned fish stared at him from their illuminated glass home. Long, green, silk curtains framed the lattice windows, and two wall-to-ceiling, polished bookshelves heaved with a selection of leather-bound books.

Harry pulled himself out of the chair and walked across to study the titles. He picked one and opened it, enjoying the smell of leather and print.

'Ah, excellent choice,' a voice boomed. 'I see you are a fan of Dickens. That one is a very rare edition.'

Harry had only ever seen Charles Brandon being interviewed on television. 'Good morning, sir. Thank you for seeing me.'

'My pleasure, my pleasure. May I offer you tea, and perhaps a little something to eat? I usually have some sustenance around this time.'

Harry accepted the offer and sank back into the comfortable chair.

Charles Brandon was clean-shaven with blond, curly hair. Harry took him to be around forty-five. He wore a light, three-piece suit, the waistcoat of which was patterned with a bold tartan.

'Have you any Scots ancestry?' Harry asked.

'Only on my mother's side. But we go there regularly. In fact, Edinburgh is one of my most favourite places.'

The mention of Scotland brought memories of the lovely Alex to Harry's mind. They'd worked on a difficult case together in London and then enjoyed a brief fling, but then she'd returned to Galashiels, citing work and personal issues. *Where was she now?*

The double doors to the drawing room swung open and

in came a silver trolley, being pushed by a woman also wearing the black-and-white uniform. She laid out a china tea service and a plate of sandwiches on a table. 'Would you like me to pour?' she offered.

'No, thank you, we can manage,' said Brandon.

The woman gave a slight curtsy as she left and closed the double doors behind her.

'Cucumber or salmon?' Brandon said, offering the platter.

Harry took a sandwich and bit into it hungrily. The crusts had been cut off. Of course they had.

Brandon dabbed at his lips with a cloth napkin.

'So, Inspector, I expect you'll be asking me how I became acquainted with Giles Cranberry?'

'That'll do, for starters,' Harry said, helping himself to another sandwich.

'We were at university together. We both studied economics and politics. Giles' politics was right wing, and I was more of a socialist.'

Harry gave Brandon a meaningful look. 'It appears Giles' politics rubbed off onto you, not the other way around,' he said, sweeping an arm around the opulent room.

Brandon laughed. 'No, no, this is all hereditary. My parents owned a string of hotels. They bought this to also be converted into a hotel but loved it so much they turned it into the family home.'

'And where are your parents now?'

Brandon's face fell. 'They're not around anymore, sadly. A couple of years ago, we were all on holiday, and they went out sight-seeing and were killed in a motor accident.'

'I'm so sorry. You must miss them desperately,' Harry said, thinking about his own recent loss.

'Very much...' Brandon said, gazing into the distance. 'Sorry, Inspector, where were we? Ah yes, so Giles and I have known each other for many, many years.'

'What about you and Peter Finch?'

'What about us? We became friends when he first came into politics. We met on a program about attracting fresh blood into politics, and then went for a few drinks afterwards, and have been pals ever since.'

'Can you think of anyone who would want to kill either of them?'

Charles Brandon's gaze went up to the ceiling. 'Giles, possibly, yes. Peter, no way. Peter's just an ordinary bloke who happens to be a politician. But Giles had a lot of power, a lot of sway. Someone could be jealous of him, or have a grudge, I don't know.'

Harry poured himself another tea. 'When did you invite Giles Cranberry out to dinner?'

'To be honest, I don't remember. I have a dreadful memory, so thankfully my personal assistant does all that kind of thing.'

'I stopped off at your office before coming here. Your PA has no knowledge of the invitation, so I assume you made the entry into the diary yourself.'

'No chance,' Brandon said. 'You've met Yvonne Martin. I wouldn't dare write anything into the diary without asking her.'

'That's a fair point,' Harry said. 'But isn't it possible that someone else could have written an entry into the diary?'

Brandon sat upright, looking horrified. 'Are you suggesting that someone who works in my department could have perpetrated Giles' death?'

'Not necessarily. According to Miss Martin, the world and his wife had access to the diary.'

Brandon sat back again. 'Actually, that's true. Our security really isn't what it should be.'

Harry found Brandon to be an excellent conversationalist

and raconteur. He could see why the politician was so popular.

After another half-hour of routine questioning and listening to Brandon's amusing anecdotes, Harry stood up to go. 'Thank you for your time, tea, and sandwiches.'

'You're more than welcome,' Brandon said. 'I'm sorry I have been of little help.'

He pressed a brass button near the door. 'Brigitte will show you out.'

The maid reappeared. 'If you'd like to follow me, sir.'

Harry followed her through the hallway and towards the front door, where she stopped suddenly and bent to pick something up. 'Excuse me, sir, I believe you dropped this,' she said, straightening up and pushing a folded piece of paper into his hand.

'Er, thank you, Brigitte,' Harry said, slightly nonplussed.

'Goodbye, sir.'

He had intended to drive straight to his office at Farrow Road but succumbed to temptation and pulled into a lay-by. He unfolded the piece of paper and read the scrawled message.

"I need to speak to you urgently. Brigitte." There was a phone number underneath.

This is dramatic, Harry thought. He folded the paper and continued his drive to the Farrow Road station.

When he arrived, he nodded to Frank on the front desk, and made his way up the stairs that led to the corridor where most of the offices were. The fact that the building was listed meant that, although no alterations could be made to accommodate the twenty-first century, there were plenty of rooms. So every rank from inspector onwards could have their own office.

Harry spent the rest of the day wading through the

reports of the shooting. They had now officially worked out the position of both assassins by the trajectory of the shots. One came from a nearby apartment and the other was from a construction site. It was confirmed that it was the shot from the construction site that had killed Giles Cranberry.

Whoever had shot Peter Finch had rented an apartment overlooking the Garrick Club. The landlord was paid six months' worth of rent in advance with cash, and as a result had waived his usual requirement for references.

The landlord never met them in person, of course. A courier had delivered the cash – he didn't know which company.

As events were unfolding, Harry knew he was dealing with professionals and would have to step up accordingly. The problem was – where to start? There was only one potential witness who had actually seen Giles Cranberry's assassin. Harry went to have a chat with him.

When he arrived at the house, little Michael was tearing up and down in a plastic dumper truck on the patio, making loud engine noises. His mother watched him proudly. 'My son was so brave. It runs in the family, you know. My brother was a firefighter and he…'

Harry wasn't listening. His eyes were sweeping over the garden and surrounding area. There had been plenty of rain recently, and he could see muddy prints on the edge of the patio.

Harry made a quick call to confirm that forensics had made plaster casts of the footprints that had been found in the garden.

'Show me where you saw the Tigerman, Michael.'

The little boy, eager to please, ran to the hallway. 'He was just here,' he said, pointing down at the carpet.

'And can you remember what he looked like?'

'He was like a tiger.' The boy clawed at the air, then ran around the lounge, making a loud roaring sound.

Harry waited patiently until he was out of breath.

'Michael, what was it that made him look like a tiger?'

The boy clumped up the stairs. Seconds later, he was back down again, holding out a book for Harry's inspection.

He looked at the image of the yellow tiger. 'The man was wearing yellow?'

Michael nodded.

'Were his trousers yellow?'

The boy thought for a second and shook his head.

'Was it a yellow jumper, or a shirt?'

Michael's face suddenly lit up, and he pulled Harry back outside onto the patio, then pointed to the little dumper truck he'd been riding. On the side was an image of a construction worker, with a yellow, high-visibility jacket and helmet.

Having already connected the shooting from the construction site near the Garrick Club with Michael's surprise visitor, Harry had been hoping for something more.

'Well done, Michael. Do you remember anything else? Did he have a moustache or beard... a tattoo, perhaps?'

The boy shook his head.

'Did he say anything?'

'He said hello, and I shot him like this, pow, pow, pow... and then he left.'

'You've been very helpful, Michael, thank you.'

'I want to be a policeman too!' Michael said, jumping up and down.

'No, you don't,' Harry said firmly.

Harry ordered the download of all the CCTV in that area for the date of the shootings, but it transpired that Sandy Sanders had beaten him to it and already emailed the files.

Back in his office, he downloaded the attachments and

watched the laptop screen intently. The house where little Michael lived only had two street CCTV cameras in the vicinity.

The first video file was hazy, showing someone walking out of shot in the far distance. However, he could make out a splash of yellow on the person's upper body.

The second video showed someone on a motorbike speeding past the end of the street. Again, there was that flash of yellow. It appeared the assassin had made his escape on a motorcycle wearing a yellow, high-visibility jacket.

That should simplify things, Harry thought. All he had to do now was to get his team to use CCTV to track the motorcyclist around the London area.

Sandy Sanders was less than impressed. 'Guv, do you know how many people ride around the city dressed in yellow jackets? Dispatch riders, takeaway delivery riders – even police officers. Needle and haystack come to mind.'

'I understand,' Harry said. 'But we have little else to work with.'

He left Sandy to it; there was something he desperately wanted to do.

He looked at the note the maid had pushed into his hand and dialled the number. It was answered almost immediately.

'Is that Brigitte?'

'Yes, who's this?' The voice sounded guarded.

'This is DI Black.'

'Who?'

'Harry Black. You gave me a message to call you.'

'Oh yes. I hope you didn't mind me approaching you like that, but I didn't know what else to do.'

Harry recognised an Irish lilt in her voice.

'That's okay,' he said. 'How can I help you?'

'It's more the fact that I can possibly help you.'

'Go on.'

'It's a bit delicate, and I might be mistaken.'

'Please go on,' Harry said, willing the woman to come to the point.

'I think my boss, Charles Brandon, had something to do with the shootings.'

9

They met later that day in a small pub in Denham village, on the outskirts of London. Brigitte was looking very different out of her work uniform. She had on a brown, leather-look skirt and a thin, white jumper that accentuated her figure.

'So, what have you got to tell me?' Harry asked, sipping from a glass of tonic water.

'It's not what I have to tell you, it's what I have to show you,' she replied, placing an envelope onto the table. Harry opened it and shook out the contents. A selection of photographs stared up at him.

'The lady featured is Petra Brandon, in case you didn't already know, Inspector.'

He whistled softly. 'Good God!' he exclaimed, recognising some faces in the photos.

Gathering up the pictures, he sifted through them one by one.

'These are interesting,' he said. 'How did you get hold of them?'

'Besides my regular duties, I do some cleaning for Mr

Brandon. He normally clears his office desk on a Tuesday so that I can polish it. However, this week I couldn't make Tuesday but cleaned his office on Wednesday instead. Mr Brandon didn't know I had changed days, so his paperwork was still on the desk, together with this envelope. I wasn't sure if it was rubbish or not, so I peeked inside and saw the pictures.'

Harry smiled. 'So you then examined the photographs one by one to check for quality control?'

She looked slightly embarrassed. 'I admit I shouldn't have done, but... What happens now?'

Harry shrugged. 'Nothing. As it stands, they are just a private selection of photographs that belong to Mr Brandon. You're the one that has technically broken the law by stealing them.'

Harry placed the envelope back on the table.

'I don't understand. What made you think that Charles Brandon had something to do with the murder of Giles Cranberry?'

'This,' she replied. She reached in her bag and handed Harry the blackmail letter.

When he'd finished reading it, his face was sombre. 'Who on earth wants Brandon to resign so much they have to blackmail him?'

'Cranberry, of course!' she said. 'It's obvious. Brandon must have had Cranberry killed because he was blackmailing him.'

Harry looked at her. She obviously hadn't thought it through. 'What about the MP Peter Finch? He was gunned down as well. Are you going to tell me he was also involved in the blackmail?'

'Perhaps he tried to kill Finch as well because he was having an affair with his wife,' she said defensively. 'Finch is in one of the photos.'

'That means nothing. We don't actually know they're having an affair. They could just be friends who were photographed together. However, these photos could still somehow be connected to the crime.' Harry tapped the envelope. 'You'll need to get these back before they're missed.'

'Don't you need them?' Brigitte asked.

'It would be tantamount to theft, and if your boss is involved, stealing these photos could compromise any case brought against him. But I'll make some copies.'

Harry used his phone to take photographs of the letter and the images. He replaced everything in the envelope and handed it to Brigitte. 'Will you be okay putting them back?'

'Mr Brandon is in London, so the house is empty at the moment.'

'How long have you worked for the Brandons?'

'About two years,' Brigitte said. 'They recruited me some time after the accident. Charles was struggling to cope after the death of his parents. Petra was less affected, but it still devastated her.'

'What's she like?'

Brigitte looked at Harry sharply. 'You certainly want your pound of flesh, don't you?'

'I'm sorry, I was just...'

She laughed. 'It's all right, I'm only messing with you!'

'So, this Petra...'

'She's all right, seems nice enough. I think she has a hard job putting up with Charles. Mind you, it looks like it might be the other way around,' she said, tapping the envelope. She sat back in the chair and crossed her legs. 'You don't believe Peter Finch was having an affair with Petra?'

'Two people eating together at a restaurant doesn't make them lovers.'

'That's a pity,' she said in a flirtatious tone. 'And I was

going to suggest a bite to eat. I've just received my pitiful weekly cash-in-hand allowance.'

Harry had found himself enjoying listening to her Irish accent and watching her sparkling, blue eyes. He thought she was actually very fanciable.

He tore the thought from his head. 'I have to get on,' he said, ignoring her not-so-veiled invitation. 'I'll be in touch. Can I offer you a lift somewhere?'

Harry ended up driving her most of the way to the mansion, dropping her off a few hundred yards up the road so that they wouldn't be noticed. He drove away, almost feeling as though he was indulging in an illicit affair. She had been friendly and flirty and was certainly attractive. However, he knew that any relationship was doomed to failure, given his track record. Besides, business and pleasure didn't always mix well, in his experience.

There was a message from Sandy to phone him. He returned the call. 'Sandy, what have you got?'

'Harry, this might be nothing, but a village police station received a visit from this extremely worried old man. He told them he'd been walking his dog in the area when his dog slipped the lead and ran towards this cottage. The man followed him into the grounds and saw a van being loaded with cleaning stuff.'

'What's that got to do with us?' Harry asked.

'When he got nearer to the property, two men came out. They were dressed like cleaners with aprons and stuff, and they were carrying what looked like a rolled-up carpet. This old boy swears he saw a human arm flop out. They apparently stuffed it back in and looked around but didn't see the old man who had ducked behind a tree freaking out with shock. He waited until they'd gone back inside the cottage and ran off to report it. When the local police went to investigate, there was no-one there. And although the weather had been wet, there were no tyre marks, and no evidence of anyone having been there for ages.'

'Perhaps the old man was imagining things,' Harry said.

'Because the old man was so insistent about what he'd seen, the local plod contacted the landlord of the property to allow them to look around.' Sandy paused dramatically. 'They could smell fresh paint as soon as they opened the door. This confused the landlord because he hadn't decorated in ages.'

'Go on,' Harry said, now very interested. 'Do we have a name for whoever rented the place?'

'No. It was some bloke who paid cash for a four-week let.'

'How many bedrooms does the property have?'

'I think it's three or four,' Sandy said.

'So, a single male rents a cottage that is much larger than his needs. He pays cash, and then disappears, leaving parts of the cottage painted, after which a wandering dog-walker thinks he's seen a dead body being carried out.'

'That's about the size of it.'

'I don't suppose we have a description of the man who rented the cottage?'

'Not as far as I know, guv, but I'll contact the landlord.'

'When you speak to him, tell him not to touch anything or let anyone into the property. We need to get over there. This could be our man.'

The cottage was situated idyllically. Trees, fields, and nature joined forces to provide a calming backdrop. The rain had stopped, and the clouds had lifted.

They walked towards the cottage where the owner was waiting. 'Am I allowed to enter my property now?' he asked grumpily.

'You can let us in, but I'd like you to stay out here,' Harry said.

The owner said something under his breath and

unlocked the door. As they walked along the hallway, the smell of paint still hung in the air. Harry went back to where the owner was waiting. 'When was this place last decorated?'

'About two years ago.'

'Are you sure?' Harry said.

'Of course. I'd know.'

'You need to see this, guv,' Sandy called from the hallway.

The walls were painted over, but the creamy colour wasn't quite a perfect match. Harry rubbed at the paintwork, staining his fingers. 'This has been recently done.'

They walked through the cottage, finding more of the same.

Harry suddenly bent down and lifted a piece of carpet from the skirting. 'Look at this.'

White powder had found its way under the carpet. Harry wet a finger and tasted it, grimacing. 'No idea what that is,' he said, 'but I don't think it's drugs.'

'I think I know what that is,' said the landlord, who had quietly followed them into the house.

'I thought I'd told you to wait outside,' Harry said impatiently.

The landlord ignored him. 'I'll bet that's plaster,' he said. 'Someone's made holes in the walls and they've tried to cover it up. They probably had a rave or something and caused damage. I'm going to ask for a bigger deposit in the future.'

Sandy looked at Harry. 'Bullet holes?'

Harry nodded. 'Perhaps. Let's get a team down here.'

By late afternoon, forensics had confirmed that a shootout had taken place, after which repairs had been made.

'Why would someone go to the bother of decorating after a gunfight?' Sandy asked. 'Why not just leave the place as it is, and get the hell away from the area?'

'I know something about this,' said a man wearing a white all-in-one. Rosko was the scene of crimes officer. He and Harry had worked together on many occasions. Rosko had a reputation for being annoying, weird, and brilliant.

He pushed his hood back, revealing a ponytail and Lennon-style glasses. 'There's been a clean-up.'

'What do you mean?' Sandy asked.

'When a professional hitman who is working for a government or a major organisation needs to hide a crime scene, they may call in a specialist cleaning department. They make any necessary repairs and clean thoroughly, leaving no traces. I've had experience of this before,' Rosko said.

'They can't be that good if they're leaving wet paint around,' Sandy said.

'Yes, but,' said Harry, 'if that old guy with his dog hadn't seen what he'd seen and gone to the police, it might have been weeks before anyone else came to the cottage, by which time the paint would have dried, and no-one would have been the wiser.'

'However, these professional cleaners don't always get it right,' Rosko said. 'Follow me.'

They went upstairs to the lounge. Harry could never get used to the idea of the so-called upside-down house.

Rosko pointed towards a window. 'There. What do you see?'

'A window with fresh paint, and putty marks around the edges of the pane,' Sandy replied.

'Good. That tells us that the window has been recently repaired. So it's reasonable to assume that it was broken beforehand. Yes?'

Harry's patience was wearing. He was in no mood for a lesson in forensic observations. 'That's pretty obvious, Rosko. Can you get to the point, please? We haven't time for this.'

'I'm coming to the point,' Rosko said with a touch of annoyance. 'In these situations, where there has been evidence of violent behaviour, one would examine the particles of the smashed glass for evidence of blood, DNA, and anything else. But because the window was repaired and the broken glass removed, we have to look elsewhere.'

'Where?' Sandy asked.

Rosko was looking smug. 'Open the window. It's all right – it's been dusted for prints.'

Sandy did as he'd been told.

'What do you see?' Rosko asked, ignoring the dark looks Harry was casting in his direction.

'Fields, trees...' Sandy sounded bewildered. 'What am I looking at?'

'Look on the walls.'

Sandy looked down at the brickwork.

'No, look up!' Rosko said impatiently.

Sandy looked up and almost immediately ducked back into the room. 'Bloody hell, guv, you need to see this.'

Harry stuck his head out and followed Sandy's example. Dried blood was spattered above the window. A lot.

Harry pulled back. 'Blimey. How did those cleaners miss this?'

Rosko smirked. 'Probably the same way as you did. They didn't look up. Maybe the light was failing, or they were in a rush.'

'It makes you wonder what else they missed,' Harry said.

'Indeed. I've something else. Come with me,' Rosko said.

Rosko had been one of Harry's instructors when he'd first started as a police officer, so Harry was used to his mood swings and occasional rudeness. Rosko's birth name was Michael Pasternak, the same as that of the seventies music presenter, Emperor Rosko, hence the nickname.

Rosko took them outside and led them to the other side of the property. Rosko pointed towards the upstairs window. 'Because there were tiny fragments of glass scattered on the ground, my guess is that someone made a leap and landed heavily.' He pointed to the ground. 'See there? Footprints. Two of them are deeper than the others.'

'Okay,' Harry said. 'My thoughts are that our man was staying here and got into a gunfight similar to the O.K. Corral. It looks like there was one fatality, given what the old man observed, probably more with all the bullets flying around, after which a van containing cleaners arrives.'

'That's about the size of it,' agreed Rosko. 'But I maintain that a major organisation is involved.'

'Why?' Sandy asked.

'Because it's unlikely that ordinary criminals would try to wipe clean a murder scene to this extent,' Harry said. 'These people weren't just trying to avoid being caught; these are people who wanted to wipe out history, which might point to a government agency being involved.'

'What, like MI5?' Sandy said.

'I don't know, but it's a possibility.'

Another of the forensic team approached them. He was clutching a bundle of newspapers.

'I found these stuffed into a dustbin,' he announced. He held one up to show the headlines to the group. 'It's all about the Tigerman.'

'It's our man, all right.' Harry said. 'The cleaners probably didn't know his nickname and possible connection and left the newspapers behind.'

Harry wasted no time. He drafted in additional officers who searched the gardens and surrounding areas, supplementing the work done by the forensic team.

'He could be dead, guv,' Sandy said. 'He might have been killed in the shootout. Or eliminated by MI5 and taken away in that van.'

The idea of MI5 or a similar body being involved seemed fanciful to Harry, but he reasoned that, if there had been a clean-up, then that might indicate the involvement of a professional entity.

It got later, and he decided to call it a day. As he drove off, a white-suited figure blocked his way, waving frantically.

'Rosko, what is it?' Harry asked.

'You told me to let you know the minute we found anything. Guess what? We found a fingerprint.'

'I'm not surprised,' Harry said. 'There's been a busload of people milling through the cottage.'

'However, no-one's been through the pile of newspapers we found in the bin. We found prints on the front pages and a colour supplement.'

'Good work,' Harry said. 'Let's hope and pray those prints belong to the Tigerman.'

10

Nick Marshall lay on the bed, his eyes closed. In his apartment high above the swimming pool, he could hear the splashing and shrill squeals of children playing.

Marshall was tired and ached all over. He'd stopped over at the safe house in London, where his friend Mike Jones had arranged proper medical treatment for his wounds. He'd then flown straight to Benalmádena.

He had an idea of the identity of "El Jefe," as the female assailant in Kuala Lumpur had called him. It had been kicking around in his head since that attack, and then had been reinforced after the incident at the cottage.

Why would someone seemingly try so hard to kill him and fail? It had to be someone who was either totally incompetent, or wanted him to know that he was being toyed with. There was only one man he could think of who would have a such a hatred of Marshall – Eddie Vance, his ex-boss. Eddie Vance had to be El Jefe.

While Marshall had been staying at the safe house, he

had called in a couple of favours and now knew Vance was somewhere around the Costa del Sol.

Although Marshall wanted to find Vance, he was under no illusions that Vance might find him. Sure, he had discovered a tracking device back at the cottage, but wouldn't put it past Vance to have an alternative hidden somewhere.

He lay for a while longer, listening to the mixture of English and Spanish voices floating in from the open doors that led out to the balcony.

A louder scream prompted Marshall to open his eyes and roll off the bed. He walked stiffly out into the late morning sunshine.

Peering down over the balustrade, he watched the people sunbathing around the poolside. Hotel staff wearing red waistcoats ran around balancing trays of drinks. Everything looked normal. He could see the beaches in the distance, multi-coloured parasols protecting recumbent figures from the heat.

There were no other buildings nearby that were higher than his apartment, so a sniper would have difficulty getting an accurate bead on him – not that he was expecting to be shot at. But his instinct to cover all possibilities was a habit.

Marshall had already gone against his better judgement by choosing a holiday apartment over a house, because he had got it at short notice, and for a good price, which had given him the idea of also renting the apartment next door under a different name. He would keep his luggage in one and sleep in the other.

He didn't feel that this paranoia was unjustified. In recent times, he had been stabbed and shot, a tracker had been hidden in his luggage, and he'd been involved in a shootout at the cottage. He had experienced many close calls in his professional life, but this felt as though unseen forces were gathering, probably headed by Eddie Vance.

Lying back on the bed, Marshal stared up at the swirly fan. Eventually, his eyes closed.

A few hours later, he awoke feeling refreshed. He looked at his watch; it was now early evening, and the noise of the children from the pool below had abated. Realising he was starving, Marshall showered and dressed, stuffing his Glock into the back of his belt.

He left the apartment, making his way along the corridor. As he entered the lobby, the lift doors opened and a man stepped out, waving something gun-shaped in Marshall's direction. Marshall reached for his Glock, but at the last minute realised the man wasn't a threat. He let his hand fall by his side.

The man smiled happily at Marshall and held his electric drill in the air. 'Hola, señor, mucho trabajo. So much work to do.'

Marshall nodded at the maintenance man, turned on his heel, and went back to the apartment. This wasn't good. Recent events had unnerved him to a point where he was permanently on high alert. He could easily have shot the maintenance man. He needed to calm right down or he would become the danger. He pulled out the Glock from his belt and placed it in the courtesy safe in the wardrobe. It didn't really matter where the pistol was hidden; he just didn't want it in his possession for the moment.

Marshall walked down to the promenade which hosted a plethora of restaurants and bars, most of which seemed to be British owned, judging by the national flags that adorned the frontages. Each of the restaurants had someone standing outside enticing new custom.

He walked past the gauntlet of offers and eventually came to a quiet, badly-lit Spanish restaurant. It was the least touristy of all the establishments. He didn't feel like rubbing shoulders with excited holiday makers.

He dined on grilled fish and salad, and the addition of a large brandy made him feel that perhaps he could relax a little. He left a generous tip and took a wander along the seafront. The night air was cooling and pleasant after the warm day.

Romantic couples strolled hand in hand. Groups of young men talked loudly as they sought their evening's entertainment. Shouts of excitement filled the air as a hen party danced past, wearing flashing devil's horns. The experience was hell, but at least Nick Marshall felt reasonably safe.

He stopped outside an English pub and peered through the open door. Inside was a giant screen on which was a game of football, watched by a noisy, jeering crowd. The bar was packed with male revellers waving euros at the harassed bar staff. He backed out hurriedly and walked along to what looked like a quiet cocktail bar, the outside of which was illuminated by a champagne glass motif.

Inside, he sat by the bar, ensuring that he had a view of the door and could watch the street through the large window.

'What will you have?' The girl behind the bar was young, dark haired, and spoke with an English accent.

Marshall thought for a moment. He probably shouldn't be drinking; he really needed all of his faculties. But he also needed to unwind.

'A large Jack Daniels with coke, please.'

The girl poured his drink, and then walked around to his side of the bar and pulled out her phone. 'It's raining in England,' she said, studying the screen. 'Is that where you're from?'

'That's right,' he said, quickly gathering a story. 'From Kent.'

'Wow,' she said. 'That's amazing. We spent some time living in a small village called Darenth.'

'Small world. That's a nice bangle you're wearing,' he said, changing the subject.

'Thank you. I like your pendant.'

Marshall looked down. His pendant had poked its way out of his shirt. 'It's very special to me. What's your name?'

'Chelsea,' she replied. 'Are you here on holiday?'

'Yes, just for a couple of weeks.'

'That's nice,' she said. 'Whereabouts are you staying?'

'I'm at–'

Another woman appeared behind the bar. She nodded pleasantly in his direction. 'Good evening.'

He smiled back politely.

'Everything all right, Chelsea?' she said.

'Yes thanks, Mum. Everything's under control. This man is here on holiday.'

The woman smiled again. 'How lovely. How long are you here for?'

'A couple of weeks. Maybe more.'

The woman stuck out a hand. 'Well, I hope we'll see more of you. I'm Rachel and this is my daughter Chelsea.' She looked at his empty glass. 'Can I get you a refill?'

Marshall considered his options. He really needed to keep a clear head, however, he'd already had a couple of drinks, and desperately needed to relax, even for one evening.

'Why not? Another JD and coke, please.'

'What do we call you?' Rachel was asking.

'Andy,' he replied. 'Andy Lincoln.' He'd prepared a name, just in case.

He looked at her properly. In the soft light, she appeared to be an attractive forty-something-year-old with long, wavy, dark hair and intelligent, soft, brown eyes.

'I'm going now,' Chelsea said, putting on a denim jacket.

'Don't be late, darling, and don't make a noise when you come in, like you normally do.'

'Yes, Mum,' she said, rolling her eyes. 'Nice to meet you, Andy.'

When Chelsea left, they sat by the bar in companionable silence, with just the sound of passing revellers wafting in.

'Are you here on your own, Andy?' Rachel asked.

'I am,' Marshall replied.

'So, no wife, girlfriend, or children?'

'None of those, and no boyfriend either,' he said, his eyes twinkling.

'Oh sorry, I didn't think about asking if you were gay,' Rachel said, looking mortified. 'That's okay,' Marshall said. 'But just for the record, I'm not. What about you, anyone in your life, apart from Chelsea, of course?'

'No husband, boyfriend, or girlfriend,' she said with a grin.

They talked softly for the next couple of hours, Rachel sharing some of her life experiences, Marshall giving an edited account of his. The Spanish breeze that wafted through the open doors and windows was a welcome relief from the heat of earlier.

Eventually, Rachel stood and picked up a bunch of keys. 'I'm going to close the doors now.'

'Okay, I'll be off,' Marshall said, picking up his glass and draining the contents.

'No need for you to go,' Rachel said quickly. 'It's just that at this time of night, most people go back to their apartments or want to go nightclubbing. All we would attract now are old guys who want to get drunk and chat up the bar staff.'

'You make it sound like a bad thing,' observed Marshall with a smile.

'Now, now.' She smiled back. 'Would you like a refill?'

Marshall pushed his glass forward and sat back in his chair. Coming to Spain had been a good idea, and although he was here to find El Jefe, there was no reason why he couldn't combine business and pleasure.

11

Harry returned to his flat, tired and hungry. He had a lot to ponder on.

His brain felt scrambled with the recent patchwork of events. So many questions. Why were two people being shot simultaneously by different gunmen? What was the link between the two men? Who would benefit from their deaths? What started the shoot-out at the cottage and was a government agency involved?

He put the kettle on, and then immediately turned it off, reaching for the bottle of whisky instead. Taking a seat, Harry gratefully gulped some of the single malt. The alcohol seemed to lend him some perspective.

Then he looked around at the mess that still haunted his flat and set to work. Two hours later, everything looked tidier, and the whisky bottle was half-empty.

He had just flopped onto the sofa when his phone rang. It was Brigitte.

'Hello there,' he said, trying not to sound as if he'd drunk too much.

'I hope you don't mind me phoning,' said the warm Irish

voice, 'but I hope I haven't caused a problem.'

'Go on,' Harry said, suddenly sobering up.

'I was replacing the photographs and letter in Mr Brandon's office, and he suddenly came in. I nearly shit myself.'

'What did he say?'

'He just asked me what I was doing. I told him I was looking to borrow his stapler. I don't know if he saw me putting the stuff back in his drawer, but he looked kind of edgy... Sort of nervous, I suppose.'

'What happened then?'

'Nothing really. I left, and he called me back. I must admit that I was frightened. He asked me if I still wanted the stapler, because I was leaving the office without it. I said yes, and then had to wait around while he tried to find the damn thing.'

Harry laughed. 'It sounds like you made a slight pig's ear of the entire episode.'

'It wasn't funny,' she said. 'Had I been pregnant I'd have given birth there and then.'

Harry laughed even more and could hear her joining in. 'Thank you for letting me know.'

'There's one more thing,' Brigitte said.

'What's that?'

'I was wondering if you'd like to come out to play?'

'I'm afraid I can't,' Harry said, and then decided to be honest. 'I'm over the limit to go anywhere.'

'Are you on your own?'

'Yes, I am.'

'I could come to your place and pick up a Chinese on the way.'

Harry suddenly remembered that he still hadn't eaten. The whisky had temporarily dulled the desire for food, but now he was starving. He also knew that his resistance was low, and it probably wasn't wise for her to come to his flat.

'Tell you what,' he said. 'I'll get a taxi and meet you at a restaurant, and I'll pay for dinner.'

'Okay, you're on,' she said. 'When and where?'

An hour later, they were studying menus in Harry's favourite Chinese restaurant. In his opinion, their chicken chow mein was the best around.

'Are you a wine drinker?' Brigitte asked.

I'm an everything drinker, he thought.

'Yes, I enjoy the occasional glass or two,' he said.

'I prefer two.' She laughed. 'What shall we have, or have you had too much already?'

'I'm slightly oiled, but I think I'll cope.'

Harry chose a decent bottle of Bordeaux that had somehow sneaked its way onto the otherwise dull wine list, and selected a variety of dishes from the menu, including his favourite chow mein.

By the end of the evening, and another bottle later, things were getting blurred, as far as Harry was concerned. He was seeing shapes of people floating towards him, and then Brigitte's face appearing close to his own. Then everything seemed to fade.

He awoke the next morning, his head doing its familiar stomp after an alcohol-fuelled evening, and stared blearily at the window. The drawn curtains were leaking in the morning light.

Bit by bit, the memories of the previous evening seeped into his consciousness. As he turned onto his back, a sudden awareness shook him wide awake.

He was naked!

He never slept naked.

Shit. What the hell happened last night? He tried to rack his brains. He didn't remember saying goodbye to Brigitte. But then again, he remembered nothing. So, had they...?

He heard the flush of a toilet and a tap running.
Oh fuck, shit, and heavenly bollocks.

The bedroom door pushed open and there stood Brigitte, a smile on her face. She was fully clothed. 'Cup of tea or coffee?'

'Tea please. Do I... do I have anything to apologise for?'

'Don't panic, nothing happened. I slept on your couch. Very comfy too.'

'But I've got nothing on.'

'I know. I undressed you and put you to bed.'

'What?' Harry didn't know which he should feel – embarrassment or shame, or both. 'Was I that drunk?'

Brigitte smiled again and went off to the kitchen.

Harry quickly rolled out of bed and got dressed. He joined Brigitte, who was rummaging for anything that could pass for breakfast.

'I was going to go shopping,' he said lamely.

'Don't worry,' she said. 'Toast will be fine.'

'I'm sorry I was so out of it. I hope I wasn't a nuisance.'

'You were the perfect gentleman,' she said. 'It was a lovely evening. The meal was lovely, and the company was great. We must do it again soon.'

'I need to recover from this one first,' he said, looking in the kitchen cupboards. 'Where's the bloody aspirin? My head feels as though there's a spear going from ear to ear, and I need to get to an urgent meeting.'

∼

THE MEETING TOOK place in "The War Room" in the Farrow Road station. It was essentially a disused canteen that had been boarded up and painted. No-one quite knew why it was named The War Room, but meetings could be held without interruption because it was tucked well away from the offices above.

Seated around the table with Harry were two of his sergeants, Sandy Sanders and Dawn Koorus, who had already proved herself to be efficient and brave, and was also Sanders' not-so-secret romantic partner.

A tap at the door heralded Sergeant Carl Copeland. 'Traffic.' He shrugged, as if to say "not my fault."

Copeland had been promoted to the rank of sergeant in recent times, although Harry sometimes wondered how. Copeland had so far shown hints of immaturity. But had also revealed flashes of brilliance.

'Carl,' Harry said, 'let's be honest. I've never known you to be early.'

Harry stood up.

'Okay, we have two incidents. The murder of Giles Cranberry and the attempted murder of the MP Peter Finch. Although they took place at the same time, I think it's safe to assume that they were separate shootings organised by the same person or persons. We need to find the connection.'

Harry took a jug from the centre of the table and poured himself a water. He downed it straightaway and poured another.

'Night on the tiles, was it, guv?' Carl Copeland asked.

'The two shots,' Harry continued, ignoring him, 'came from two different locations. In fact, they were almost opposite each other. One was from the construction site, the other came from a block of flats.'

'Perhaps both shots were aimed at Cranberry, but one missed and wounded Finch,' Dawn Koorus observed.

'It's possible, but unlikely. Professional hitmen rarely miss their target.'

'How do we know for certain they were hitmen?' Copeland asked.

'I think it's a safe bet to make that assumption, given the high profile of both victims and the distance from which they fired both shots,' Harry said, taking another sip of water, silently vowing never to drink that much alcohol again. 'Also, the shootout at the cottage could indicate rival gangs or a group of people who were after the so-called Tigerman. Either way, these are people who are used to handling firearms.'

'Talking of which, guv,' Sandy said, 'if the body that was removed from the cottage belongs to the Tigerman, then surely we're wasting our time.'

'We can't assume anything at the moment, because we actually know nothing. The circumstantial evidence points to an assassin making his escape from a construction site and turning up in a semi about a mile away, where he speaks to our one and only witness, a four-year-old boy.'

Harry looked around the table.

'And the man the child witnessed may not even be the Tigerman. It may just be an assumption by us, and the press.'

'In a court, that would be worse than circumstantial,' Dawn said. 'Flimsy, in fact.'

'I have a question, guv,' Carl Copeland said. 'What happened to the Tigerman's yellow construction helmet? He couldn't have worn it to ride the bike. He would have had to swap it for a proper crash hat.'

'Carl, there are times when I know that your promotion to sergeant wasn't just a fluke. Uniform searched everywhere – bins, wastage containers, gardens, high-sided vehicles, and shrubbery. It's possible that his bike had a carrier on the back, and he swapped the headgear.'

Harry paused and drank some more water. He was perspiring and feeling washed-out. 'We've now identified some footprints at the cottage as being the same as ones found in the little boy's garden.'

'Has that helped us in any way?' Dawn asked.

'No, unfortunately. There were also several sets of tyre marks in the outside vicinity of the cottage, one set of which was definitely that of a motorcycle. Another set possibly belonged to the van that took the body or bodies away. Whilst they cleaned the surrounds of the cottage well, they couldn't erase all the tyre marks leading to their ultimate destination.'

'But in real terms, we have nothing,' Copeland said.

Harry looked at Carl Copeland.

'That's right, we have nothing, at the moment. We have a jumble of potential leads that might take us somewhere, or nowhere. Think of this as a giant game of Jenga. If we can pull out one good bit of evidence, then the whole lot will come crashing towards us.'

∼

THAT EVENING, when Harry arrived back at his flat, he was in good spirits and feeling better than he had earlier. It had been a good meeting, and now everyone was up to speed.

He put the kettle on and wandered into his lounge, suddenly aware that the flat was neater and cleaner than usual, with books and CDs in their proper places.

The carpet was freshly vacuumed and there was a smell of polish in the air.

When he fetched milk from his fridge, he saw that it too had been thoroughly cleaned, and was freshly stocked.

He frowned. Brigitte? Why would she?

But he'd left her alone in the flat earlier when he'd gone to work. So who else could it possibly be?

Harry went through into the bedroom, where he saw a feminine-looking overnight bag sitting on the bed. His clothes were in a neatly folded pile, not strewn on the floor as they had been earlier.

In the bathroom, he found a strange toothbrush sat next to his own. Surely Brigitte hadn't moved in. Perhaps having witnessed his drunkenness the previous night, she had decided that he might need a carer.

Just as he was pondering this latest development, he heard a key opening the front door. He stiffened. Then, to his relief, he saw the welcome figure of Alex Jackson. She hadn't changed – the Annie Lennox looks, complete with the short, boyish hairstyle still warmed his heart.

'What a surprise,' he said. 'What are you doing here?'

She looked at him, her green eyes piercing and cold.

'You gave me a key, remember?' She certainly wasn't happy.

He and Alex had got together after successfully catching a serial killer who targeted cheating husbands. They had grown close and Harry had thought it may turn into something special. But things got in the way, as they always did in Harry's life. Alex had returned home to Scotland for personal and career reasons.

They hugged, but within the embrace, Harry could feel a tenseness. 'Are you okay?' he asked.

'Yes,' she replied, but the tone of voice didn't match the reply.

'Are you sure?' Harry pulled away, looking into her eyes.

'Yes, I'm fine,' she almost snapped.

Harry moved on. 'So, what are you doing down here? When I hadn't heard from you for a while, I decided to…'

'Get another woman into your life double-quick?'

Ah, there it is, he thought.

'Alex, there's no other woman in my life, and even if there was, it wouldn't–'

Suddenly, there was a confident rap on the front door.

Surely not, he thought. *Please God. Fate wouldn't be that cruel to me.*

He opened the door and there she stood.

'Brigitte, come on in. Brigitte meet Alex, Alex meet Brigitte.'

Harry motioned for her to enter, shut the door, and then stuffed his hands into his pockets resignedly.

12

He awoke the next morning to more splashing and shouts of joy from the pool area.

Staring up at the fan, he watched it cast its spinning shadow around the room. He was alive. That was good. He hadn't been murdered during the night. In this profession, you had to be thankful for things that others took for granted.

He sat on the edge of the bed, contemplating his next move. His well-thought-out plan now had a hole. A very large, gaping hole.

His machine-like existence had kept him safe over the years. He didn't do intimate relationships – at least not proper ones. His sexual needs were met, almost mechanically. No names, no attachments, no succumbing to shallow emotion.

Sex was sometimes paid for. Afterwards, a little distant small talk. Then she would be gone, probably onto her next client, leaving him with an emptiness that he knew couldn't be filled. Instead, that void was taken up with the energy of planning each job. This was his chosen life.

However, last night, something unusual had taken place.

Perhaps it was because there was a strange and unwelcome vulnerability that had been thrust on him because of recent events. Or maybe it was just time for change.

Meeting Rachel had thrown him off course.

They had sat together and talked well into the night. Most of the talking came from Rachel simply because she had an authentic life to talk about.

He had hung onto her every word, nodding and smiling encouragingly when she paused. Marshall caught himself studying her and enjoying her every movement – the way she flicked her long hair back over her ears with her thumb, how she covered her mouth delicately with her fingers when she laughed, which was often.

Her life had been tough. Rachel had brought Chelsea up on her own after an abusive, controlling marriage. She told him how she had walked out of the relationship with two-year-old Chelsea cradled in her arms and had run down a street in the middle of the night with her drunken husband hollering after her.

Her Uncle Thomas had taken them in and looked after them for the next few years.

The husband had contested the divorce, but Uncle Thomas had gone around to his house, after which the husband had gone quiet. All Uncle Thomas would tell Rachel was to always play bullies at their own game.

They had pooled their resources, moved to Spain, and bought the cocktail bar, which originally was a run-down, shabby tavern with a reputation to match.

Over the years, that had changed. Now they had a good solid business looking after their regulars and welcoming new clients, most of which were holiday makers. Rachel and Uncle Thomas ran the business between them, with Chelsea doing shifts behind the bar in between college and a varied teenage social calendar.

Rachel had impressed Marshall with her quiet determination, her refusal to be upset by her past, and her insistence that her ex-husband hadn't been all bad. She clearly had strength and fortitude, and also had intelligent, blue eyes that had seemed to look into his soul.

Several times, she had tried to turn the conversation towards him, and he had to deflect her questions without appearing evasive. It hadn't been easy, and there had been a part of him that had screamed out to him, "Tell her everything. Tell her the truth!" But obviously he couldn't. He couldn't even tell her his real name. Instead, he trotted out his standard blurb that he had been in sales.

'What did you sell?' she'd asked.

'Intelligence software to governments,' he'd told her, feeling unusually guilty and shabby, almost as though he were sullying her with his lies.

They had talked for hours until the sound of Chelsea arriving home from her evening out prompted them to call it a night. They, however, planned to meet the next day. It was Uncle Thomas' turn to be on duty, so she was free to see him for lunch.

The thought of the appointment spurred Marshall into action. He only had a limited amount of luggage with him and only one set of decent clothes, so he went into town and kitted himself out with some new gear.

It turned out to be worth it.

'You look nice,' was Rachel's greeting as they met up. She kissed him on the cheek and slid her arm through his as they walked to the restaurant.

They sat at an outside table and enjoyed a seafood lunch whilst watching the world go by.

The streets of Torremolinos were busy, and as they looked on, Marshall couldn't help feeling that they were being watched. He ignored the thought and concentrated on the woman opposite.

She was even more lovely than he had remembered from the night before. That daylight had replaced artificial lighting did nothing to diminish her beauty. The soft Spanish breeze was blowing her hair into her face, and her almost familiar habit of flicking it back endeared her to him even more.

They finished with coffee, accompanied by a glass of Ron Miel, a honey rum.

After their lunch, they took a walk through the markets, Rachel stopping occasionally to feel the quality of the cloth of the garments that were on sale and making general comments. Marshall was barely listening to a word. He was too wrapped up in the unfamiliar feeling of intimate togetherness. He found it bewildering, but wonderful. It was as if a being from another planet had taken him over.

They strolled down to the beach and, taking off their shoes, walked along the soft sand. Rachel skipped in and out of the water's edge, laughing as the sea ran over her bare feet.

At the end of the beach, there were steps carved out of grey stone, but erosion by the sea had taken its toll and navigation back to the promenade was treacherous. She smiled delightedly as he took her arm to steady her as they navigated the uneven path.

When they reached the promenade, they carried on holding hands. He noticed that her grip was firmer. They walked along without speaking. Marshall was lost in his own thoughts and enjoying this new experience.

'Shall we have a drink?' Rachel suggested.

They sat down at a beachside bar and ordered a couple of glasses of Tropical, a Spanish beer.

'Salud,' she said, raising her glass at him.

At that point, a large, swarthy man with a cap and sunglasses appeared, wielding a camera.

'A photo of the lovely couple?' he asked.

As Marshall looked up, behind the photographer, he could see a figure in a dark shirt and jeans watching them. The man had an intent expression on his face that set him aside from the passing holidaymakers. The man looked away quickly, but Marshall was on his feet.

'I'll make a lovely picture for you,' the photographer was saying, his body obscuring Marshall's view.

'No, thank you,' Marshall said.

'Andy, why not? I'll pay,' Rachel said, fumbling for her purse.

Marshall glared at the photographer. 'No photos. Please go away.'

The photographer shrugged and went to the next couple.

Marshall looked around for the man who'd been watching them, but there was no sign.

'Andy, what was the problem? It would have been nice to have a photo together,' Rachel asked, looking puzzled.

But now Marshall's mood had changed from flighty romance to harsh realism.

He was a killer, a hitman; that was his job.

He felt stupid to have allowed soft emotions to get the better of him.

'We have to go,' he said. 'I have things to do.'

'What's going on?' Rachel said, dismay on her face. 'We were having such a lovely time.'

Marshall's insides were in turmoil. He was also putting this lovely woman at so much risk.

'We must go,' he said firmly.

They walked in silence along the promenade, Rachel looking miserable and dejected. They took a taxi back to Rachel's bar, where there were people waiting outside the entrance. Some were peering into the window.

'That's strange,' Rachel said. 'It's closed.'

'Why is that strange?' he asked.

'We always open at four.' She looked at her watch. 'It's now nearly five. Uncle Thomas is never late opening.'

'So he's late today. These things happen.'

Rachel shook her head. 'The lights are off and the doors are still shut. Something's happened.'

An alarm bell rang inside his head. He pulled her around the corner of the building, out of sight of the waiting customers.

'What are you doing?' she asked.

'Listen to me,' he said. 'You're saying this has never happened before?'

'No. Never.'

'Who would normally be behind the bar now – apart from Thomas?'

'Just Uncle Thomas. Chelsea is out with her friends.'

'Good, that's something.'

'What do you mean?'

'Look, Rachel, I know things are probably seeming strange to you, with the photographer and everything else, but I can explain... Well, sort of. Would you please trust me for the moment?'

She looked up at him for a few seconds, then nodded, fear appearing on her face.

'Good. Now listen, but don't be alarmed. I'm going into your bar, and I want you to stay here. I'm sure there's no reason to worry, and I'm probably being overcautious.'

Rachel was now looking even more anxious. 'Andy, you're really frightening me.'

'Just trust me for a few minutes.'

Marshall approached the bar and let himself into the private entrance at the side of the building. He stopped and listened, his senses on alert. There was silence. He moved quietly through the room, noting the crates of beers lying behind the bar ready to be put into the bottle fridges.

Someone's started to open up for business and stopped, he thought. There was a bag of money on the side ready to be counted into the till, next to which was a ceramic mug half filled with tea, on which was inscribed "Best Uncle in the World!"

Marshall felt the mug. It was stone cold.

There was an opening that led to a hallway, beyond which were stairs. He presumed they led to the living quarters. He suddenly felt a waft of freezing air. It was coming from a half-open door, which opened into the walk-in beer store, where bottles of wine and beer were being chilled.

There, propped up against the wall, was a man who Marshall assumed to be Uncle Thomas.

He'd been stabbed in the throat.

His sightless eyes were still open, and one arm trailed by his side. The other lay across his chest, as if someone had placed it there. His clenched hand held a piece of paper.

Marshall prised open the fingers and unfolded the note.

It was a message. "Kilroy. You have evaded us, but your new lady and her daughter won't. The boss wants to speak to you. If you refuse, you know what will happen. This is a one-time offer."

He read the note a second time, trying to adapt to this sudden change of events. He knew that by allowing himself to be captured by them, he might save himself. But Rachel and Chelsea? He didn't want to think about it.

They had to act quickly.

He looked down at Uncle Thomas. 'I'm sorry I never got to meet you,' he said, before closing the man's eyes.

13

Harry put the kettle on for the second time in an hour. It was as if he wasn't in the flat. Peals of laughter came through from the lounge as the two women talked loudly and animatedly.

They're getting on so well, they'll be on the wine before long, he thought.

After the initial awkwardness, the women had quickly established that there was nothing to worry about and had busied themselves getting to know each other.

However, Harry knew it wouldn't end there. The idea of another woman putting him to bed whilst drunk and then waking up hungover and naked would be a permanent source of amusement as far as Alex was concerned.

He took the tea through to the lounge.

'I'll take you both out for a bite to eat shortly,' he said.

'What, you want to go out to a restaurant two nights running?' Brigitte asked. 'Couldn't you remember what happened first time around?'

They collapsed into giggles.

'Anyway,' said Alex, 'there's plenty of food here. I filled up your empty fridge, which was absolutely minging, by the way.'

'I can't stay to eat, anyway,' Brigitte said. 'I have to get back and prepare for breakfast duty tomorrow morning. I only popped round to make sure you were okay.'

'That was very kind of you,' Harry said. 'But as you can see, I'm fine.'

Brigitte said her goodbyes and gave them each a hug as she left.

'See you soon,' called Alex, as they waved her off.

'You both seemed to get on well,' remarked Harry.

'Yes, she seems lovely. I'm sorry I got the wrong idea. Even though I had no right, anyway,' Alex said.

'No, you had no right. We hadn't spoken for weeks. You even missed my mum's funeral.'

'I sent flowers. Didn't you notice?'

Harry hadn't noticed. On the day of the funeral, he hadn't really taken anything in.

'I also sent you a card. You probably haven't opened it yet.'

Harry looked at the mantelpiece, where there was still a stack of unopened envelopes.

He smiled at her apologetically. 'Fair enough. But why haven't you been in touch?'

'I could ask you the same thing!'

'Okay. Touché. I see you have an overnight bag with you.'

'Yes, a bit presumptuous, I suppose. I'll obviously sleep on the couch,' Alex said.

'You'll do no such thing. If anything, I'll sleep on the couch.'

Alex leaned forward. Harry couldn't be sure, but her green eyes seemed to hold a trace of mischievousness. 'Are you seeing anyone, Harry? You know, having a relationship?'

'No.'

'Then I'm sure we can share a bed again, can't we? We

could top and tail, couldn't we?' This time, her eyes were definitely sparkling.

The two shared a basic supper and a few glasses of wine, and swapped memories of a previous case.

'Did you hear Mainwaring got promoted to superintendent?' Harry asked.

'No, we hear nothing north of the border. Good for her, though. I think she had an awkward start but came good in the end.'

'True enough,' agreed Harry. 'She seemed to act like a dictator at first, then she suddenly turned into a mother figure. How long are you down for?'

'Just a couple of weeks. I took some holiday that was owed to me, and as I didn't get down for the funeral, I thought I'd pay you a visit, and visit friends down south at the same time.'

'You can stay as long as you want. Use this place as a base, if you like.'

Alex looked at him softly. 'I'm sorry I haven't been in touch.'

'Me too. I was guessing you and your cheating ex-boyfriend had got back together again.'

'That would never happen. Anyway, he and that tart he took up with are married now. Good luck to them. They deserve each other.'

Harry smiled at the venom in her voice. 'As long as you don't bear a grudge!'

Alex laughed. 'I don't, actually. I look back and realise that I had a really lucky escape.' She gave Harry a look. 'Do you think that if I hadn't come down, you and Brigitte might have got together?'

'Don't go there,' Harry said. 'She's very nice, but she's a potential witness.'

'A witness?'

'Well, a sort of witness. She's actually put me in a bit of a difficult situation,' Harry said, rubbing his head. He was still getting itchiness on his scalp from the fire, even though it was a long while ago.

'Tell me more.'

Harry told Alex about the photos of Charles Brandon's wife that Brigitte had shown him in the pub, and then showed her the images of the photos that he had taken.

'Okay, does this make Charles Brandon a suspect?' Alex asked.

'Not exactly, but he might be a person of interest. Although he was with Cranberry and Finch at the time of the shooting, he could still have organised the hit.'

'But why would Brandon have Cranberry killed?'

'There could be two reasons. Cranberry might be the blackmailer. Or Brandon could have the oldest motive in history, jealousy. He may have discovered that Cranberry was one of the many men that Petra was seeing behind his back.'

'Petra?'

'Yes. The woman in those photos is his wife, Petra. As you can see, she seems to like the intimate company of men.'

'Intimate is the right word,' she said, looking at the photo of Petra naked with Nigel Kendall.

'Yes, that was a strange one. Everyone thought he was gay.'

'Perhaps he's a bit bi.'

'How can someone be a *bit* bi?'

'I don't know how it works.' Alex laughed. She looked at the photo again. 'Interesting position.'

Harry couldn't be certain, but Alex sounded flirty, so he pushed it further. 'It does look interesting. Based on evidential research, I think we need to ensure that the position is physically possible.'

He waited for her to take in what he was proposing, trying his best to look innocent.

She looked up at him. 'I thought you'd never ask.'

The next morning, before the alarm went off, Harry was already awake and had his arms folded behind his head. He was lost in thought. He looked at the recumbent figure next to him, and gently pulled the sheet away from her face, watching her breathe.

She opened her eyes and smiled. 'Hello.'

'Will you be here tonight?' he whispered.

'Would you like me to be?'

'Of course,' he said. 'Perhaps I could show you some other photos.'

She giggled and pushed at him playfully. 'You sound like a dirty old man when you say it like that.'

Harry put on his best leer. 'Who says I'm not?'

Later that morning, Harry was behind his desk. He'd already dealt with a mountain of emails and paperwork, but now he was just staring out of the window, lost in thought.

Alex's arrival had once again turned his personal life upside down. He hadn't expected to see her again, and her reappearance into his life was very welcome. But at the back of his mind was the fact that she'd left without warning a few weeks after they had first got together.

Was that because of him? Had her situation in Scotland become a dilemma for her? He'd always been very careful to not put pressure on her and knew she needed space and time to think. Christ, they both did. He'd seen two sides of Alex. At work, she seemed clear-sighted, determined, and talented. At home, she was soft and vulnerable.

There was part of Harry that had been pleased with her jealousy at the thought of someone new in his life, despite her having disappeared for a while.

Would he and Brigitte have got together had she not arrived?

He would like to have thought not. However, after his drunken night at the restaurant with Brigitte, he wasn't so sure. Especially after shamefully waking up naked in bed the next day.

He focused his mind on Brigitte.

She came across as a fun-loving, impish character who seemed to have scruples, but she had been so quick to want to cast aspersions on Charles Brandon's character – particularly with such little evidence. Yes, the photos were damning, but not for Brandon. He was the victim. Or was he? Harry knew better than to take things at face value.

The person who would most be adversely affected was Petra Brandon, whose reputation was at stake. Harry could understand how that also could affect Charles Brandon's reputation, and could see how that could lead to him being blackmailed. But he couldn't understand why Brigitte had gone to such great lengths to put the Brandon name in the frame.

He rang her number; it went straight to voicemail. Of course. She was probably working and wouldn't be allowed to have her phone switched on.

Harry picked up the phone again, this time dialling the number for the Brandon household.

14

The sturdy gates swung inwards as he arrived, and minutes later, the door was being opened by Charles Brandon. Harry was once again standing inside the grand hallway.

'Inspector, so nice to see you again. Please come on through.'

Brandon led the way into the ornate drawing room. Harry went for the same comfortable chair he'd sat in on the previous visit.

'I should leave you that chair in my will, Inspector. Would you like some tea?'

'Thank you,' Harry said, sitting back and getting further enveloped by the leather-clad padding.

A maid appeared almost immediately, dressed in her black-and-white uniform. Harry was disappointed it wasn't Brigitte.

'Would you like something to eat, sir?' she asked.

'Not for me, thanks,' Harry replied, patting his stomach. 'I need to cut back a bit.'

The maid smiled. 'You're looking fine, Inspector.' She turned to Brandon. 'And sir, what will you have?'

Brandon looked at his watch. 'Yes, I'll have a little something. Perhaps some of your home-made scones.'

When she'd gone, Harry remarked on how well the staff had been trained.

'Thank you for saying so,' Brandon replied. 'I must admit it is a matter of pride.'

'However, you answered your own front door today.'

'I did,' admitted Brandon. 'We're short staffed at the moment. One of our team, Brigitte, who I believe you met on your last visit, had to fly back to Ireland today. Something to do with looking after a sick mum. So we are on the lookout for a replacement.'

Brandon stood up and gazed out of the window, his hands folded behind his back.

'So, Inspector, what's on your mind? You didn't come here to discuss my staffing situation.'

'No, I didn't,' Harry said. 'I'll be honest with you, I'm a bit stuck at the moment, and you seem to be the key that might unlock a few things.'

'How?'

'Giles Cranberry was murdered and Peter Finch was wounded. You were present at the shootings. You were friends with them both. You must know something that might help us.'

'Inspector, I have been through the whole scenario a thousand times. I can't make head or tail of it myself.'

'Someone must have had a grudge against Cranberry,' Harry said.

'Well, I suppose he wasn't the most liked person in the world. But that's the world of journalism.'

Harry nodded. 'I suppose. And what about Finch?'

'Finch is a good MP. They should have him stuffed and mounted. He actually cares about his constituents.'

'Don't you?' Harry asked.

'Yes, of course I do, but Peter will always go the extra mile. There have been plenty of times when he's put his hand in his own pocket and helped someone financially, like an old person or someone living on the streets. He hasn't tried to claim it back on expenses like his colleagues, either.'

They paused as the tea trolley arrived. Despite Harry's protestation, sandwiches, scones, jam, and cream were laid out in front of him, and he was given a bone china plate and a linen napkin.

'You certainly do things in style,' he said, helping himself. 'To get back to my question, if Cranberry was a man just doing his job and Finch, who by your reckoning is a bit of saint, why would someone want to kill them?'

'I don't know. The whole thing is deeply distressing.'

'Yes, but somehow, everything seems to centre around you.'

The maid put her head around the door. 'Is there anything else I can get you?'

The men shook their heads. 'We're fine, thanks,' Brandon said.

'I'll be off then, Mr Brandon. Are you sure you'll manage this evening?'

Brandon waved her away. 'I'll be fine, Monica. I've cooked for myself before. You enjoy your night off.' When the door shut, Charles Brandon leaned forward and whispered, 'There's no way I'm cooking my own dinner. I can't cook to save my life. I'll be going to a restaurant.'

'What about Mrs Brandon?'

'Petra? Oh, she's away just now. We have another house in South Wales, near the Brecon Beacons.'

'Wonderful,' Harry said. 'What does she do with herself down there?'

His face seemed to darken for a second. 'I suppose she entertains, goes for walks, relaxes... That sort of thing.'

'When is she due back?'

'I don't know. May I ask the reason for your interest?' Brandon asked. He had a slight edge to his tone.

'No reason,' Harry replied. 'I was just thinking about you coping on your own.'

Brandon laughed. 'It wouldn't make any difference if she was here or not. She doesn't exactly contribute to the household chores. She does the hiring and firing, and that's about it.'

'Then you'll be the one doing the hiring whilst she's away.'

'I guess so,' Brandon said, putting a dollop of jam on a scone. 'Although Brigitte will be hard to replace.'

'She did seem very efficient. What was her story?'

'Nothing to tell, really. She just arrived out of the blue wanting a job. We were desperate and took her on as live-in staff.'

'What did she do before?' Harry asked.

Brandon stroked his chin. 'To be honest, I'm not completely sure. Petra might know.'

'Does Petra keep details of all the employees?'

'No,' Brandon said. 'I keep them in my office.'

'And what about references?'

Brandon smiled. 'Petra has a thing about employing Scottish or Irish staff. She reckons they are the most hospitable and trustworthy. Brigitte and Monica are both Irish, as is the gardener.'

After Harry had left the Brandons' house, he tried Brigitte's number again, but with no luck.

He arrived back at his flat that evening to be greeted with a pleasant waft of cooking.

'That smells good!' he said.

Alex poured Rioja into an over-sized glass and handed it to him.

'Good health. How did you get on today?'

This feels wonderfully normal, having someone cook for you and enquiring about your day, he thought as he took a sip.

Over dinner, Harry filled Alex in on the day's events, including his visit to Brandon's mansion.

'So, Brigitte has gone back to Ireland, then?'

'Apparently so,' Harry said, helping himself to more spaghetti. 'Although it's very sudden. I'd have thought she'd have dropped me a text or something.'

'Why would she?' laughed Alex. 'You've only known her for five minutes.'

'True. There's one other problem, though. I can't now get my hands on the original photos and blackmail letter, should I need to.'

'You should have kept the original photos when Brigitte showed them to you.'

'Perhaps. Except there may have been a legal issue if Brigitte was actively involved, and I was concerned about her getting caught by Brandon.'

'Are you sure you didn't have a soft spot for her?' Alex asked.

'Having a soft spot is very different from fancying someone. Now get on with your spaghetti.'

After a minute, Harry put down his fork. 'I've had an idea of how you can help.'

'Oh dear.' Alex put down her fork and sat back. 'Your ideas in the past have ended up with me being locked in a room and then pretending to be a nurse in a hospital.'

Harry was getting excited. 'This'll be easy for you. I need

you to apply to be a maid at the Brandons' mansion. I remember Brigitte telling me when we first met that they paid her cash-in-hand, so you're not officially there. All you've got to do is find the photos and dig out what you can on anything else.'

'How do you know they'll take me on?'

'Brandon said that his wife normally did the hiring and firing, and she normally went for staff who were Scottish or Irish. You'll get the job.'

'Are you stark-staring bonkers?' Alex asked. 'What happens when the Brandons ask me about references?'

'We can make sure you have a written reference with you when you apply for the job. Honestly, you'll be fine. Judging by the way Charles Brandon was acting, he would take anyone on.'

'Oh, thanks!' Alex said, pretending to look offended.

'Will you do it?' Harry asked.

'Do I have a choice?'

15

They sat, facing each other on the twin beds. Rachel's eyes were red-rimmed, but now the crying had stopped. Chelsea, sitting next to her, was looking at Marshall with undisguised loathing. 'Why did you have to come into our lives? Uncle Thomas is dead, and now we've lost everything.' She put her head into her mother's shoulder and sobbed.

Marshall knew what to do in most situations, but this was different. His appearance into these women's lives had created massive upheaval and the death of the uncle.

After finding Thomas dead, on Marshall's insistence, they had fled the area. His only thought was to get them to safety. He knew that if he was going to have to deal with El Jefe, it would have to be on his own. If the two women were captured, he would be completely compromised. His plan was to get the two women to safety and then do what he had to do.

Before leaving the bar, the police had been called, and Rachel had made a statement saying she had discovered the body but knew nothing more.

The police had been sympathetic; apparently a fast-food vendor had been robbed and killed in the same region some days earlier. It seemed the authorities were taking the view it might be the same person.

Marshall had hired a car and driven them to a hotel in the Montes de Málaga, then booked them in under assumed names.

Much to Chelsea's disgust, Marshall had taken their phones from them. He reasoned that if El Jefe was powerful enough to have him tracked halfway across the world in Kuala Lumpur, then having their phones tracked would be easy.

It had suddenly hit him that there was a possibility the police could be in on it. After they had reported the uncle's death, he thought at the time that they were spectacularly incompetent. He realised that he possibly was being paranoid, but he trusted very few people at the best of times.

He had booked two rooms. His room was next door. He and Rachel hadn't had a chance to talk yet. Her immediate grief had overtaken everything. Uncle Thomas had been a major influence in both their lives.

The opportunity for them to have a proper talk came with Chelsea saying she didn't want dinner and was going to stay in the room.

They went down to the restaurant and sat together in silence.

The appearance of the wine server seemed to galvanise Rachel. After ordering, she looked hard at him. 'All right, Andy, as my daughter said, you have cost us everything. I suppose an honest explanation will be impossible for you.'

The verbal sting hurt. He felt like his armour had been penetrated.

'Listen, Rachel, I can't tell you everything, for your own safety.'

'Rubbish, Andy, or whatever your actual name is. It's the very least you can do. Today, I saw someone who I thought might be my Mr Right suddenly turn into Mr Wrong. When that photographer appeared, you changed character. You became unrecognisable to the man that I thought I might have a future with.'

He could see the glistening in her eyes as more tears appeared.

'Then my lovely uncle is murdered, and I have to give a statement to the police as if I'd found the body, keeping you out of the picture. If I didn't know better, and I'm not completely sure I do, I'd think that you had something to do with his death.'

'I know you don't really think that,' he said. 'Otherwise you wouldn't be here.'

They sat back and allowed the wine server to top up their glasses.

Then she leaned across the table. 'Just start talking. Otherwise Chelsea and I will be out of here, and trust me, I will go to the police and amend my statement.'

'You can't,' he said. 'And I'm not worried about me or the police. I'm worried about you.'

'Bullshit.'

Marshall was silent for a moment, painfully aware that her soft, brown eyes had hardened into pinpricks of distrust. He sighed, knowing that what he was about to say might change everything. But she deserved answers.

'Rachel, listen to me carefully.' His change of tone caught her attention.

He fished in his pocket and brought out the piece of paper that he had retrieved from Thomas's body, and then passed it to Rachel.

'This was from your uncle's killers.'

She read it. 'You're Kilroy?'

He nodded. 'Sort of. We all had code names.'

'Oh, for Christ's sake, now what are you talking about?'

'I'm about to tell you something which will make you look at me differently.' He cleared his throat. 'Rachel, this isn't the easiest conversation I'm ever going to have. We spent some wonderful time together, and despite only having met you a couple of days ago, I know that I have never enjoyed the company of a woman as much as I have with you.'

As he was saying this, Marshall felt exposed and, to his surprise, embarrassed.

'I'm going to lay my cards on the table. What you do afterwards is up to you. I won't blame you, whatever you decide.'

At that point, the server appeared for their order.

Marshall ordered a steak. Rachel said that she couldn't eat anything. After a little cajoling from the waiter, she accepted the offer of a special omelette made just for her. The waiter went off with a smile, and she once again fixed Marshall with a glare.

'You were in the middle of laying down your cards.'

He took a sip of wine and placed the glass carefully on the table, as if the action would help him with what he wanted to say next.

'My actual name is Nick Marshall.'

'Are you sure?' she asked tartly. 'Will you be someone else tomorrow? Perhaps Ed Sheeran or Prince William? If you've already lied about something as basic as your name, how can I believe anything that comes out of your mouth?'

'Rachel, I can't blame you for feeling like this, but there's little I can do about it. I used to work for an agency employed by the government. Our job was to ensure that some of the politically based requirements of our country were carried out smoothly. So, for example, if the UK brokered a peace deal with another country, it was our mission to ensure that everything went without incident.'

'Why wouldn't it?' Rachel asked, looking confused.

'Because there are people in the world who don't want the earth to turn smoothly. There are those who want to disrupt peaceful events because they have their own agenda.'

'Like who?'

'Like people that sell arms illegally. It's not in their interests to have world peace, is it? How would they survive? So we covertly monitored all aspects when a deal was being struck, and if we found someone who wanted to upset the UK government's plans for their own evil agenda, we would step in and remove the problem.'

'Remove the problem?' Rachel asked. 'Do you mean that you'd have to kill someone?'

He ignored her question. 'We were an extremely successful unit, and then I discovered something that changed everything.'

At that moment, the food arrived. Her dish was covered with a silver dome, which the waiter removed with a flourish. 'Your special omelette, madam. Your steak, sir.'

Rachel smiled her thanks at the waiter and turned back to Marshall. 'Go on.'

'I discovered my boss was crooked. He was leaking details of any potential investigations to the very people who were being targeted by the British government in exchange for money. When I made the discovery, I gave him the opportunity to put things right. He refused, thinking that I wouldn't dare, because if the agency would be shut down, I'd also be out of a job. But I went ahead with my threat, because I discovered that besides running the agency, he had his fingers in many other crooked pies.'

'What happened then?' Rachel asked, looking astonished.

'After I'd handed over unshakable proof to the Home Office of his illegal and dangerous activities, the agency was closed down immediately, and Vance was out of a job.'

'Vance?'

'That was my ex-boss's name. Eddie Vance.'

'So now Eddie Vance is in prison?'

'Unfortunately, not. The Home Office was in a bit of a predicament because the agency didn't officially exist. So instead, they did a deal with Vance and told him to leave the country.'

'Where did he go?' Rachel asked.

'I'll give you three guesses.'

'Surely not here, in Spain?'

Marshall nodded. 'That's the reason I'm here. I believe that Vance and his men have been tracking me for some time and want to get revenge because of my actions. My plan was to get to them before they got to me.'

'And now they are punishing you by going after us? And that's why Uncle Thomas is dead.'

Her eyes filled with tears again. Marshall handed her his serviette and gently rubbed her shoulder. The restaurant had emptied out. Marshall could hear the clatter of plates, as the clearing-up process took place. He could hear the excited chatter of two waitresses as they set out tables ready for breakfast. People doing ordinary jobs, living ordinary lives. His life could never be ordinary again.

'So, when the agency shut down, what did you do?' Rachel had picked up her knife and fork and was cutting into her omelette.

'I went freelance, but still get all my work through the government. The government contacts me though a handler, so I'm anonymous as far as the rest of the world is concerned. Then, out of the blue, I was attacked in Kuala Lumpur a few weeks ago. And recently, something strange happened during my last job, which resulted in two people being shot instead of the one I was allocated.'

Rachel had stopped chewing. Disbelief followed by

understanding was spreading across her face. 'Am I right in thinking that you are a hired assassin – like a hitman?'

'Sort of.' He had a bad feeling that his admission was going to backfire.

She retched and spat a bit of omelette back onto her plate.

'Bloody hell. Last night when we met, I'd made plans to make love to you! We could even have had a relationship. Jesus Christ... You're nothing but a mass murderer!'

She pushed her chair back and ran across the restaurant towards her room.

The waiter was immediately over to the table, looking concerned. 'Did madam not enjoy our chef's special omelette?' he enquired.

∽

MARSHALL AWOKE the next morning with a feeling that something was wrong. His sleep had been interrupted throughout the night with dreams of being chased by demons, unseen forces waiting around a corner. He hadn't had such nightmares since he was a child.

After showering and dressing, he tapped on the adjoining door. No answer. *Perhaps they're downstairs having breakfast*, he thought. His instinct made him enter the room anyway.

Their bags were gone.

He ran downstairs and checked with the hotel staff.

The Spanish receptionist said, 'Ah yes. The lady and her daughter went earlier this morning. I booked them a taxi.'

'How long ago?' Marshall asked, looking at his watch.

'About an hour,' he said.

'Did they say where they were going?'

The receptionist paused, looking agitated.

'What is it?' Marshall asked.

'Please, the ladies said that if you ask their destination, I wasn't to tell you.'

'I know you're just trying to do your job,' Marshall said, kindly, 'but their lives are at stake. Do you want to be the person responsible for any harm that comes to them?'

The man shook his head. 'No, but I have to–'

'Look, I'll make it easy for you.' Marshall put his hand in his pocket and pulled out two twenty-euro notes. 'This is all the cash I've got. Now tell me where they went. Quickly!'

Minutes later, Marshall was in the hire car speeding down the mountain roads towards Malaga Airport.

After a delay, primarily caused by a broken-down school bus that had blocked most of the narrow road, he eventually arrived at the airport.

He ran into the building, his eyes scanning the terminal for the two women.

At the far end, there was a line of people waiting to check in. He ran towards them and almost skidded to a halt as he realised that Rachel and Chelsea weren't amongst them.

The people in the queue stared back at him.

'Has anyone seen two women...' He stopped short, knowing how ridiculous the question would sound.

Marshall looked up at the boards marked *Salidas* – Departures. There were no flights for another two hours.

He ran to the next floor where a glass partition showed the interior of the departure lounge. There was no sign of Rachel and Chelsea.

He forced himself to calm down. He knew he was behaving out of character and was probably being irrational. Their flight might already have gone. But where to? Perhaps they couldn't get a flight today and were staying locally. He had to find them. Wherever they went, their lives could be in danger.

Maybe they'd taken a detour and hadn't yet arrived at the

airport? Perhaps they'd bluffed the receptionist back at the hotel and weren't actually heading here at all? There were too many variables.

He had to think.

He ordered a coffee from the cafeteria, at the same time keeping an eye out for any new arrivals. Then Marshall heard a chair scraping on the floor beside him as someone sat down.

The next thing he heard overturned his world.

'Kilroy – or should I say, Nick Marshall?'

He froze. Nobody had called him that for a very long time.

'Mr Vance would like to have a word with you,' the voice continued.

He turned to look at the man.

If this had been a film, he would have expected a Humphrey Bogart type character to be sitting there wearing a pinstripe suit and a fedora hat. Instead, he was looking at a well-built, youngish man, with dark, curly hair and a full beard, wearing a T-shirt and shorts.

'I don't particularly want to meet Mr Vance,' Marshall said casually. 'I have plans for the day.'

'Those plans have just altered, Mr Marshall. I am not carrying a gun, but I have something that will persuade you to come with me right now.'

Marshall's heart sank. He knew what was coming next.

'They are a charming couple of ladies, your girlfriend and her daughter. Shall we go now? Mr Vance is so looking forward to seeing you again.'

16

Alex thoroughly enjoyed her first day working at the Brandons' mansion.

As Harry had predicted, getting the job had been easy. At her job interview, Alex had told Charles Brandon she had worked for much of her life in a small hotel in Galashiels which had recently closed down, because of the owner passing away. It had been left to the children who wanted to sell it on.

She had pulled out a crumpled envelope containing a personal reference from the family, which she handed to Charles Brandon.

Harry had actually written the reference and done the crumpling.

Brandon had asked her how soon she could start.

She wasted no time in getting to grips with her various duties, which included meeting and greeting anyone who came to the house, breakfast service, and office cleaning duties. Monica, the other maid, would help her with the morning kitchen duties, and afterwards, she would help Monica with the beds upstairs.

Alex was used to hard work, and so took it all in her stride. It was a pleasant change from her police work in Scotland; she knew what she had to do, and when to do it. It would have been easy to get into a routine, but Alex knew she had one purpose – to find the photos. Anything else would be a bonus.

Monica was a lively soul, five-foot-nothing and an Irish bundle of energy.

'How long have you been here?' Alex asked as they made the beds.

'I came here about two-and-a-half years ago,' Monica replied.

'Then you started here around the time that Charles' parents died?' Alex asked, remembering Harry's briefing.

'How did you know about that?' Monica asked.

Damn, thought Alex, *I was too quick off the mark.* 'I think Mr Brandon mentioned something about it at my interview. Did you get to meet them?'

'Yes, very nice people,' she said. 'Tragic accident. Terrible. Mr Brandon was very upset.'

'Is he married?' Alex asked innocently. 'He didn't mention a wife at my interview.'

'Yes, his wife is quite a forceful person. I think she wears the trousers.'

'I love your accent,' Alex said. She knew she was asking perhaps too many questions for a new recruit and should act a bit more normal.

'Thank you. I'm from Kilkenny in Ireland.'

'Ah, the Kilkenny cats,' Alex observed.

'You've heard of them? I'm impressed.'

'Yes, folklore says something about two cats having had such a vicious fight, that at the end, only their tails remained.'

'That's one of a few versions, but I'm even more

impressed! I haven't met any other English people who knew any of the stories.'

'Don't forget, I'm a Scot.'

'That explains it,' laughed Monica. 'Some of the English are so far up their own arses, they don't know what's going on in the rest of the world.'

They both laughed. 'Where's Mrs Brandon now?' Alex asked.

'She's away at the moment in Wales. They have a place there.'

'How lovely,' Alex said. 'How long is she there for?'

'I don't know. She's been there for ages.'

'Maybe she's got a fancy man,' Alex laughed.

'You say that jokingly, but there might be truth in that,' Monica replied, looking around to see if anyone was listening.

'Really? Tell me the gossip!'

'Nothing to tell, for sure. But there are rumours she sees plenty of men behind Mr Brandon's back.'

'So, when you say she wears the trousers...'

'Except for when she doesn't,' Monica finished.

They both laughed.

The next day was Monica's day off, but she came in to make sure that Alex was coping okay. She gave her a hand with some chores and then went home after Alex had reassured her several times. 'I'll be fine,' she said. 'Enjoy your day off.'

As soon as Monica had gone, Alex had a look around. Brandon had already given her a tour after the interview, but only showed her a small part of the grand house. There were sixteen bedrooms, all of them empty apart from the one that Brandon was clearly occupying.

Alex went through each of the rooms noting the beautifully styled furniture and expensive carpets and rugs. The beds were permanently made up for any last-minute guests, and each of the bed coverings matched the decor of the rooms.

Alex was impressed. She walked into one of bedrooms and looked into the ensuite, which was equipped with the most expensive of toiletries. She looked out of the bedroom window and could see Charles Brandon standing on the patio next to some flowerpots, pointing something out to the gardener.

She ran downstairs and went to Brandon's office. The door was locked. *Damn.*

There was another room opposite, which had been missed off Brandon's grand tour. That door was also locked. From what Brigitte had told her, Brandon hadn't seemed to be that security conscious. Perhaps this was a new policy. She saw an ornamental wooden chair leaning against the regency-style wallpaper. She pulled it over, and was about to stand on it to look for a key above the door frame when she heard voices. She replaced the chair, quietly ran back up the stairs, and listened.

It was just Brandon and the gardener talking about the petunias and whether to get some more seeds. She could hear the gardener complaining about the pond and how some bloody idiot had thrown a load of rocks in and killed some fish.

Looking at her watch, Alex saw it was time to end her shift. What a waste of a day. She had nothing to show for it. Nothing that would help the investigation.

Alex returned to Harry's flat and went into the bedroom. She was about to take off her maid's uniform when she heard a sound. She went through to the lounge and saw Harry lying on the sofa, snoring.

She smiled to herself and tiptoed back to the bedroom, where she put on stockings and suspenders, and hitched up her skirt so the stocking tops were revealed, St Trinian's style. She put on her coat and buttoned it, concealing what she had on underneath. Alex giggled at what she was about to do.

Very quietly, she opened the front door, and then banged it shut, loudly, as if she'd just arrived. She stomped loudly through the hallway, shouting, 'Hello, I'm home!'

A sleepy Harry sat up on the settee as she came into the lounge. 'Hi, how did it go?'

'Hello, sleepy-head,' she said, unbuttoning her coat. 'I've got a bone to pick with you. You didn't tell me about their unconventional uniform policy, did you?'

'Unconventional uniform policy?' he repeated. 'What are you talking about?'

His eyes suddenly widened as the coat came off to reveal the stocking tops showing under her skirt.

'You had to work like that?' Harry asked disbelievingly, now sitting bolt upright, his sleepiness vanishing quickly.

'Oh, it's much worse than that,' she replied. 'They have a very strict policy about personal hygiene.' She sat on the chair opposite and pulled her knees up, revealing her lack of underwear.

Harry laughed, now fully awake. He gave her a leery look. 'Tell you what,' he said, 'I think I should give you a further interview for the job.'

'Go for it!' she said with a big grin.

∽

THE NEXT DAY, Alex was back working at the mansion. The breakfast dishes were long cleared away, and Alex and Monica were sitting in the staff area having coffee.

'Are you enjoying it here?' Monica asked.

'Very much,' replied Alex. 'It made me wonder why Brigitte left so suddenly.'

'It's a mystery to me too,' Monica agreed. 'One minute she was saying that she'd happily work here forever, the next, she was gone.'

'Did she tell you she was going?'

'She didn't tell me anything,' Monica replied. 'I first found out when Mr Brandon told me. He said she had gone back to Ireland, something to do with family.'

'Did you think it was strange that she didn't confide in you?'

Monica looked at Alex strangely. 'Why do you ask?'

'Well, you had things in common, like both coming from Ireland, doing the same job. That sort of thing.'

'I see. We shared a few girly secrets, and if I'm honest, when Mr Brandon told me she'd gone, I actually had the hump with her. But then I reasoned it was her business, and well…' Monica shrugged.

'I'm only surprised that Mrs Brandon hasn't come back from Wales to make sure that Brigitte's replacement is up to scratch.'

'You think Petra would come all the way here just for that? No chance.'

'Pity. I'd love to meet her. What's she like?'

Monica laughed. 'It depends on who she's talking to. If it's a man, they fall to her knees. If it's a woman, well…just be careful.'

'What's the story with her and Charles?'

'They met about three years ago. She had moved over here from Russia and was a model. Her real name is Petrova, but it got shortened to Petra.'

'Was she a fashion model?'

'Not quite. More glamour than fashion. She had been seeing someone for a while. In fact, I think they were engaged. And then she met Charles at a garden party, and bang, that was that.'

'How did you discover that she'd been a glamour model?'

'Her face, and her body, were plastered all over the internet. There were even rumours that she did favours for money.'

'What? You mean she...'

'Exactly.'

Alex sat back. 'Shit, who am I working for!'

'Don't worry, I'm sure you'll get on fine with her. She's nice enough, and I think you're similar ages.'

'So there's quite an age gap between her and Charles?'

'At least thirty years, I would say.'

'What was the attraction, do you think?'

'I'll give you three guesses.' She looked at the clock. 'Anyway, we'd better get on with our work. I've really enjoyed chatting with you. It made a pleasant change.'

When Alex got back to the flat that evening, she recounted the conversation with Monica.

Harry frowned and pulled out his phone. 'Sandy, do something for me urgently.'

'Guv?'

'I want you to check all flights to Ireland for a Brigitte Walsh. She would have travelled in the last twenty-four hours. Check the ferries too, just in case.'

'Will do.'

'What are you thinking, Harry?' Alex asked, as Harry finished the call.

'I was getting a bad feeling about Brigitte and her return to Ireland. One minute you're her new bestie and then she's gone. And then it turns out that Monica did not know about her departure either. Of course, it's possible that her mum is so ill that Brigitte had to tend to her, but you'd think she'd have time at the airport, or ferry terminal, to send a quick text.'

Sandy got back to Harry within the hour. No person of that name had landed in Ireland in the last seven days.

'Are you certain?'

'A hundred percent, guv. Could she have gone under a different name?'

That made Harry think. Was Brigitte as innocent as she had made out?

'Good point. We can tighten our search and also put together a timeline. She's obviously left the Brandons' house by foot or by car. There are CCTV cameras at both ends of the road outside. Sift through the footage and see if you can see anything.'

'Okay, guv.'

Harry got a phone call back a few hours later, just as he was going to bed.

'I have news, of sorts,' Sandy said. 'The road outside the Brandons' house isn't particularly busy, and there are two CCTV cameras – one a hundred yards to the left, and another about a mile on the right. There are no turnoffs, so I could cross reference all the cars in both directions. I also timed them to see if any of them could have stopped outside the house. Nothing for that twenty-four-hour period. Charles Brandon's car didn't leave the house, and the only way that Brigitte could have left would have been by foot, which would have been ridiculous if she's rushing to get transport to Ireland.'

'Are you sure?' Harry asked.

'Guv, any car that came out of the Brandons' house would have appeared on one camera but not the other,' he continued. 'But no car left that house in that twenty-four-hour period.'

'So, either Brigitte cut across the fields next to the house, or she's still there.'

'That's it exactly, guv.'

'If you are right, we are going to need a search warrant, which won't be easy, considering who Charles Brandon is. If we get this wrong, we will be in the shit, big time. So, I want you to do all that you've already done once more, and list and time every action taken. This will probably be the most important search warrant we've ever applied for.'

∽

GRAVEL SCATTERED into the air as the police cars ground to a halt on the driveway.

As Harry stepped out of his vehicle, Charles Brandon ran down the steps of his mansion, looking as though he was about to blow a fuse.

'What the fuck is going on?' he demanded, tightening the belt of his dressing gown.

'Your maid, Brigitte Walsh, has disappeared,' Harry said tersely.

'She hasn't disappeared. She's in Ireland. What's that got to do with me?'

'According to our enquiries, Miss Walsh never left these premises, which indicates that she's still here.'

'Would that be a crime if she was?' Brandon asked sarcastically.

'It would be if she was dead, Mr Brandon.'

'Dead? What are you talking about?' Brandon exclaimed, taking a step back.

'Mr Brandon, we are here to find Brigitte Walsh. Do you know where she is?'

'Christ, I've already told you. She went to Ireland because her mother was ill. She texted me, I can show you.'

'Anyone can get hold of someone's phone and use it to send a text. Did you actually see her leave?'

'You're being ridiculous. I can't be expected to monitor the comings and goings of everyone.'

'Then I am really sorry, Mr Brandon, but we must conduct a thorough search of these premises, ideally with your cooperation,' said Harry.

The team went through the house quickly and then concentrated their efforts on the grounds around the mansion. After a couple of hours, the officers were still searching, and Harry was getting frustrated.

He phoned Alex, who was on a day off from her domestic duties, and relaxing at the flat.

'Harry, how are you getting on?'

'Not very well. Alex, you know these premises better than us. If you had to hide someone, dead or alive, where would you put them?'

'I don't know... Does it have a cellar or loft? It's a big old place.'

'It certainly is. We've searched the entire house, cellar and loft included. We're looking around the grounds at the moment. If we find nothing, by this time tomorrow I'll be lucky if I have a job writing parking tickets. Even the gardener is leaning on his spade, looking at us as if we are stupid.'

Alex exclaimed as though remembering something. 'Harry, I heard the gardener complaining to Charles Brandon about rocks being thrown in some pond. Maybe there's a connection?'

'I thought the pond had been checked, but I'll take another look.'

The pond was at the far end of the estate, right on the perimeter. It was rectangular and stretched lengthways between two giant hedges, making it impossible to cross without getting wet.

Harry peered into the murky depths of the pond but

could see nothing. However, he could see that a whole load of rocks that had been thrown into the water.

'Are you all right, guv?'

He turned to see Dawn Koorus.

'I should ask you that question,' he said, eyeing the mud stains on her uniform and wet sleeves.

'All in the line of duty, sir,' she said with a grin. 'I was also investigating the pond.'

'It does seem strange that there are so many rocks in it.'

The pond was shallow, about a metre or so deep, and the rocks underneath the water had just broken the surface, making a sort of stepping-stone pathway to the other side. Had someone thrown the rocks in for that very reason? Or was something or someone buried beneath them?

He looked at the grass verge on the other side. It seemed as though the vegetation had been disturbed by something. A fox or a cat... a person?

Harry estimated the distance between him and the far side of the pond – about two long strides. A fit person could leap it thanks to the man-made steppingstone in the centre. He took a chance. His reasoning was that if he fell into the pond, it would just add to the whole sorry situation, making it even easier for the board to sack him. He could see Charles Brandon standing outside the house, arms folded, looking in his direction.

Taking a breath, he performed a two-step jump to the other side of the pond, nearly skidding on the damp surface as he landed. Standing still for a second, he sent grateful thanks heavenward. Then Harry carefully followed the trail of disturbed grass and squeezed through a prickly hedge, scratching his hands and neck. He stood on the other side, dabbing at his skin with a tissue.

'Can you see anything, guv?' called Dawn.

'Nothing yet,' he shouted back.

There was a steep ditch at the bottom of a long, grassy bank. Harry could see that the shrubbery had been disturbed. *Someone has been here recently.*

There was a disturbance behind him, and Dawn appeared, brushing off bits of hedge.

'Well done you, you pond-hopper,' Harry said. 'Let's just hope that we can both get back without falling in and getting soaked.'

Suddenly, some half-dozen officers joined Dawn.

'Did you all leap across?' Harry asked, looking impressed.

'No, guv,' replied Dawn sheepishly. 'The gardener found a long plank of wood in his shed and laid it across the pond. So we all just walked over.'

The officers scrambled down the bank, slipping and slithering on the mud. They reached the ditch and searched, beating down the long grass. A sudden shower of rain made the conditions even more difficult.

Eventually, there was a shout from one of the officers.

'Over here!'

Harry quickly clambered over, using his hands to steady himself.

The officer was looking ashen. 'I think it's her.'

17

They drove through the mountains; the engine screaming as the jeep strained its way up the narrow road. Marshall and his friends had visited the Sierra Nevada as teenagers, but this time, the experience wasn't as pleasant.

He was sitting next to the driver, his hands tied, and a cord securing his wrists had been pulled up onto one of the roll bars.

'Why bother?' he'd asked, when the man had produced the rope. 'You know that I'll come with you, given that you hold all the aces.'

'With your track record, Mr Marshall, no chance.'

They arrived at a plateau and came to a halt. The driver pulled out his phone and dialled a number.

'What are you doing?' Marshall asked.

'If I don't phone ahead, they will blast us to kingdom come. They do not take any chances.'

After speaking in rapid Spanish to someone, he put the vehicle into gear and carried on driving until they came to a gravelly clearing. There were stone steps hewn into craggy rock, under which was parked a battered, old Suzuki.

The driver untied the rope from the roll bar but kept Marshall's hands bound. He gestured for Marshall to go first and then gave him a shove, sending him sprawling into the dust.

The driver yanked him up and pushed him towards the stone steps.

They climbed up, the man keeping a firm grip on Marshall.

At the top, a guard aimed his rifle at Marshall's head. 'Don't give me an excuse to use this. El Jefe would prefer you alive, but...' He turned to the driver. 'I'll take it from here. You can go now.'

'Be very careful,' the driver said. 'He has a reputation.'

The guard spat on the ground. 'So do I.'

He unlocked a steel gate, which swung open to reveal comparative paradise.

A group of palm trees provided the backdrop for a stunning villa that looked out onto a huge terrace. A fountain sprayed water high in the air and was surrounded with copies of some of the world's best-known statues. Marshall recognised the Venus de Milo and Christopher Columbus, normally seen at the top of the famous monument in Barcelona.

A huge, kidney-shaped swimming pool took centre stage, at the side of which sat two figures that Marshall instantly recognised.

They both looked at him, but neither moved. Chelsea turned her head and faced the other direction as if she was disinterested, whilst Rachel looked at Marshall almost sorrowfully.

'I don't think they are very happy with you,' the guard commented.

He prodded Marshall to move away from the terrace and towards a group of outbuildings. The guard ushered him into a barn.

Marshall looked around. Although it looked old and worn on the exterior, the inside had been reinforced with concrete and steel.

'Where's Eddie Vance? I thought he wanted to see me,' Marshall demanded.

'Does it matter?' the guard said. 'Perhaps he changed his mind and just wants you dead.'

'Then why am I not dead now? You've had plenty of opportunity.'

The guard gave an unpleasant smile. 'Mr Vance wants to talk to you first. I understand that he wants to make you an offer.'

'What kind of offer?'

'I believe that there is some job that needs doing. Mr Vance will speak to you when he arrives. He is flying over from England and will be here soon.'

'Okay, that's fine,' Marshall said. 'I'll do the job. Now let the women go.'

'Let them go?' the guard said. 'Why would we release two good-looking women without having some fun with them first? You see Miguel over there?' He nodded over at a man with a pock-marked face and yellow teeth, who had taken over guard duty. 'He hasn't had a woman for months. Maybe a year, who knows? Perhaps when we have had our fun, it will be his turn.'

Marshall kept his face impassive. What he did for a living sometimes pushed his moral boundaries, but these people were at the bottom of the heap.

He was a little surprised. Eddie Vance had shown himself to be crooked and immoral, but Marshall had him down to at least to be stylish, certainly not someone who would employ people from the bottom of the gutter.

'Move.' The man pushed Marshall forward suddenly, again causing him to sprawl forward onto the filthy ground. *I wonder how many years of animal dung I'm breathing in*, he thought, as he used his bound wrists to push himself upright.

'Get in there,' the man was saying.

Marshall's eyes were adjusting to the gloom; he could make out a small cage in the corner of the barn. It looked like the ones used in the sheriff's office in westerns he had seen as a kid.

He looked at the man. 'Seriously?'

The guard nodded. He held a pistol in his hand. 'I'm not going to ruin a day lazing around a pool with two lovely ladies. This will save me from having to keep an eye on you. When Mr Vance arrives, you'll be let out then.'

'Can I at least have a drink?' Marshall asked.

'Of course.' The man laughed sarcastically. 'Would you like champagne? We'll give you all the home comforts we have!'

Marshall started to get to his feet, but the guard pushed him back onto the ground with his boot.

'Animals crawl into cages. They do not walk,' he said.

The guard padlocked the cage and left the barn. He arrived back a few minutes later holding a can of coke. He pulled the ring, squirting foamy spray towards Marshall, and tipped the can into his own mouth. He slurped noisily, and then threw the can at Marshall.

'There, you can have my leftovers.'

'I thought you might have a bit more class than that,' Marshall said, picking up the can with his bound hands.

The guard laughed. 'Look at you. I have tamed the Tigerman in his cage.'

He padlocked the iron door again, and then closed the big barn door, plunging the cage and the barn into darkness.

Marshall hunched forward and contemplated his situation.

The two women he had come here to save were almost certainly unaware of the danger they were in and were understandably perceiving Marshall as the bad guy. He reasoned these guards couldn't be part of Vance's inner circle. They'd probably been hired just to keep the place ticking over whilst Vance was away.

They certainly weren't professionals, that was for sure. They had already made several mistakes, one of which was keeping Marshall alive.

This so-called offer that the guard spoke about could only mean that Vance wanted Marshall to do something for him – most likely a hit that was considered impossible, but probably worth a king's ransom as far as Vance was concerned.

Even with the threat on the two women's lives, this would put Marshall into a quandary. He only ever worked directly or indirectly for the government, and only took on sanctions on people who were a threat to security or British lives. He considered himself a soldier, not a murderer. If Vance had a task for him, then it was almost certainly a job that was considered 'No Return.' That meant you were going to be unlikely to be alive afterwards.

Vance would keep the two women as hostages until the job was done and then probably kill him, anyway. Why wouldn't he? Nick Marshall had ruined his lucrative business.

Marshall had to get the women safe before he took any action against Vance.

He looked at the coke can he was still holding. When he asked for a drink, he couldn't believe his luck when the guard returned with it. He'd no intention of drinking the remainder of the contents. He just wanted the can.

He flattened it in the middle and then bent it backwards and forwards until eventually it weakened and tore in half. It left him with two halves of the can, both with sharp edges. One of those edges, he used to rub against his bonds, until eventually the ropes frayed, and then broke away, leaving his wrists free. He rubbed them whilst looking around his prison.

There was a sense of urgency within him. He knew that if he was going to make a move, it would have to be whilst there were only a couple of guards around. When Vance arrived, he would probably bring more men, and Marshall preferred the odds as they were now.

The iron bars of the cage went from floor to ceiling and looked as though they had been concreted in. The door to the cage was made of vertical iron bars welded together.

I wonder how many poor souls have been locked in here, Marshall thought, as he examined the padlock.

He heard someone approaching and sat back down in the same position as when the guard last saw him, wearing an expression of resigned defeat.

The light from outside was blinding as the heavy door to the barn was pushed open. The same guard was back. He stood, silhouetted against the brightness, and looked through the cage bars at Marshall, who sat hunched over, hiding the fact that his hands were no longer bound.

'Okay,' he said waving his gun, 'the boss will be here soon. Time to get ready.'

He inserted the key into the padlock of the cage. The door swung open with a clang.

'Let's go.'

Marshall made as if he was getting up, and then, in a single movement, rammed the sharp edge of the can into the soft bone under the guard's nose, then twisted the gun from his grasp.

The guard fell back and made a squealing sound, blood spurting down his chin.

Marshall brought the butt of the gun down hard on the man's head, and there was silence.

Marshall peered out to see if the noise had attracted any attention, but the thick, stone walls of the barn had deadened any sound. He could see the two women were still sitting on the edge of the pool, their legs dangling in the water. They looked more like holiday makers than captives. The other guard, who he now knew to be Miguel, was in his position, on a platform above the swimming pool. He had a commanding view of the mountainous area and all routes leading to the villa, including the stone steps that led to the front gate.

Below him was an ornate wall that surrounded the pool. Marshall estimated that if he kept low, he wouldn't be seen by the guard.

Miguel had his hand over his eyes as if searching the horizon. Marshall guessed that Vance and his team couldn't be far away.

Marshall stealthily made his way along the ornate wall, stopping to check that Miguel's attentions were elsewhere. He stopped behind the two women, still concealed from the guard.

'Ladies, please don't make a sound.'

Despite the request, the two women gasped when they saw him. Marshall glanced over at Miguel, who was still gazing into the distance.

'We need to leave now, and quickly,' he said urgently.

'We're not going anywhere with you,' Chelsea said. 'You've ruined everything. Uncle Thomas is dead, and we've lost our business and home. Just leave us alone.'

'Yes, it's my fault you're in this situation,' Marshall said. 'However, I wasn't the person that killed Thomas. That was one of Vance's men. Vance wanted to prove that he could get to me anywhere, and up to now, he couldn't force me to do anything.'

'Up to now?' Rachel repeated.

'The only reason we are all alive is because they probably want me to do a job for them. Without me, they have no further use for you. You will both be raped and murdered.'

The two women looked at each other.

'How do we get out of here?' Rachel asked.

'There seems to be only one guard on duty,' replied Marshall. 'Unless you've seen any others.'

'What happened to the guard who brought you in?' Rachel asked.

'He's having a lay down,' Marshall said.

Her daughter was still looking sullen.

'Look, Chelsea, I can't bring your uncle back, much as I'd like to. But I can protect you and your mother. All I'm asking you to do is to trust me for the moment, and when this is over, I will disappear from your lives forever.'

'How do we know we can trust you?' Chelsea asked.

'That's easy,' Marshall replied. 'Ask yourself, why am I still here still talking to you?'

Marshall looked up. The guard was taking a final drag from a cigarette before flicking it over the side of the rock.

'We need to move,' Marshall said urgently.

'What do you want us to do?' Rachel asked.

'I need the guard's attention to be over here so that I can get around to the other side of the platform. Can you help?'

Rachel whispered something in her daughter's ear, after which they nodded at Marshall.

'We've got an idea.'

THE GUARD SQUINTED into the far distance. He could see dust swirling and a vehicle glinting in the sunlight. The boss would soon be here. Glancing down at the far side of the swimming pool, he saw that the barn door was open. He frowned. Where were Jan and the prisoner? They had planned it so that when the boss arrived, the prisoner would be strapped to the chair, with Jan pointing a gun at his head. The boss would be pleased with their efficiency.

He peered again at the barn, his frown deepening.

Then he heard laughing and a swashing sound coming from the two women. One was dabbling her hand in the swimming pool. When he looked properly, he could see she was completely naked.

He was completely transfixed.

Miguel noticed that the younger one was also naked, but lying face-down on the lounger, exposing her firm buttocks.

He watched the older one scoop water from the pool and sprinkle it across her breasts, the rivulets running down her tanned stomach and towards the area between her legs. Miguel strained his eyes to glimpse her hidden treasure and moved towards the women to get a better look.

Suddenly, his ankles were being held in a vice-like grip, as he was pulled down from the platform, banging his head on the iron support. Before he had time to think, his rifle had been removed from his grasp, and an arm around his neck was cutting off his air supply.

∽

MARSHALL LAID the unconscious body on the ground and looked into the distance. A dust cloud was coming towards them. *Vance will be here in minutes.* He waved frantically at the two women, who quickly dressed and scrambled up towards Marshall.

Then he heard a phone ring. He rifled through the guard's pockets and found the device. The display read "El Jefe."

He took a chance and answered it. 'Sí?'

'Miguel, has Jan arrived with Marshall?' The voice was unmistakably Vance's.

'Sí.'

'Good. We'll be there in a few minutes.' The line disconnected.

'Right, we need to get as far from here as possible,' Marshall said.

'How?' Rachel asked.

'That's a good question.' Marshall once again turned his attention to Miguel's inert body, grabbing the keys that hung from his belt. 'By limousine, I hope,' he said. 'Come on, let's leave this paradise of evil.'

Marshall locked the iron gate behind them and hurled the key into the distance. They scrambled down the stone steps that led to the clearing where Marshall had been brought earlier that day. The battered Suzuki was still there.

'All right, not quite a limo,' Marshall said. 'But it'll have to do.'

'Where are we going?' Rachel asked.

'We don't want to bump into Vance and his men, and we can't go back to Malaga Airport because that's the first place they'll look for us. We'll have to head east and hope for the best.'

Marshall gunned the Suzuki into action, and with a cloud of dust, they were on their way. The car groaned its way up the track. When they reached a small clearing further up into the mountains, Marshall stopped and got out. He could see Vance's villa down below. The air was hot and dusty.

As he watched, two Land Rovers came to a halt below the villa. Both vehicles were the same shade of dark green. The occupants got out and walked up the steps. When they reached the top, he could see them attempting to open the iron door, and then bang it with their fists.

Marshall was pleased he'd thrown away the key but cursed himself for not having hidden the guard properly. After finding the body, they would be after them in no time. There was a sudden flash of light.

'Let's get going,' he said. 'One of them has binoculars. We may have been spotted.'

He got back into the Suzuki and drove as fast as he dared along the narrow, hazardous roads, praying that nothing would come in the opposite direction. The thought that Vance and his men were after them spurred him on.

They sped through a series of small villages, after which the track twisted and turned as they got deeper into the mountains. The road widened into a clearing. Marshall stopped and looked over the edge. Way down below, he could see the winding road on which they'd driven.

'What are you looking for?' Rachel asked.

'I not sure if Vance's men saw us. If we're not being chased, we can take it easier.'

A cold mist was descending onto the track as darkness started to fall. The women only had tunic dresses over their swimming costumes, which made them look respectable, but cold. They huddled together on the back seat of the car.

As Marshall studied the roads below, he could see the two green Land Rovers travelling at speed.

'Shit!'

'What's up?' Rachel asked.

'That's them,' Marshall said, quickly getting back behind the wheel.

'Can't we turn off somewhere?' Chelsea asked. 'We could turn off the headlights and they'd go straight past us.'

'Great idea,' Marshall said. 'However, we're on the side of a mountain, with a sheer drop on the right.'

He turned to look at her. Despite the darkness, he could see that her young face looked white and frightened.

'Don't worry,' he said with a forced grin. 'We'll be fine. I've got out of worse scrapes.'

He put his foot down and the vehicle surged forward. After a few miles, they drove up a steep incline, the Suzuki engine whining. The road had straightened, and Marshall could see the twin sets of lights behind them in his rear-view mirror. He estimated they were about two or three minutes ahead of their pursuers. They were now very high up. Just as the road levelled, the engine coughed and stopped.

'What's the problem?' Rachel asked.

Marshall could tell that she was desperately trying to appear calm in front of her daughter.

'I think we've run out of petrol,' Marshall replied, his foot going back and forwards on the accelerator as he tried to restart the engine. He turned off the Suzuki lights. 'Everybody out!'

'What are we going to do?' Chelsea asked.

'We're going to try and shorten the odds.' Marshall pointed to the side of the road. 'I want you two to climb up that slope and hide behind the boulders at the top.'

The women scrambled up the steep incline and huddled together behind a boulder.

Marshall pushed the vehicle, turning it so it was now facing the opposite direction, and then adjusted the steering wheel so that it would track the road in a straight line.

He could hear the throaty roar of the Land Rovers coming towards him. He waited until the first set of lights were closer, then gave the vehicle a push.

He watched the Suzuki slowly gather speed as it rolled down the hill and held his breath as it veered towards the rocky wall, expecting it to grind to a halt. But, like a ball in a pinball machine, the Suzuki bounced back into the middle of the road and went straight into the path of the leading vehicle.

The driver couldn't possibly have seen it until the very last minute, and swerved sharply, smashing through the thin barrier that protected vehicles from going over the edge of the sheer drop.

The Land Rover hung, half of the vehicle in mid-air, the other on the road. It swung like a seesaw before finally toppling over the edge and smashing onto the road far down below.

There was no explosion; just an eerie silence.

The Suzuki ground to a halt against the rock face, its job done.

The second Land Rover had stopped.

Under cover of the darkness, Marshall took the opportunity to quickly clamber up and join the women in their hiding place behind the boulders. He could hear the shouts of the men from the second vehicle, as they looked over the edge of the road and saw what had happened to their comrades.

Marshall noticed a solitary figure move away from the men and light a cigarette. The glow from the flare showed it was Vance.

'Damn,' he said under his breath.

He had been hoping that Vance had been in the car that had gone over the edge.

The men got back into their vehicle, but Vance remained standing, staring down at the carnage below. He suddenly looked up towards the boulders where Marshall and the women were hiding. It almost seemed Vance knew they were there.

Marshall ducked down instinctively.

'Marshall!' the man roared. 'If you can hear me, you know I can find you anywhere. Anywhere at all.'

From their position behind the boulders, Marshall held a warning finger to his lips.

'You have one chance to give yourself up. I'll allow the women to live. They can go free.'

Time stood still and hearts thudded as Marshall and the women waited, barely drawing a breath. After what seemed an eternity, there was the sound of a door slamming and a vehicle revving as they drove away.

Chelsea started to sob, her shoulders shaking.

Her mother put an arm around her. 'Don't worry, darling. It'll be all right... Won't it?'

The last couple of words were aimed at Marshall, who tried to smile reassuringly. 'Had they actually known we were here,' he said, 'they wouldn't have gone. They'd have combed the area until they found us.'

'What did that man mean? When he said he could find you anywhere?' Rachel asked.

Marshall shook his head. 'I'm not sure.'

But given what had happed so far, it was a fair question.

'We need food and rest,' he said, standing up and looking around.

'And where are you going to magic that from?' Chelsea asked.

'I have a sort of idea,' Marshall said, scrambling back down the slope.

When the two women caught up with him, he was examining the battered Suzuki.

'Lucky it didn't go over the edge as well. It means we have wheels,' he announced.

'Are you serious?' Rachel said. 'The front end is smashed. There's no way you can drive this thing.'

'I said we have wheels,' replied Marshall. 'I said nothing

about an engine. We're on a mountain. Providing we can steer and use the brakes, we might be able to freewheel down to the nearest village. Or at least get closer to it.'

The two women looked at him.

'Don't waste time,' he said. 'Get in.'

Marshall put the Suzuki into neutral and placed his foot on the clutch. The vehicle didn't move. He opened his door, put his foot on the ground, and pushed. The Suzuki started to lumber forward, slowly picking up speed.

Rachel said later that she'd been on many fairground rides in her life, but the experience of freewheeling down a winding, narrow slope at night, without lights, and a sheer drop to one side, was one of the scariest things she'd ever done in her life.

Marshall managed to cover a lot of ground in what was effectively little more than a go-cart, and eventually the ground levelled, where the Suzuki came to a halt.

'Everybody out. All change,' Marshall said jovially.

'How can you be so cheerful?' Rachel asked, clambering out of the vehicle, and suddenly realising her legs had turned to jelly.

'We're alive, aren't we?' Marshall replied. 'And look,' he said, pointing to a signpost. 'We're only a kilometre from the nearest village.'

Chelsea helped Marshall push the Suzuki off the road and into undergrowth. Together they covered it with branches and leaves.

What they'd thought was a village turned out to be nothing more than half-a-dozen Spanish fincas in a cluster. As they passed the first building, they saw the shutters were open, and the lights were on inside. They could hear a football match on a television, along with loud Spanish voices and cheering.

'That one looks like a possibility,' he said, pointing at a

finca at the end of the row. 'The shutters are closed, top and bottom. Perhaps the occupants are away.'

'What? Are you thinking of breaking in?' Chelsea asked.

'I'd say that was nothing compared to what we've seen and done today,' Rachel said.

Marshall grinned at her and went around to the back of the house. He prised the shutter open, unlatched the window, and climbed in. After a glance around, he opened the front door and waved the women into the finca.

'Mi casa es tu casa. It's not much, but it's home for the night.'

'You got in quickly,' remarked Rachel.

'It was quite easy. I don't suppose there is much crime around here, so everyone is quite trusting. Or there's nothing for people to steal.'

The fridge was switched off, indicating that the occupants might be away for a while. Marshall hunted in the cupboards and found a couple of tins marked fabada, a kind of Spanish bean stew.

'This'll do,' he said, pouring the contents into a saucepan.

'This will do even better,' Chelsea said with a smile, holding up a bottle of red wine. 'I don't care how cheap and nasty it is, I need it!'

They sat eating their basic meal, each alone with their thoughts. It was the first piece of normality they'd enjoyed for a while.

Marshall awoke the next morning with a sore neck, having slept on a small, uncomfortable sofa. Rachel and Chelsea had shared the only bed and looked rested, despite their recent traumatic experiences.

They breakfasted on more stew, washed down with bottled water, and left the finca. Marshall doubted that the property owners would miss some wine and a couple of tins, and would probably never know that their home had been invaded for one night.

He remembered the story of Goldilocks and the Three Bears. *Who's been eating my stew?*

'What are you smiling at?' Rachel asked.

'Nothing,' he replied. 'We need to keep going east. We'll try to flag someone down.'

'Who's going to stop for us?' Chelsea asked.

They walked past the fincas and nearly jumped out of their skins when a cockerel suddenly squawked its morning greeting.

As they reached the road, they heard a diesel engine.

'Be careful. It could be Vance's men,' Marshall said.

'No,' Chelsea said, shielding her eyes. 'Not unless they've taken to travelling by bus.'

As the vehicle pulled up, Marshall realised that he only had credit cards in his pocket. He turned to Rachel, who rummaged around looking for cash.

'What's the matter?' Chelsea asked.

'We need Euros.'

'No problem.' Chelsea pulled out a twenty, and after a brief exchange with the driver, sat down looking pleased with herself.

'Well done. You've saved the day,' Marshall said. 'Where did he say this bus was heading?'

'Almería. Apparently there's an airport there.'

Perfect, thought Marshall. His primary concern was the immediate safety of both women. After that, he could do what he needed to do.

The journey was long and hot, and after a few hours of discomfort, they were finally inside Almería Airport, enjoying the coolness of the air conditioning.

At the check-in counter, Rachel looked at Marshall. 'Where are we going?'

'You're going to safety. I have something left to do.'

'What are you talking about?' Rachel exclaimed. 'I thought you were coming with us. Where are we going?'

'The worst is over, as far as you are concerned,' Marshall said. 'You should be safe from here on. It's me they are after. You're flying to Gatwick. When you arrive, get the train to Victoria and then go to this address. When you get there, you'll need to show this.' He pulled a gold chain from his neck and handed it to Rachel. 'The pendant on this chain is very special to me and will prove to the person you give it to that you are who you say you are. Just answer his questions honestly. His name is Mike and he will look after you.'

Rachel took the chain and examined the pendant. Under a depicture of an eagle, there was an inscription that read, "To one brave man."

'What's this about?' she asked.

Marshall smiled and shook his head. 'That's not important. Just keep it safe.'

Rachel put her arms around his neck and gave him a hug. 'Nick, whatever you are about to do, be careful.'

He hugged her back. 'I'm sorry that I brought all these problems to your doorstep. I will try to make amends.'

Chelsea gave him a slightly self-conscious hug, and the women headed for the departure area. Marshall kept watching them until they were safely through airport security. Then he walked back outside into the sunlight.

His priority was to purchase a disposable phone. After making a couple of calls, he hired a car and set off for Malaga.

Although his mind was busy, he still enjoyed the views of the Mediterranean, with people on their sailing boats living very different lives than his own. Not for the first time, he wondered how he would fit into a different lifestyle.

When he arrived back at his holiday apartment, he was pleasantly surprised to find that the rooms he'd booked hadn't been trashed or searched. However, that wasn't to say they didn't know where he was.

After showering, he sat on the edge of the bed, enjoying some final quiet moments of normality. He thought of Uncle Thomas, who had selflessly done so much for his girls, and had been brutally murdered just so that Vance could make a powerful statement to Marshall.

He could hear children screaming with joy down by the pool and thought to himself that it could have easily been one of them. It was becoming clear that, these days, Vance didn't care about the divisions between innocent people and those who were in the same game.

Marshall's thoughts had turned to a dark place. He was now quarry-turned-hunter, and determined to bring the walls of justice crashing down on Eddie Vance's existence.

This was going to be a long night, and he was very much looking forward to it.

18

As hardened to death and violence Harry had become over the years, he felt deeply affected by the murder of Brigitte Walsh.

It surprised him, particularly as he'd only know her for such a brief time. He put it down to the rawness he still felt after the death of his mother.

He knew that the memory of discovering Brigitte's body would haunt him and his colleagues for a long time. He could still visualise her bluish-white skin, almost highlighting the marks around her neck where someone had forcibly ended her life.

He felt saddened that he'd never enjoy her company again. Her humorous wit and bluntness had engaged him. He was angry that anyone should have the power to end anyone's life, particularly someone as fun-loving and carefree as Brigitte.

Standing by his office window, gazing almost unseeingly at the traffic outside, he heard a knock on the door that interrupted his thoughts. It was the desk sergeant; he was carrying a package.

'Good morning, sir,' he said. 'This just came for you.'

Harry looked at him. 'Doing the office postal deliveries nowadays, are we, Frank?'

Frank tapped the package with a knowing look. 'I think you'll find this is special.'

'Special?' Harry said with a trace of annoyance. Frank was the station gossip and could rub Harry up the wrong way just by being in the same room.

'If you look on the reverse, you'll see it comes from beyond the grave,' Frank said.

'Just hand it over and get on with your business.'

An hour later, Harry was standing outside the gates to the Brandon mansion, speaking into the intercom.

'I can't see anyone. I'm busy today, Inspector,' Brandon's voice answered.

'Yes, I heard that's what you told my sergeant when I asked him to phone ahead. I'm afraid you're going to have to un-busy yourself. Now open these gates immediately.'

There was a pause. Harry heard the mechanism switch on, and the sturdy gates swung open. As Harry pulled up outside the mansion, a side gate was unlocked, and the gardener stood there.

'Mr Brandon asks if you would mind following me,' he said.

The gardener led him to the rear of the house, where Harry paused to look over the palatial lawns to the pond area, beyond which Brigitte's body had been discovered.

'This way, sir,' the gardener said, prompting Harry.

They entered a conservatory. Brandon was sat in his dressing gown, newspapers open before him.

'I can see that you are very busy,' Harry remarked.

Brandon ignored the thinly-veiled sarcasm. 'Look at this.' He held up the front page of one of the papers. The headline read, "Could Charles Brandon be the Keeper of the Tigerman?"

'They're suggesting that I'm in the frame for the murders of Giles and Brigitte. Am I, Inspector?'

Not for the first time, Harry wondered how the press got its information.

'Mr Brandon, you shouldn't be surprised. After all, Brigitte's body was discovered in the vicinity of your property.'

'But I had nothing to do with it.'

'That's something we are going to need to determine.'

'What do you mean?'

'Well, you're either very unfortunate, or in this up to your neck.'

Brandon said nothing but sat back in his seat. Harry thought he was suddenly looking aged.

'Mr Brandon, you were present at the shootings of Giles Cranberry and Peter Finch. The next moment, one of your members of staff is found murdered on the perimeter of your property. What do you have to say?'

'I agree it looks somewhat peculiar, Inspector, but surely you don't really think that I–'

'Mr Brandon, it really doesn't matter what I think. My job is to establish the facts and then try to link them together with the intention of identifying the guilty. My problem is that the vast majority of the people on this planet will go through their entire lives and not be present at a shooting. Most people will never ever have a murder take place on the boundaries of their property. And yet, here you are, amazingly having achieved both within a short space of time. I'm sure you can see my problem, Mr Brandon.'

Brandon nodded. 'I suppose so. I admit it doesn't look good.'

'Now,' Harry continued, 'if you can tell me anything that

may be relevant, now would be a good time. Think of it like a one-time offer. You tell me everything you know, and I'll take the view that you are trying to help. If you bullshit me now, I'll treat you like any other suspect.'

Brandon raised his arms expansively. 'Of course, I'll tell you anything that might be relevant.'

'No, you won't,' Harry said brusquely. 'You'll tell me anything and everything that may or may not be directly related, and you'll start now by telling me the events leading up to you being blackmailed.'

Brandon's face changed. 'What? I don't know what you're talking about.'

'You are a stupid man,' Harry said. 'That was your only chance. Now I'm afraid we'll have to make it official.' He stood up. 'Charles Brandon, I'm arresting you on suspicion of the murder of Brigitte Walsh...'

As Harry read him his rights, he could feel something withering inside the man.

'All right, all right,' Brandon said, putting his hands up in surrender. 'You don't have to do this. I'll tell you everything.'

Harry was grateful that there were no witnesses; he was hardly doing this by the book. He sat back down and waited.

'You're right,' Brandon said. 'I am being blackmailed. However, it has nothing to do with the shootings outside the Garrick Club or the tragic murder of Brigitte.'

'You can't know that,' Harry said. 'But please continue.'

'I received an envelope in my in-tray at the Commons containing photos and a blackmail note. I presume you've seen these?'

Harry nodded.

'They want me to step down or the photos will become public. That's it, Inspector. That's all there is. I have received no other form of communication. I promise, there's nothing more to tell.'

'Who else knows about the blackmail threat?'

'Just Peter Finch. I had to tell someone. Petra is in Wales – not that I'd have worried her, anyway. Nobody else knows, apart from the blackmailer and whoever gave you the information.' Charles Brandon gave Harry a quizzical look. 'How *did* you get to know about the blackmail?'

Harry smiled thinly. 'I received a package from, as my desk sergeant put it, beyond the grave. It's actually from Brigitte, and it contained the pictures and the letter. She took it upon herself to remove it from your office and send it to us.'

'But why would she do that?' Brandon asked.

Harry reached into his inside pocket and took out a small envelope. 'This is a letter that she sent with the package. The back of the envelope reads, "From Brigitte Walsh. Please give to DI Harry Black urgently." Without even reading the contents, you can see that she has concerns.'

He unfolded the letter and cleared his throat.

'"Dear Harry, I have the feeling all is not well. I think CB saw me returning the envelope, and I am worried that he'll hide it somewhere else, and I know that you'll need it. Hope to see you again soon. Brigitte, x."'

'So that's what she was doing at my office desk. I thought there was something amiss.'

'She obviously didn't trust you to do the right thing, Mr Brandon. An opinion which I now share, given your reluctance to come clean.'

'With respect, you're not the one being blackmailed. It's impossibly hard to determine the best way forward in my situation.'

'But you're a senior politician, someone who is supposed to be a champion of the legal process, and yet here you are, almost muddying the waters of our investigation by not telling the truth. Even Brigitte thought the blackmailing was somehow linked to the shootings. She had come across the evidence in your desk, but she worried perhaps it might get into the wrong hands. So she guaranteed it got into the right hands by sending it to us before her murder.'

'Do you think she knew that her life was in danger?' Brandon asked.

'No,' Harry replied, 'otherwise she would have said as much in the letter. However, it raises an interesting point, doesn't it?'

'What's that?'

'Motive, opportunity, and means – the three components of a murder. That Brigitte's body was found near your premises shows opportunity and means, which just leaves motive. Perhaps you discovered Brigitte had removed the photos, and you confronted her. Maybe things got out of control and you inadvertently killed her. Or you deliberately murdered her to shut her up.'

Brandon's mouth dropped open. 'You surely don't seriously believe that I had anything to do with Brigitte's murder?'

'It's not about what I believe. It's about the facts. You'll be put on trial by the media anyway, like it or not.'

'What happens now?' Brandon asked.

'In the light of your confirmation that you were being blackmailed, you're going to need to come down to the station and make a formal statement.'

'Do I have to come with you in your car?' Brandon asked.

'Not necessarily. Why?'

'Because as I'm not under arrest, I'd appreciate it if it looked as if I were helping the police and not being coerced.'

'Who would ever know, one way or the other?' Harry asked, confused.

'I'll show you.' Brandon led Harry to the drawing room and pointed through the lattice windows. 'Look.'

Harry could make out a man perched in the upper

branches of a tree outside of the gates of the mansion. He didn't need to take a closer look to know that there would be a telescopic camera lens pointing in their direction.

He shook his head in wonder. 'Sometimes I think the people who work for the press take more risks than we do.'

Harry looked around.

'Where are all your staff today? I've only seen the gardener.'

Brandon laughed humourlessly. 'Staff? What staff? It seems Monica and the new girl have both left my employ. Monica told me she was leaving because of the upset about Brigitte's death, and I'm assuming that the new girl left for the same reason.'

Harry breathed an inward sigh of relief. He knew he'd been stupid to use Alex as an undercover worker. It could have blown up in their faces.

'That's a shame,' he said. 'I'm only sorry that I can't reciprocate your kind hospitality down at the station. I think we're low on salmon and cucumber sandwiches. However, I might be able to rustle up a meat pie from the canteen. They're very good.'

19

The next day, Harry sat reading through Brandon's statement. It seemed full and concise. However, Harry was mindful that without the official evidence relating to Brandon's blackmail, they would have been no further forward. He leaned back in his chair. Were they actually further forward? Had anything in Brandon's statement helped?

He re-read part of the statement.

"CB. 'I came into my office to see Brigitte nosing around in my office. She was by the open desk drawer. When I challenged her, she seemed sheepish, and made some excuse about looking for a stapler. And that's it. I've absolutely no idea if she saw the contents of the envelope. I'm guessing now that she may have done.'

HB. 'Did you mention this to anyone else?'

CB. 'I wasn't sure how to handle it, so I mentioned it to Peter.'

HB. 'Peter Finch?'

CB. 'Yes. He basically said not to worry about it, because there was nothing that could be done either way.'

HB. 'So? I understand he's a close friend, but why tell him?'

CB. 'Because when I initially received the blackmail pictures and note, he was the only person I told. I had to tell someone.'

HB. 'I'm surprised you told him, given he's in one of the photos with your wife.'

CB. 'I actually wound him up over it and insinuated there was something going on, but I knew there couldn't be. Finch is too refined for Petra. She doesn't want polite conversation. She just likes the occasional bit on the side.'

HB. 'How do you feel about that?'

CB. 'I'm a realist. Petra is beautiful to look at and that makes me feel good. I like it when other men give her admiring glances. As you can see, I am much older. She needs people more her own age when it comes to physical activity.'"

HARRY PUSHED the statement to one side. It had felt strange interviewing someone so prominent about something so intimate.

Brandon had seemed without embarrassment throughout the process.

'What about you?' Harry had asked. 'Have you been totally faithful during your marriage?'

Brandon had smiled. 'Of course. Why wouldn't I? As I've said, she is stunningly attractive. I have everything that satisfies my needs.'

Harry stood up and went to the window, his hands clasped behind his back. Was Charles Brandon involved in this situation? Had he commissioned the murders of Giles Cranberry and Peter Finch? If so, for what reason?

But, apart from his initial evasiveness, Brandon had seemed to open up, even revealing some of the lurid details of his wife's behaviour. He had appeared calm and forthright. There again, Harry mused, he was a senior politician, possibly used to spinning events and portraying himself as the good guy in all situations. He could hear his father's words from when he was a boy. They'd been watching a party-political broadcast. His father had stood up and abruptly turned off the television.

'What did you do that for?' Harry's mother had demanded.

'He was lying. I always know when a politician is lying,' his father had responded.

'How?' Harry had asked, intrigued.

'Because their lips move,' his father had replied, a twinkle in his eyes.

To this day, Harry couldn't be completely sure if his father meant it, or had just said it for comedic effect, but it had stayed with him.

There was one person heavily involved in all this who wasn't a politician – Brandon's wife Petra. A trip to Wales was becoming increasingly essential.

Harry put on his coat. Before going to visit Petra Brandon, it might be worth getting some extra background knowledge about her from someone other than her husband.

They met at a coffee shop near the King's Road.

Peter Finch was looking pale and drawn, his arm still in a sling.

'How are you feeling?' Harry asked, giving his coffee a stir.

'Fine, I suppose.' Finch looked down at his arm. 'There have been complications which have meant extra treatments, but I'm grateful to be alive.'

'I'm sure,' Harry said sympathetically. 'Now I need to ask you some questions. You'll know from the press that there is speculation surrounding your friend Charles Brandon.'

'I've read the papers. They are completely wrong. I've known Charles a long time, and he is the most honourable man you're ever likely to meet.'

'I'm sure,' Harry said. 'But what can you tell me about his wife?'

'Petra?' Finch asked with a surprised look. 'What has she got to do with it?'

'Mr Finch,' Harry said in a deliberately formal tone, 'I know you are completely aware of the blackmail attempt on Charles Brandon, and I understand you want to protect your friend. But I'm afraid we are further down the line. So honesty, please.'

Finch looked at the remnants at the bottom of his cup, as if in thought, and then put it down again. 'On the night of the shooting, Charles and I had drinks at the Garrick and Charles showed me a letter that revealed that he was being blackmailed because of his wife's indiscretions.'

Harry nodded.

'There were also several photos,' Finch continued, 'that, shall we say, offered evidence as to those indiscretions.'

Harry nodded again. 'Yes, I know.'

'Okay, so you know I was in one of those photos.'

'I do.'

'I just want you to know that I wasn't having a sexual relationship with Petra Brandon. We were like...well, mates, I suppose.'

'What were you doing with her, then?'

'Just having lunch. That's all.'

'That's all?'

Finch went quiet for a moment and then looked directly at Harry. 'You said that the best thing I could do to help

Charles was to be completely honest. I'm not sure that it will help. The reason we met was because she wanted to confide in me about Charles.'

'Please, go on.'

'Well, that's it. Surely you don't expect me to break a confidence, do you?'

'Mr Finch, please understand that this is a serious murder enquiry and not some prank pulled at a grammar school where everyone involved keeps quiet and doesn't tell the teacher about their friend's involvement.'

'All right, Inspector. Essentially, she wanted to express her unhappiness within the marriage.'

'In what respect?'

Finch signalled to the server for attention. They were both quiet as she came over and refilled their cups.

'I so prefer the personal touch in these places, don't you?' Finch said. 'I hate modern coffee shops where you have to get up and queue when you want another drink.'

'Yes, I agree,' Harry said with a trace of impatience. 'So why was her marriage causing unhappiness?'

'She said that he made her life hell and abused her mentally. Apparently, he's a control freak, and she was thinking of leaving him. She wanted my advice about what to do next.'

'And what advice did you give her?'

'It was difficult because I felt caught in the middle, but I told her that if she was that unhappy, she must find a solicitor and start divorce proceedings, and yes, it was the right thing to do. Common sense, really.'

'Why did she want your advice in particular?'

'Perhaps she wanted someone to use as a sounding board, I don't really know.'

'And you and Petra never ever had any sort of sexual liaison?'

'Good God, no! She's good looking, and flirty, and she has that feminine capacity to draw you in. But no, that's apart from the fact she's married to my friend.' Finch stared into the distance, a faraway look on his face. 'I can't tell you how sad this makes me feel. You and the press may perceive Charles as being the stereotype politician surrounded by dark secrets, but I can assure you, you're wrong about him. He's a good man through and through, who seems to want to change the world for the better. Remember, I say this as someone who is sitting on the opposite side to Charles in the House of Commons.'

'All right,' Harry said. 'You've had plenty of time to ponder, since the shooting. Have you thought of anyone who might want you dead? Someone from the past? An ex-partner, perhaps? Anyone?'

Finch looked sombre. 'I've done nothing else but ponder. I've wracked my brains trying to think of anyone I've upset, and there are plenty, but they are all contained within the political world I live in. I suppose I've been lucky enough to have led a clean life. Inspector, I genuinely don't know who would want to kill me. And as for ex-partners, there's been no woman in my life for quite a while now.'

'Not even Petra Brandon?' Harry asked with a hint of mischief.

Finch smiled. 'Not even Petra Brandon, Inspector.'

20

'Wales?' Liz Mainwaring sat back in her chair, cleaning her spectacles, and then holding them up to the light. 'Well, if you think it's the best use of your time. Petra Brandon doesn't seem to be involved in any of this, so what are you thinking?'

A few months ago, Mainwaring wouldn't have given him the time of day, let alone have any respect for his thoughts.

'I want to get a different slant on this investigation,' Harry said. 'I have this feeling that somehow we are being jollied along, which could be wrong, of course, but I think that interviewing Mrs Brandon might shine a different light on the investigation. For example, we don't have her own thoughts on her relationship with Charles. Let alone the other men in her life.'

'It just seems a long way to go just to gain perspective,' Mainwaring said.

'It is. However, I am curious, and any gleaned information could be valuable.' He looked at Mainwaring. 'If you had a husband who was being questioned by the police over his alleged involvement with the death of a member of your staff, wouldn't you want to be by your husband's side?'

Mainwaring nodded. 'Yes, I suppose so. Although it might depend on what the marital relationship is.'

'That's right,' Harry said. 'At the moment, we've only got what other people are telling us about their marriage. I'd like to see for myself.' Harry pulled an envelope from his breast pocket. 'I intend to show Petra Brandon the photos and see what her reaction is and discover more about her other relationships. You never know, it could unearth a suspect.'

'You don't think Charles Brandon is a suspect?'

'He's definitely one suspect, given the facts we have so far. Brandon has an involvement in all this, but to what extent remains to be seen.'

'I'm learning to trust your instinct,' Mainwaring said, 'but please tread carefully. Where's Brandon now?'

'He's given a statement and is presumably back at his home. There's nothing more we can do, as far as he is concerned. On the bright side,' Harry said, 'there surely can't be any pressure on you from the Home Office. The Tory party must love the fact that the Labour leader seems to be involved in something that could cause him damage.'

'That's true,' Mainwaring smiled. 'It might be a different matter if it were a Tory minister. No, there is pressure, but only because Brandon is high-profile, and therefore all our ducks must be in a row. The media are always looking for an excuse to crucify us. As well you know.'

A few months prior, their team was accused by the newspapers of allowing dead bodies to pile up. When Harry had successfully brought the killers to justice, he had seen no headlines along the lines of, "Well done to our wonderful police force." It just didn't work that way.

Later that day, Harry was holding a team briefing in The

War Room. His laptop was connected to a large screen, on which was a still image of Peter Finch and Petra Brandon.

'This is the first of a few that we will be going through and discussing. Some images are quite explicit, so I'm giving you fair warning.'

Carl Copeland looked pleased. 'That's okay, guv, I'm sure we'll cope.'

Harry gave him a look and continued, 'You'll know by now that this is Peter Finch. MP for Middlington. Finch is unmarried, with no children. He lives alone in a flat in the Middlington area. He says this photo was taken at a meeting with Petra Brandon, during which she sought his advice about her marriage. She alleged to Finch that her marriage was shaky and that she was considering her options. Now we haven't spoken to her yet, and it seems that she doesn't have any involvement in any of this. However, I will be interested to hear what she has to tell me about these liaisons.'

'One of them could be the person behind the shootings and the murder of Brigitte Walsh,' Copeland said.

'That's correct,' said Harry.

'So, do we still suspect Charles Brandon, or not?' Dawn Koorus asked.

'He is very much in the thick of it,' Harry said. 'But how involved in a crime, we don't yet know. Charles Brandon was present when one of his friends was shot, and the other killed. A maid that worked for Mr Brandon turns up strangled to death near the grounds of his estate, after him telling us he thought she'd gone home to Ireland to look after her sick mother.'

Harry put up the next image.

'This is Gavin Smart, pictured with Petra. He has been an MP since the last election, and lives with his wife and two boys.'

'They look to be friendly with each other,' observed

Dawn. 'They're holding hands and looking into each other's eyes like a honeymoon couple.'

'The degrees of friendliness increase further with the man on the next slide. I am giving you fair warning!' Harry said, putting up the next image.

Suddenly the screen was filled with the picture of a naked Petra on her knees with the MP Nigel Kendall behind her.

'But he's supposed to be gay!' Copeland exclaimed.

Harry nodded. 'That seems to be a consensus. Whether or not he's gay isn't the issue. The fact is someone has taken a photo of the two of them having sex.'

'Is it possible that others are being blackmailed?' Dawn asked. 'By the same blackmailer, using the same photos?'

'It's a possibility,' Harry said. 'I think we should certainly look into it.'

'Could someone have photoshopped any of the photos?' Sandy asked.

'Our techies say definitely not.'

The next few photos were agency publicity shots showing a younger version of Petra in various poses.

'Do we know who took any of these photos?' Dawn asked.

Harry grinned. 'If we knew that, I think we'd be further ahead. The photos could have been taken by the blackmailer, or someone working for the blackmailer. But whoever it was knew exactly where these people would be.'

'They could have been lucky,' Copeland remarked.

'Maybe,' Harry said. 'However, in the photo that features Nigel Kendall, you can see that they pushed the camera through curtains into a bedroom to get the shot.'

'At every step, we are getting more questions than answers,' Sandy said. 'There are so many tangles. We need something to knit it all together.'

Harry rubbed his eyes. 'Perhaps the trip to Wales will unearth something.'

'Ah yes, you're going to meet the famous Petra. You be careful, guv,' Copeland said.

'Why do I need to be careful?' Harry asked.

'You don't want to end up being featured in a photo!'

~

'I'LL BE a day or maybe two, depending how I get on,' he said to Alex as he packed an overnight bag.

'Are you looking forward to meeting the man-eater?' Alex asked, mischief in her voice.

'I suppose so,' he replied.

'You be careful. I don't want her chewing on you.'

'I think she has enough on her plate already,' Harry said, folding a shirt. 'Anyway, you know you can trust me.'

'Yes. But can I trust her?'

A few hours later, as he drove over the Severn Bridge and across the Welsh border, Harry's thoughts were scattered in many directions. Sandy had been right. There were so many tangles.

He hadn't even started probing the activities of Gerard Tournier. That meeting with Jimmy McNeal in the pub now seemed like months ago because of everything that had happened since. He had googled Tournier on a few occasions and was getting the image of a respectable family man who was one of the president's right-hand men. He felt he was being led on a wild goose chase. But why? What was in it for McNeal?

However, it wasn't a priority. Finding Brigitte's murderer was, together with whoever had shot Cranberry and Finch.

In what way was Brandon involved? Aside from his initial reluctance, Brandon had been helpful and courteous throughout the process. Anyone could have written the blackmail note, Brandon had said, although it had been written on his own official headed paper. Apparently, it was easy for anyone to slip it into his in-tray.

When Harry told Brandon about his intention to question his wife, Brandon had become defensive. 'Look, Inspector, just because she's in a few photos, doesn't necessarily make her involved. Is there really any point in questioning her?'

Harry guessed they'd all find out soon enough.

He had booked into The Imperial Hotel in Merthyr Tydfil. It was a small, functional hotel that offered a cooked breakfast and a bar, and, he noticed with anticipation, they served real ale.

After checking in, he went to his room and changed into a suit and tie. He didn't feel like questioning someone while wearing the same shirt and jeans that he'd worn to drive down in. He tried to smooth back the stubble on his head. When Harry had attempted to grow it, it had looked tufty and patchy, so the barber had cut it very short, which, according to his team, made him look like a hard man. He supposed that might be useful when operating undercover.

Harry smiled at a memory. The last time he'd been undercover was when he'd literally been undercover. A bedcover, to be precise, whilst wearing a false beard and bandages. The man in the next bed was a target for a suspected killer. When the suspect turned up wearing a fake nurse's uniform, Harry had leapt out of bed to arrest her. But she'd taken off out of the window, and Harry had chased her around the hospital grounds, with bandages and bits of beard in his wake. Afterwards, he'd been mercilessly teased, with observers saying all that was missing was Benny Hill and some 1930s comedy-style music.

He put on his jacket and took a last look in the mirror. It was time to meet Mrs Brandon.

21

Petrova Brandon sat across from Harry and delicately poured tea from a china teapot. Harry wouldn't have been surprised if it had been from the same set of china as the one used at the mansion. Everything around her oozed the same class and quality. White Regency doors and windows added style and complimented a crystal chandelier.

His eyes were drawn to a Welsh dresser which was serving as a display unit to many blue and white dishes. Harry was no expert, but they looked expensive. In the middle of the dresser was a wedding photo of Petra and Charles.

'What made you buy a place down here in Wales?' Harry asked.

She waved a hand at the rolling hills and forest through the French windows. 'That's why. Beautiful, isn't it?'

Harry nodded. It was a far cry from the view from his office in London, where there was wall-to-wall traffic wherever you looked.

He could see why she'd found it easy to entice men into her life. She was indeed very attractive and had a haughty way about her that might make her seem out of reach for many. Her long, flowing, dark hair framed an oval face and dark eyes that were sparkling with amusement. She was tall, about five foot ten, and carried herself erectly. Harry guessed that she may have been a dancer earlier in life. Or perhaps an actress?

She was wearing a dark blue dress that finished well above her knees, accentuating long, shapely legs. When she spoke, it was with a soft Russian accent. 'Do you like the view?'

'I do, very much.' He realised she was being flirtatious, and quickly added, 'It must be wonderful to stay in such a tranquil, peaceful place.'

She smiled, as if reading his mind. 'So, Inspector, I assume you've come all the way down here to ask me about my husband?'

'Yes, that would be one of my reasons.'

'Why didn't you just phone me? It would have been much easier for you. Or did you just want to witness my beauty first-hand?'

Harry searched her face for signs of humour or sarcasm but found none. 'When we investigate a murder, Mrs Brandon, we tend not to just sit in an office making phone calls to people who may be suspects or witnesses. We visit them in person. You can read a lot from actually seeing a person.'

'And what are you reading from me, Inspector?' Her dark eyes flashed at him.

He took a sip from the china cup and set it down gently. 'I haven't come down here to read you, Mrs Brandon,' he said, side-stepping a possible trap. 'I'm here because you are married to Charles and I want to further my enquiries. That's all. If you were staying in the same house as your husband, it would certainly have been easier for me.'

'I think what you are trying to ask, Inspector, is why am I not with my husband at our home?'

'That would be one of my questions, I suppose.'

'Have you ever married, Inspector?' Petra asked, looking down at Harry's left hand.

'Once,' he replied. 'It didn't work out.'

'I am very sorry, Inspector, or may I call you Harry?'

'Yes, call me Harry.' He could see why she seemed to make such an impression on the male species. Perhaps females too. He suspected that a relationship with one man was simply not enough for her. Maybe she needed different parts of a few men to make the perfect one for her.

'If you are married, or you even if you just live with someone, you sometimes need space. I just seem to need more space than most.'

'Are you fully aware of your husband's situation?' Harry asked.

'Yes,' she said, the amused look disappearing from her face. 'He phones me every day, so I know everything that's going on.'

'Including the blackmail attempt?'

'I am.' She stood and went to the window. 'I suppose you will have seen the photos, Inspector. Please don't judge me, you don't know me.'

Harry thought it interesting that she'd reverted to calling him "Inspector," and he followed suit. 'Mrs Brandon, I'm not here to judge, or condemn you. I'm simply here to do my job. Would you mind sitting back down and looking through these photos?'

Harry took out the envelope and shook out the contents.

'You are featured in each of these.'

She examined them one by one and eventually looked up at Harry. 'I didn't sleep with all these men.'

'No, but the blackmailer is inferring that you did. The

photos are certainly compromising, and this one shows you actually in the act.' He pointed to the one with Nigel Kendall. 'Have you any idea who might have taken these photos?'

She didn't seem embarrassed as she looked at the explicit photo. 'I have no idea who took that particular photo, or the ones with the other MPs. The others are just shots from years ago.'

'Someone doesn't want your husband to continue as the leader of Her Majesty's Opposition. That "someone" wants your husband to step down, otherwise these photos will become public.'

Harry looked at Petra Brandon questioningly and waited.

'Inspector, you realise these photos will most probably be published, whatever happens?' she said.

'What do you mean?'

She smiled. 'The blackmailer has a double-edged sword, getting my husband to step down from his position, and the money that he will make from the newspapers and magazines when they're sold.'

'He?'

She looked at him and smiled. 'Or she. Just a figure of speech, Inspector. In which case, it seems a waste of time for my husband to resign from his position, don't you think?'

Harry nodded. 'That certainly makes sense. Taking it a stage further, it's possible that this is just one big publicity stunt to then sell the photos to the highest bidding newspapers. The blackmail attempt could be a red herring. Perhaps you're both in on it. I would be taking that as a strong possibility, except for the fact that there is the small matter of two shootings and one dead body.'

Petra looked shocked. 'Inspector, I swear I know nothing–'

There was a sudden crashing sound, and into the room

arrived a smart looking man wearing a dark blue suit. He stopped short when he saw Harry.

'Oh, sorry Mrs Brandon. I just accidentally stepped on the dog's bowl. I didn't mean to interrupt you.'

He looked in Harry's direction questioningly.

'This is Inspector Harry Black. He's come down from London to investigate the murders. Inspector, this is Stephan. He does some jobs for me and also drives me around.'

Stephan nodded affably. 'Ma'am will you be travelling in the car this afternoon? If not, I'll have it valeted.'

'No, I think I'll probably stay in. You carry on. The inspector and I will probably have some more tea and chat for the rest of the afternoon. I'll see you in the morning.' She smiled at him.

As Stephan left the room, Harry noticed him turn to look back. It wasn't a pleasant look. Had he been listening from the kitchen before the accident with the dog bowl? Or perhaps it was jealousy? Perhaps Petra and Stephan were having an intimate relationship. After all, he was a good looking, young man, much better than some of the craggy, old Whitehall politicians Petra had been photographed with.

That evening, Harry sat at the bar in The Imperial Hotel. He took a sip from his pint of Brains bitter and stared through the large window at the stationary traffic outside. It was a narrow, one-way street, and it only took one badly parked car to cause a jam.

It concerned him that his journey to Merthyr might be a waste of time. What had he learned? After Stephan had left, they had lapsed into small talk, during which Petra had asked him if he wanted to dine with her. He'd politely declined, but the invitation had started a rumbling in his stomach.

'Same again?' asked the man behind the counter.

'No, this time I'll have a pint of Reverend James,' Harry replied after a quick scrutiny of the hand pumps. He was determined to inject some enjoyment into his visit to Wales. 'Are there any good places to eat around here?' he asked. 'Although I'm sure your own offer is great,' he added quickly, after noticing a big menu on the wall.

The man behind the bar laughed. 'No offence taken,' he said, in a deep Welsh accent. 'There's plenty of choice in Merthyr. There are pubs like the Lantern or the Spoons that will do you an evening meal, or there's an excellent Indian restaurant just down the road.'

After downing another pint of Reverend, Harry made his way towards the restaurant. It was getting dark, and the traffic had turned in for the night.

After a hearty Indian meal and a few brandies, he made his way back towards The Imperial. The street was so quiet and empty, he could hear his feet echo between the buildings. He glanced into the window of an estate agency, marvelling at the difference in property prices compared to where he lived.

Harry carried on walking up the street. He could feel the effect of the evening's excesses and was looking forward to his bed.

As he passed a passageway, a fist shot out, knocking him sideways. As he fell to the pavement, a kick to his stomach doubled him over, and he vomited the evening's food and drink into the street.

He could hear footsteps running away, back through the passageway. His brain wanted to give chase, but his body was adamant that it was going to stay where it was.

From the pavement, he looked up at the passersby who had seemed to appear from nowhere, and was aware of what he must look like. He drew his hand across his face and looked at it. *Great, vomit and blood.*

He waved away the offers of help and got to his feet, wondering why he had been targeted.

Back at the hotel, he was thankful it was in darkness, so he wouldn't have to make any awkward explanations.

The mirror in his room revealed nothing more than a bloody mark on the side of his face that would heal over the next day or so. He noticed more vomit down the front of his jacket, which he took off and rinsed under the tap. He had a sudden thought and felt around the inside pocket.

The envelope containing the photos had disappeared.

Shit. He had been deliberately targeted; it hadn't just been some random assault.

The realisation wiped away the last vestige of his mild drunkenness. He sat on the edge of the bed, a bunched-up piece of wet tissue held against his cheek.

As far as the photos were concerned, it wasn't a problem; they were copies. But whoever had stolen them didn't know that. There were very few people who knew he was down here, and he was willing to take a punt on who might be behind the attack.

The next morning, Harry was impatient to get on with the day, but as he passed the dining room, the smell of breakfast reminded him that everything he had eaten the night before had probably found its way into a local drain.

He ate heartily, before phoning to make an appointment to speak to a fellow inspector at a local station.

A thickset man welcomed him into a small, poky office. 'Welcome to Merthyr. I'm Phil Morgan. It's good to meet a fellow inspector, even if you are English. No offence.'

Harry laughed. 'None taken, I'm just grateful for your help.'

Morgan waved Harry into a seat. 'Sorry about my workspace. We don't have a big shared office area like you lot in London.'

'We're in exactly the same situation,' Harry said. 'Ours is a listed building, so our shared office space is limited too.'

'What happened to your face?' Morgan asked. 'That wasn't one of our Merthyr boys, was it?' He spoke with a distinct Valleys accent.

'Funny you should say that,' he replied. 'I'm hoping you'll help me find out.'

'Let's get some coffee down you.'

Phil Morgan led Harry to an office where various screens showed live images from around the town centre.

'This is our control room,' he explained. 'We get our fair share of Friday night and weekend problems, normally at pub closing time, so these cameras are a blessing.'

Morgan pulled a couple of chairs on wheels towards one of the monitors. Within minutes, Harry could see himself on screen, walking up the deserted High Street. It was a long-distance shot. He felt slight embarrassment as he saw himself stumble at one point.

'Had a few, had we?' Morgan chuckled.

Harry watched himself be knocked to the ground, and saw a figure lean over him and reach into his jacket. The person stood up and seemed to vanish.

'Can we get a closer look?' Harry asked.

'I don't think you'll get a clearer picture. It'll just look grainy. We might have a better chance if we switch cameras.'

Morgan pressed a couple of buttons, and the view on the screen changed to a carpark.

'This is the other side of the passageway. Your boy has to reappear here.'

Seconds later, they could see a man running out of the passageway, carrying something. Another man joined him, and the pair ran into the carpark. Morgan pressed another button, and a different screen showed the two men approaching, their faces becoming increasingly visible.

One face became familiar to Harry. 'That's Stephan,' he

said. 'He's a sort of chauffeur for someone I know.' Harry wasn't surprised. He would have put money on it being him.

'No. His name's not Stephan,' Morgan said. 'It's Steve, Steve Butcher. And the other guy is his brother Terry,' Phil said. 'I first nicked them for violent behaviour at a football match a few years ago, and then repeatedly for similar offences around the Gurnos area where they live. They've both been in and out of prison a few times. That's probably why your boy changed his name slightly, to get the chauffeur's job.'

Harry shook his head. He was going to make a revisit.

If Petra Brandon was expecting to see Harry again so soon, she didn't show it. Her face screwed up as she looked at the mark on his cheek. 'Oh, you're hurt. What happened?'

'Someone mugged me. Two men, to be precise.'

'Did they take much?' Her concern seemed genuine.

'Only the photos that show you in all your glory.'

Petra actually stepped back. 'No!'

'Yes, and guess what? One of my attackers has been identified as your chauffeur, Stephan.'

'No!' she exclaimed again.

'Stephan's actual name is Steve Butcher. He and his brother Terry stole the photos from me last night.'

Petra sat down. She suddenly looked pale and shaken, and even, Harry thought, a little vulnerable.

'I don't care if his name is Stephan or Steve. He wouldn't do this to me. He is too gentle. He wouldn't hurt a fly.'

'I'm afraid the evidence says otherwise, Mrs Brandon,' Harry said. 'He and his brother have both served prison sentences for violence. Are you expecting him today?'

Petra Brandon appeared to ignore the question. 'Why would he steal photos of me? It makes little sense. I'd have given him a photo of me if he'd asked.'

She put her hand to her mouth as if realising what she'd said.

'Don't worry, Mrs Brandon. I'm not interested in your personal affairs. I just want to find this Steve Butcher. The police already have a warrant out for his arrest and have been to his home. Both he and his brother have gone.'

Petra Brandon stood up. She looked tearful and a little angry. 'I have done so much for him. I've bailed him out of financial problems. Why would he do this to me?'

'It could be my fault,' Harry said. 'Do you remember yesterday's conversation, when we spoke about the blackmailer selling the photos to the highest bidder? I think it's possible Steve Butcher overheard the conversation and decided it might be a good way to make some money for himself aided by his brother.' Harry paused. 'The other possibility is that he stole the photos to protect you, Mrs Brandon. After all, he wasn't to know that the ones he stole from me were copies.'

'That's very kind of you to even consider the possibility, Inspector, and to give me a ray of hope. However, I think your first thought was definitely the more accurate.'

'Why do you say that?' Harry asked.

'Because he was due to take me shopping in Cardiff this morning, but he hasn't turned up, and he's not answering his mobile.'

22

Harry almost fell through his own front door he was so exhausted. The combination of events over the last couple of days had taken their toll.

'My God, you look awful!' Alex exclaimed. 'What happened to your face?'

'Oh, I bumped into one of the local lads,' Harry said. He filled her in on the details.

'Jesus Christ! Are you sure you're okay?' she asked when he'd finished. 'You only went down there to interview a politician's wife. How did it go so wrong?'

He looked at her. She had an impish look on her face.

'Have a shower,' she said, 'and I'll make you some supper.'

When he awoke the next morning, Alex was already frying breakfast. She knew that the smell was enough to get him scrambling out of bed in anticipation.

'You've got a free day today,' she remarked, looking at a planner on the kitchen wall. 'Shall we do something together? Or have you already made arrangements?'

Harry looked out of the window. 'No, I have a free day. It

looks nice out there, let's go somewhere and do something enjoyable.'

Later that morning, they hired a narrowboat from Little Venice and took it along the canal to a waterside restaurant, where they had lunch. Harry was looking better, and his face was less swollen, although the bruise was still visible.

It could have been worse. The Butcher brothers had clearly been desperate to get the photographs, so who knew what lengths they might have gone to? They had put out a search for them, but Harry knew it was just a matter of time before the photos were made public.

After lunch, they came back to the boat and shared a bottle of wine.

'What are your plans for the future, Harry?' Alex asked.

'What do you mean?' he asked, looking nonplussed.

'What are you going to do when you leave the force?'

'I don't know, Alex. I might become a private investigator like Will.' Will Kidman was one of Harry's closest friends and was currently touring France with his family. 'What about you?'

Alex wrinkled her nose in thought. Her work life had been placed into turmoil after she'd discovered that the man in her life, also a colleague, had cheated on her. She had kicked up a fuss, after which they had sent her to London in an advisory role, where she had helped Harry to catch a serial killer.

As a result, Harry's boss, the then Chief Inspector Liz Mainwaring, had written to the local superintendent in Scotland formally praising Alex, which had made it awkward for her ex-fiancé, and his new partner, who would probably have loved for her to just disappear into the ether. When Alex had returned to Galashiels, she had received a warm welcome from everyone, and then was summoned to a meeting where they'd talked about the possibility of transferring her to another area in Scotland.

Alex refused, as she felt she had done nothing wrong.

The bosses had then invited her ex-partner, now himself a chief inspector, to a meeting and offered him the same deal. He'd also refused. So there was now a sort of stalemate.

Because her ex-partner was more senior within the force, Alex could guess which way the wind would blow if her bosses were pushed to make a choice.

As a result, she was having a couple of weeks holiday down south to consider her options, and one of those was to apply for a position within the English force, if they would have her.

She stretched an arm out and dabbled her hand in the water, sending ripples across the canal. Two ducks looked in her direction, hoping for titbits.

Alex was no nearer to reaching a solution to her problem. She regarded the man next to her with something akin to love, but it had to be reciprocated before she would consider it a proper relationship.

She watched as the two ducks swam near the vessel, side by side, almost in synchronicity, until one duck plunged its head into the murky water, and at the same time, the other flew off. *Typical*, she thought whimsically.

After a lazy afternoon, followed by a pleasant dinner, they returned to Harry's flat and relaxed on the sofa, listening to music. She sat with her legs tucked under her, her head on Harry's shoulder, her thoughts swirling around in her consciousness. Perhaps they should discuss it.

She lifted her head. 'Harry?'

But Harry was asleep.

Nigel Kendall was a short man with wavy, brown hair that barely concealed a bald patch.

'Come in, come in,' he said, holding the door wide.

Harry entered the mews house with interest. It wasn't too far away from where he and Alex had been boating the day before, and they had passed properties similar to this, wondering what they were like inside.

Kendall ushered Harry down a hallway, which featured a narrow, oak staircase and pint-sized furniture that matched the size of the house. There was a separate lounge and dining room, but both were tiny, separated by a set of double doors, which were latched open. On the wall, there were tiny shelves showing china ornaments.

The place was compact, clean, and very well-kept.

Harry sat gingerly on the edge of a two-seater sofa, slightly concerned that his weight might break it.

Kendall sat opposite. He leaned back and crossed his legs. 'So, Inspector, what did you want to see me about?'

'Mr Kendall, would you tell me about your relationship with Petra Brandon?'

'What relationship? I don't know what you're talking about.' Nigel Kendall seemed genuinely puzzled.

Harry brought up the image of Kendall and Petra on his phone and showed it to him.

Kendall's face transformed. 'What the fuck? How did you get this?'

The shrill outburst must have stirred something in the house. Harry heard a door opening in a room above, followed by a clip-clopping down the wooden stairs.

The door opened, and a man with a blue and white floral shirt stood and stared at Nigel. 'Are you all right? I heard a screech.'

Kendall's face changed again, this time from outraged

shock to innocence. 'Malcolm, this is Inspector Black. I'm sorry I disturbed you.'

Harry diplomatically replaced the phone in his pocket and stood, his hand outstretched. 'Pleased to meet you, Malcolm. I'm just making routine enquiries about the murder of Giles Cranberry, together with the shooting of one of Mr Kendall's fellow MPs, Peter Finch. Is this something you can also help with?'

Malcolm totally ignored Harry. 'Nigel, the next time that you invite someone to my home, would you do me the courtesy of at least letting me know?'

Kendall looked abashed. 'I'm sorry, Malcolm, I'd forgotten the inspector was coming.'

'Is that so?' Malcolm seemed to force a pleasant look towards Harry. 'Nice to meet you, Inspector.'

Malcolm left the room, leaving an awkward silence.

Kendall lowered his voice. 'I'm so sorry about this. Inspector. You deserve an explanation, but this cannot be made public. This has to be off the record, otherwise I'll lose everything, and I mean everything.'

'Please go on,' Harry said, intrigued.

'It's simple, really. I and a couple of other MPs used to play poker secretly in friends' houses.'

'Why?' Harry asked. 'Couldn't you have gone to a casino?'

'In normal circumstances, yes. However, the Prime Minister doesn't like us to gamble because he reckons we would be a poor example to others, especially those with addiction problems. If the paparazzi filmed us coming out of a casino, our careers would be finished. So we used to have many poker sessions at a private house in the countryside, where no-one could point a finger. The rules were that we had to hand in our mobile phones so that no-one could secretly take a photo of a colleague, and then use it to incriminate them. It was great. There was no press intrusion. When we finished playing, our cars would take us back to our homes.'

'And other people assumed you were just having a good old drink up, I suppose,' Harry said.

'Something like that,' Kendall said. 'At first, all the stakes were quite modest, you know, a tenner here, twenty there. No more than a couple of hundred in the same evening.'

'A couple of hundred? Phew!' Harry said with a surprised look.

'Anyway, I got carried away and lost an enormous amount of money, and tried to get it back by gambling more and more. You can guess what happened. I lost everything. My home, my car, everything. I was at the point of bankruptcy.'

'That was tough,' Harry said.

'It really was. My party couldn't know, and neither could my constituents. Malcolm took me into his home and covered all of my debts. I was very grateful to him. I don't know what I would have done without him.'

Kendall dabbed his eyes with his sleeve.

'He really was a saint. That led to Malcolm and I living together as a full-time gay couple. But the problem is, Inspector...' Kendall lowered his voice. 'I'm probably more bisexual than gay. I need to have women in my life as well as men.'

Harry nodded. 'I think I get it. I'm guessing you having sex with Petra Brandon was a way of gratifying the other side of your sexuality.'

'I suppose so.'

'Do you have any idea who it was that took the intimate photos of you and Petra?'

'No, no idea. We had sex several times. I think she came on to me initially because she thought I would be a challenge. But obviously I wasn't. I was really up for it.'

Kendall suddenly rose from his seat and quietly went out into the hallway. He listened for a moment and came back, resuming his seat.

'I was just checking that he wasn't listening,' Kendall said. 'I'm terrified he'll find out about this.'

'What do you think he'd do?' Harry asked.

'He'd kick me straight out the door.'

'Really?'

'Oh yes, Inspector, I'd be thrown out of this house immediately.'

'In that case,' Harry said, 'I'm afraid you may have one hell of a problem.'

That problem materialised a little sooner than Harry expected. The next day's headlines were damning for Kendall.

Harry believed that the Butcher brothers might take their time and sell the photos to the highest bidder. However, they'd gone to an agency, struck a quick deal, and as a result, the tabloids were full of it.

Pictures of Petra Brandon and Nigel Kendall were splashed across the front pages. Whilst the images used had been doctored for the sake of decency, it left the readers in no doubt as to what was going on, with headlines such as "Sex Scandal Rocks Commons," "Is Kendall Standing For Parliament?" and "Party Leader's Wife Has No Opposition To Gay Lover!"

There were also the pictures of her with the other MPs including the one of her holding hands with Gavin Smart. Harry had tried to reach Smart, to warn him that the story might leak, but his phone had gone to voicemail. Harry later found out that he and his family had booked a last-minute holiday in Florida.

Later editions of the same newspapers featured additional pictures of Nigel Kendall dragging his suitcases away from the mews house, some of them featuring the headline, "Bi-Bi Love!"

There was a back story about Petra Brandon's past, and the picture of a younger Petra posing with the maid's outfit.

Harry threw the paper to one side in disgust. The Butcher brothers had done exactly what Harry had suspected and were wrecking lives in the process. Although he suspected that Nigel Kendall would now sell his side of the story to the press.

He also felt for Charles Brandon. Whether or not he was innocent, the man's life seemed to be tumbling around him. Questions about his wife's affairs, about his involvement in the shootings, the death of Brigitte. Even if Brandon knew about his wife's indiscretions, it certainly wasn't the best of times for him.

Harry got up from his desk. There was a rest room down the corridor, and sometimes Harry would pop in and enjoy a bit of banter with his colleagues as they had their refreshment break, or "refs," as it was known.

Unusually, the television was on, and the officers in the room were watching the Prime Minister squaring up to Charles Brandon in the House of Commons.

Prime Minister's Questions, or PMQs, was a weekly event looked forward to by anyone with any interest in politics. Normally the popular leader of the opposition would verbally dismantle the PM, but today current events surrounding Charles Brandon had given the Prime Minister renewed vigour and a chance of revenge.

The Prime Minister looked as though he was salivating with delight as he looked across the dispatch box at the man opposite.

'Oh, what a tangled web we weave!' he said, pausing to accept the laughter from his benches. 'I just hope that Her

Majesty's opposition still has the ability to hold my government to account, with everything else that is affecting my honourable friend.'

He turned to his left.

'Mr Speaker, how can my honourable friend be able to speak with any conviction about crime and punishment in his situation?'

Then he looked straight at Brandon.

'In fact,' he said, holding out his arms theatrically, 'how will he be able to speak with a conviction?'

His colleagues howled delightedly at their leader's witticism and waved their papers.

'Order, order,' the Speaker of the House commanded. 'The Prime Minister is being presumptuous about the legal circumstances surrounding the leader of the opposition and should withdraw any inference to the matter immediately. I'm sure he would want to apologise for this lapse in his behaviour.'

The Prime Minister stood up and faced the man opposite. 'I do indeed apologise. I'm sure that the many events surrounding my honourable friend have nothing at all to do with him.'

The Prime Minister sat back down. A close-up of his face revealed it was all he could do to contain his delight.

The officers watching the screen were silent. Harry could sense the big question. What if Charles Brandon was guilty? What if he were hiding in plain sight? The evidence against him was pretty much circumstantial, certainly not enough to get him off the streets.

Harry watched as the camera closed up onto Brandon's face. Everyone expected the usual witty retort, but none came. The leader of the opposition just sat in his seat and stared back across at the PM.

That parliamentary session was possibly the easiest the

Prime Minister had ever known. Charles Brandon looked like he'd had the stuffing knocked out of him. He rose to his feet and make some half-hearted attacks on government policy.

As he and the officers watched the lights diminish in Charles Brandon's eyes, Harry had a strong feeling that there was more to come, more revelations, and hopefully, more evidence.

Harry went back to his office and sat back in his chair, his hands behind his head. He still faced with the big question – who would actually gain from the deaths of Giles Cranberry, Peter Finch, and Brigitte Walsh?

It couldn't be ignored that the only link between the three was Charles Brandon himself.

His mind flitted to Brigitte and the night they'd spent at the restaurant. Perhaps he'd have gleaned more information if he hadn't drunk so much.

The post-mortem report of her death was on his desk. They may as well have just sent him a text on his phone saying they'd found nothing. There were no signs of any transference of DNA suggesting that the killer had worn gloves. The report asserted Brigitte had been murdered at another location and then dumped where they'd found her.

Harry rubbed at his head, his fingers once again feeling the scar tissue amongst the tiny curls of hair.

He was frustrated. There were so many unanswered questions. Why were Finch and Cranberry targeted? Why was Brigitte murdered? And why leave her body so near to Brandon's mansion? Was someone trying to implicate Brandon? Or was he playing the "I'm-being-framed" card? Using smoke and mirrors to divert everyone from the truth?

Whatever the truth was.

Was Petra involved? And what about the Butcher brothers? Did their involvement go beyond theft and greed?

Yes, Brandon was certainly the chief suspect. But at the conclusion, would the finger of justice still be pointing towards him?

23

Nick Marshall put the night-scope to his eyes and scanned the rocky terrain ahead of him. The peaks of the Sierra Nevada looked foreboding against a sky that was darkening further as the rain clouds amassed. Marshall thanked his lucky stars for the weather conditions that would hopefully help keep him concealed.

He moved slowly and purposefully; he wanted to strike while his target was off guard.

Having left a motorbike hidden in foliage a couple of miles back, he was now on foot, a single purpose in his mind.

As he got nearer, he put the scope back to his eye.

He could make out a solitary guard. Just one? Marshall was surprised. With everything that had happened recently, he'd have thought that Vance would have put an army around his villa. Perhaps Vance had no more men to put out. After all, he'd recently lost a carload over that cliff edge.

Marshall was taking no chances. The villa was high up ahead of him. The climb up the mountain side looked daunting but do-able without climbing gear.

As he got nearer, the rock face confronting him was

looking more treacherous. For a moment, he was tempted to change his mind and approach the front side of the villa, where he and the women had so recently escaped from. But experience told him that this was the best way to enter Vance's kingdom.

The clouds looked darker and heavier. He hoped torrential rain wouldn't make the climb an impossibility.

He took it carefully, step-by-step, knowing that one slip could be life-ending.

On reaching the top, Marshall stopped to recover. Ahead of him was the villa. He could see lights on, indicating someone was home. The surrounding trees afforded him extra cover. He circumnavigated the building and headed towards the guard.

Divide and conquer was always a good plan.

As he drew nearer, it seemed the guard had disappeared into the darkness. Then a tell-tale, red glow caught his attention. *Smoking is bad for your health*, he thought with amusement, as he edged forward stealthily.

~

EDDIE VANCE FELT he had every reason to be content, as he looked across at the naked figure stretched out on the silk sheets of the bed. She lay on her back, long, blonde hair tumbling across the pillows.

He watched her from his chair, a satisfied smile on his face.

He swished the brandy around the bottom of the glass and knocked it back, then looked at the bottom of the empty vessel as if making a decision. Standing up, he walked naked into the lounge, where he poured more brandy from a crystal decanter and added a handful of ice-cubes.

Vance opened the glass sliding doors and looked out with

pleasure at the lit-up swimming pool, casting its moving reflections as the night's breeze caught the water. He wandered outside into the seating area, enjoying the air on his nakedness, and sat on one of the cushioned, wicker chairs. He took a sip from his drink and put his feet up on the glass table.

Yes, life was good.

He should spend much more time here, he mused. This was the place to be. Much better than congested London with its pollution and tourists. Here, it was secure and comfortable; he didn't need lots of security staff. It was in the middle of nowhere and easily guarded. He could almost relax.

Vance set the glass on the table. Thinking about London turned his thoughts towards Nick Marshall. Marshall had exposed Vance's activities to the British government. Now the scales of justice were being righted, and Marshall would soon be out of the game.

Marshall had cost him dearly, and that wasn't including the recent loss of some of his men over the side of the mountain pass.

He could feel the droplets of rain on his skin, and got to his feet.

Finishing the rest of his brandy, he padded to the glass doors. He took a last look outside; the weather had turned, and the rain was getting heavier.

He felt relaxed. It was nice knowing exactly where Marshall was. All his plans were on track.

∽

THE GUARD WATCHED as the villa door closed behind Vance, and he grunted with satisfaction.

Vance didn't like his guards leaving their posts for any reason. He ran to some nearby bushes, where he unzipped his trousers and exhaled with pent-up relief, as the spray made an arc which shimmered from the lights of the pool area.

It was possibly the last moment he ever enjoyed.

Marshall allowed him to finish and zip up before crunching the back of the guard's head with a rock. The man fell forward without a sound.

Marshall turned his attention to the villa. He couldn't understand why everything seemed so relaxed and laid back. Could it be a trap? There was no way Vance could know he was here. However, Vance had seemed to know Marshall's every move so far.

He kept to the shadows, thankful for the combination of the sounds of the water feature and the rain that was streaming onto the patio.

Peering through the glass doors of the villa, he saw a single side lamp illuminated the inside. The lamp was switched off, suddenly. Now there was a chance he could now be seen from inside the room.

He swiftly moved away from the villa and made his way around the perimeter of the pool area, keeping well out of sight. Marshall saw the barn where he had been held captive. Its iron roof was almost next to the tiled roof the villa, which gave him an idea.

Yanking the movable steps out of the swimming pool, he placed them against the side of the barn, where he climbed up. Then he pulled himself onto the roof and walked to the edge. After jumping the gap between the two buildings, he gently walked along the tiles of the villa. A skylight was left slightly ajar, so he swung down into one of the rooms.

He looked around. He was in a small bedroom. The lights from the pool area enabled him to look around without using his torch. The room was basic, probably used by one of

Vance's guards, he thought, noticing a bottle of cheap whisky and an over-full ashtray on the table.

The door opened out into a corridor, where he passed a few other rooms before pausing at the top of a stairwell.

He strained his ears for the slightest sound. Nothing.

Softly, he went down the steps.

The downstairs was open plan except for one door that was shut, but he could see by the light around the edge of the frame that it was another bedroom and there may be an occupant. The lounge area looked opulent and well-furnished. He slid open the glass doors that led to the pool area. It was one of the first things he'd been taught. Always prepare your exit.

As he turned to go back, Marshall was blinded by a torch light being shone in his face.

'Don't make a fucking move,' a voice growled.

The main lights switched on, revealing a large man with thinning, red hair, clad in a green, silk dressing gown. He was holding a gun.

Eddie Vance looked at Marshall, astonishment appearing on his face.

'Marshall? How the fuck are you here? You're supposed to be in London.'

Vance's eyes settled somewhere on Marshall's chest, as if looking for something. In a flash, Marshall understood how Vance had been able to identify his every move and location.

'The pendant,' Marshall said slowly. 'You put a tracker in my pendant.'

Vance nodded and grinned. 'I knew you'd probably discover other bugs that were placed amongst your things, but I reckoned you'd never guess the pendant was your problem.'

Marshall's mind was racing. Giving Rachel that pendant at the airport may have cost her and Chelsea their lives.

Vance and his men could track them wherever they were. He had another thought. Rachel and Chelsea were on their way to his friend's house, which meant Vance could find them as well.

'The tracker shows you to be in London,' Vance said, as if reading Marshall's thoughts. 'However, if you're here, and the tracker isn't, then you must have given the pendant to your lady friend. So she must be special to you. You should be careful about people who are special to you. Who do you think planted the tracker in your pendant in the first place?'

'No idea.' Marshall said. 'Why don't you tell me?'

'Do you remember who gave it to you?'

Marshall remembered. Julie was a lovely lady Marshall had known during the time he'd worked for Vance. He'd saved her boyfriend's life under extreme circumstances, and as a thank you, she'd presented him with the pendant.

'I told her I'd organise the inscription and had the device inserted at the same time. From then on, I always knew exactly where you were.'

'But why?' Marshall wasn't just playing for time; he was genuinely curious. 'Haven't you better things to do with your life? I can understand you being pissed off with me after your nasty little sideline was closed down, but why target me?'

'I had all the connections set up, everything virtually on autopilot, and then you ruined it all for me. However, it wasn't just me you ruined things for.'

Marshall looked puzzled. 'Go on.'

'Where do you think I got the names of the various contacts in the Far East? How do you think I knew who to contact, who to warn, who would pay? Did you think I was a one-man operation?' Vance laughed. 'Why do you think I'm not behind bars? I know you were fed different stories, but this went much higher than me.'

It was dawning on Marshall that he'd been duped all

along. It was becoming clear that the people he'd reported Vance to were actually in on it, and the removal of Vance from his position had been a token gesture. No wonder Vance hadn't been prosecuted.

Marshall was feeling naïve and stupid. But how could he have known who to trust?

Christ, if this went right to the very top, was a government minister in on it?

The unwavering gun muzzle focused his attention. He wanted time to think, but it didn't look as if he was going to be afforded that luxury. There was a look of intent on Vance's face as the gun moved slowly towards Marshall's head.

'Sorry, Nick, but it's the end of the line. You could have done some work for me, and saved yourself, but it's become clear that's never going to happen. The Spanish police will cart away your body as some nameless intruder.'

Marshall could almost feel the squeezing of the finger on the trigger.

They were both startled by the bedroom door opening, as a sleepy figure emerged. 'What's happening?' she said, her eyes widening as she took in the situation.

The explosion of the shot was deafening, but the bullet went past Marshall's ear. The interruption allowed him to somersault through the open glass door and into the pool area, where he ducked behind the stone water feature.

The second shot shattered chunks of the ornate sculpture over Marshall. He pulled out his own weapon and fired back several times, trying to predict Vance's movements but not willing to wound the woman. He wasn't sure of her innocence in this situation.

Marshall stopped firing and waited, his ears still ringing from that first shot, his senses on high alert.

There was a very long silence. That was okay. Marshall

was used to playing the waiting game. He kept very still, breathing slowly and quietly.

Suddenly, he heard a car starting in the distance. He scrambled up and ran towards the sound. *Shit, they're getting away.* But then he had an instinctive thought and hurled himself to the ground as a hail of bullets sprayed over him.

Very clever, he thought. Vance had obviously got his girlfriend to start the car to make Marshall think they were both escaping, enticing Marshall to break cover and make himself an easy target.

He'd forgotten how devious Vance was – a mistake that he mustn't allow to happen again.

Elbowing his way along the ground, he got back to the now decimated water feature. A statue, which was supposed to be a depiction of the Venus de Milo, had also been shot to pieces and stone fragments lay next to him.

He had a thought. The statue's head was within reach. He stretched out his legs until he could get both sides of his shoes around the head and pulled it towards him. Hoping that in the poor light Vance would mistake it for his own head, he raised the stone above the water feature.

The ruse worked. The stone head exploded as the bullet hit its target, but the process had enabled Marshall to pinpoint where the firing was coming from.

He fired several shots back in rapid succession and waited.

Nothing.

He was loath to make a move after what had happened, but he took a chance and ran towards the building, keeping his profile low. When he neared the villa, he ducked down and peered through the shattered glass doors.

He could see a body on the floor, face down, the green silk dressing gown billowing over the body.

Marshall ran in and turned the body over, pulling away

the silk covering. His stomach lurched. It wasn't Vance who was lying there with blood spreading across the floor. It was his female companion. The lousy bastard had escaped, and a left a woman to defend him to the last.

Although it was Marshall who had killed her, he consoled himself with the thought that, given the accuracy of her shooting, she was clearly a professional who was hell-bent on killing him.

Marshall went back outside. He could hear the car was on the move. He ran towards the sound and stood at the top of the steps, watching the departing vehicle down below. It was going to be difficult to stop Vance now. Firing a gun into the night would be like throwing pebbles at a fish in the sea.

He pulled out his night-scope. He could make out Vance in the distance, driving an open-top vehicle. There were wooden boxes in the back. Focusing the scope, he could make out the letters on the side of the boxes – M72.

Shit. An M72 was a rocket launcher used by the Americans during the Vietnam War. What the hell was Vance doing with them? He took the rifle from the guard's body and scattered some bullets towards the departing vehicle, hoping that one of the shots might hit the ammunition. He held little hope at a strike at this range. But he was gratified to see the vehicle come to a stop.

He peered through the night vision scope. His gratification came to an abrupt halt when he saw Vance getting out of the vehicle and pulling out one of the rocket launchers.

Fuck, thought Marshall. He ran full pelt to the far end of the villa. He had misjudged Vance yet again.

The first rocket wiped out the guard's sentry point, together with the stone steps, cutting off any chance of Marshall giving chase. Marshall knew enough about military weapons to realise that these rocket launchers were single fire only, which he hoped would give him time between shots to make his escape before being blown to pieces.

Quicker than he expected, a second rocket destroyed much of the villa, sending chunks of masonry into the swimming pool.

Marshall kept his head down. The explosions had caused a mini-dust storm, sending choking clouds swirling around what was left of the building.

He took a chance and ran towards the rock face that he'd used to access the grounds of the villa. It felt like it had been hours ago since he'd made the ascent.

Although he'd made the climb earlier, it seemed a longer way down now. But he knew he had no choice. He gritted his teeth and hurled himself down the stone face just as another rocket landed. The resulting explosion sent him tumbling in the air for what seemed like forever until a painful wrench in his back told him he'd landed on something.

As the dust settled, he could see that he'd been saved by a small tree jutting out from the rock face. He looked down at the ground below. There was still a long way to go, but it looked possible to get to a slab of rock that was at a gentler angle than the rest of the face. It was smooth and flat, which had made it impossible to climb. However, if he could jump across to it, the surface would enable him to reach the ground below. It would be like going down a children's slide. Almost.

As he contemplated the dangers of his plan, another explosion tearing up chunks of rock above him made up his mind.

He leapt across to the slab. As he landed, he scrambled for a handhold but could only grab thin air. He slid down the slab of rock, with nothing to slow his descent, until everything came to a sudden stop as he hit the ground.

He lay, trying to catch his breath. His heart was beating double time, and there were aches all over his body.

Marshall looked up at the night sky. The rain had stopped, the clouds had gone, and the stars were shining. There was a quietness in the air.

He was alive.

Wriggling his fingers and toes, he prayed there was nothing broken.

He seemed to be okay except for scratches – cuts and bruises where ridges of the rock had torn through his clothing.

Tentatively, he stood up, rubbing at the soreness in his back, and looked up at the rock face. It had been a longer way down than he'd realized. He'd been lucky.

He was annoyed with himself at the way he'd approached the situation. Vance had outwitted him and had escaped.

Marshall now had to alert his friends in London. He pulled out his phone. Of course, there was no signal; he was surrounded by mountains.

An hour later, Marshall had pulled his motorbike out from its hiding place and was on his way to the airport. He knew it was imperative that he warn his friends in London about Vance, but also realised they were going to need his help.

24

'We've found the Butcher brothers.'

Harry scrambled out of bed, nearly dropping the phone. 'What? Where?'

'In Cardiff Bay,' Sandy said. 'They were in a cafe about to have breakfast when they were arrested.'

'Serves them bloody right,' Harry said, remembering how his own meal had turned out that night in Merthyr Tydfil. 'Where are they now?'

'Being questioned at Cardiff nick. They'll send over the video files when they are finished.'

'I'll look forward to it,' Harry said.

It wasn't long before Harry was watching the screen with interest.

The brothers initially denied assaulting Harry, saying that they had found the pictures in the carpark at Merthyr. However, that claim was dispatched when shown the implicating CCTV images.

Eventually, the brothers admitted the assault.

Steve Butcher said that he'd overheard the conversation

between DI Black and Petra Brandon, and had decided to capitalise, roping in his brother.

When asked about a relationship with Petra Brandon, Butcher flatly denied it, saying that he'd rather "turn gay than shag an old tart like that."

They'd contacted an agency they'd found online, and quickly reached a deal, for which they were paid £2,000. Harry winced in disgust. These boys clearly weren't business minded. The agency probably broke out the champagne after the brothers had signed on the dotted line.

The brothers flatly denied any involvement in anything else connecting them with the Brandons, and judging by their demeanours, Harry was inclined to believe them, although he was unconvinced about Steve Butcher's denial of a relationship with Petra Brandon.

He found it incredible that for the sake of a couple of grand – less, after whatever he'd given to his brother – Steve Butcher had thrown away his job, his relationship with Petra, and was going to be charged with assault. Hardly a profitable experience.

A rumble in his stomach reminded him he hadn't eaten. As he walked into the canteen, Harry saw Dawn Koorus and Sandy Sanders looking into each other's eyes. He coughed, and the two sprung apart from each other, looking guilty.

'Oh, for God's sake, you two,' he said, hearing a fatherly tone in his own voice. 'You are allowed to sit close together when you're on refs. No-one minds about your relationship. Sandy, did you find any new information about Cranberry?'

'I had a good poke around, guv, but nothing seems to be amiss. I spoke to a few of his employees and they wouldn't hear a bad word about him. I'm going to see his sister later on. She's staying at the Cranberry house.'

'I'll come with you,' Harry said.

The door to the Georgian terraced property was opened by a stooped, elderly man. 'May I help you, sir?'

Harry showed his identification, and they were welcomed into a hallway.

A musty smell hung in the air. It brought back memories of visiting his granny when he was a small boy. The smell of mothballs, cabbage, and the fact she had a huge eiderdown on her bed was all he could remember about her.

'Good afternoon.' A woman had seemed to materialise from nowhere into the hallway.

She had blue eyes that peered over rimless spectacles and was blessed with huge curls of dark-grey hair. 'I'm Sally Goldsmith, Giles' sister. Please come into the living room.'

They sat on striped, Regency style chairs. Along the length of the living room were identical packing boxes, all labelled neatly. Goldsmith noticed Harry looking at them. 'Yes, I know, it might seem a bit soon to be packing up his life, but it's got to be done at some stage.' She shrugged.

Harry cleared his throat. 'I'm here because–'

'You don't have a clue who murdered my brother, have you? And you're here to ask more questions and then you'll go away, and you still won't catch anyone.'

'Mrs Goldsmith, I know my colleagues have already spoken to you, and I apologise for turning up with yet more questions, but we are–'

He was interrupted by the loud chime of the clock, which had been ticking noisily.

'Sorry about that,' she said. 'I'm waiting to pack that, but the clockwork hasn't run down yet. You can't have a cardboard box with the sound of ticking coming from it, can you?' She laughed apologetically and motioned for Harry to continue.

'We're just trying to get a flavour of your brother's character, in order to try and establish who'd want to kill him.'

'His character couldn't have had anything to do with his murder,' Goldsmith said. 'He was the sweetest, gentlest person, who would do anything for anyone.'

Sandy nodded. 'His staff members I spoke to said the same thing.'

'What was he like in business?' Harry asked. 'After all, you surely don't get to become a newspaper owner without stepping on someone. Did he have any business enemies?'

'The newspaper was the family business, which he took over. He was terrible at business,' Goldsmith said. 'If a supplier told him he owed them money, he would just pay it, there and then. What he was good at was sniffing out stories. Giles should have been an investigative reporter. He had a nose for it. Giles and the editor had many a row over what news to headline, and who or what should be investigated.'

'There we are,' Sandy said. 'There's an employee who might have a grudge against your brother.'

'No, I'm afraid not. Whilst they may have disagreed on editorial matters, Robert thought the world of Giles. Giles was Robert's best man at his wedding and godfather to his son.'

'We'll have a chat, nevertheless,' Harry said. 'So what's in the boxes?'

'Old paperwork, clothes, ornaments, junk.' She stood up. 'I'm not sure that I can help you any further, Inspector, but you are welcome to go through the boxes of Giles' personal paperwork. Your colleagues took a load of stuff away, but I found these two other boxes in the loft when I was clearing it out.'

Goldsmith looked around the room.

'I shall miss this place. We grew up here, but I can't afford to keep it going.'

Harry nodded appreciatively. 'It's exquisite. I hope it sells quickly for you.'

Back at the office, he examined the contents of the boxes. But after an hour of sifting through what he considered meaningless documents, he enlisted the help of Dawn and Sandy, both of whom he knew to be far more paperwork-orientated.

Dawn immediately systemised their approach and labelled everything into piles.

Their efforts were rewarded a while later when Sandy came across a thin, brown envelope, which had been attached to a bundle of photographs with a thick rubber band. He carefully unfolded the envelope and studied the contents. He looked up.

'Guv, I think you're going to want to see this.'

25

It rains in Wales – a lot. But when the clouds disappear and a deep, blue sky emerges, the green hills, interrupted by the grey crags of rock, make the Brecon Beacons worthy of a visit.

Harry had stopped to admire the view, as well as exercise his aching back and shoulders. It shouldn't have been such a long drive from London, but it had been, thanks to some hapless idiot who had collided with the central reservation and found himself facing the oncoming traffic.

The resulting mayhem had put an extra two hours onto Harry's journey, and he was now feeling the physical effects.

He returned to his vehicle and drove the remaining few miles to Mrs Brandon's house.

As he pulled into her driveway, the front door opened and she appeared wearing a thin nightdress, loosely covered with a white, silk dressing gown. When Harry got out of the car, she flung her arms around him and placed a kiss on his cheek.

'Good morning, Mrs Brandon,' Harry said, disentangling himself from her hug. He was conscious of the boozy smell that emanated from her, and that her open dressing gown revealed more than he really wanted to see.

They went into the living room.

'I am so sorry about my driver Stephan, or Steve, or whatever his real name was,' she said. 'I did not know he was such a thug. Is your face better now?'

'I'm fine,' he said, quickly taking a seat so that she wouldn't wrap herself around him again.

He noticed a gin bottle and a half-empty glass on the side.

'Was this your breakfast?' he asked.

She gave a slightly drunken laugh. 'More like I was continuing last night's supper.'

'I see,' Harry said. 'Is it possible I could ask you some more questions over a cup of coffee?'

Her eyes seemed to focus more. 'Coffee. Yes, good idea.'

She arrived with the tray ten minutes later, her dressing gown now pulled together, Harry noticed, to his relief.

Thankfully, there were biscuits on the tray. Harry had left London at an absurd hour that morning and hadn't yet eaten. He grabbed a couple and sat back and appraised Petra Brandon.

He was disappointed. She had known that he was coming, and had still drunk herself into a state, which meant that he had to field his questions carefully, so as not to provoke any booze-driven emotions.

'How did Steven Butcher come into your life?' he asked.

'Steven? Oh Stephan, yes. I just advertised locally and someone recommended him. I didn't realise that he would turn out to be a nasty little bastard. Those pictures of me all over the newspapers. Now when I go into the village, I can feel other people's eyes on me, and I know they are talking behind my back.'

Tears appeared in her eyes, and Harry saw her glance in the direction of the gin bottle.

He quickly stood up and refilled her coffee cup from the jug on the tray, while helping himself to another ginger nut.

'It must have been very hard for you, Mrs Brandon.'

'You have no idea,' she said, wiping her eyes with a tissue.

'Were you aware of the pictures being taken, at any stage?' Harry asked.

'No, I don't think so. You must understand that when you are married to a political leader, you get photographed almost daily.'

'But the photos that were published in the press showed you with other men, and when I originally showed them to you, you didn't seem bothered.'

'I am what I am,' Petra said with a defiant look. 'I like the company of men. Charles isn't too bothered about what I get up to, providing I keep it discreet.'

'But it isn't discreet, is it? Everyone now knows that–'

'That I'm some sort of cheating slut? It's all right, Inspector, you can say it. God knows the rest of the country is probably thinking it.' Tears streamed down her cheeks. There was a box of tissues within Harry's reach. He handed her one, and she blew her nose noisily. 'Sorry,' she giggled. 'Not very ladylike, but then again, I'm no lady.'

The sun shone through the patio window, catching her face like a spotlight. Harry could see lines etched in her face that hinted she had a story or two to tell from an interesting past.

A couple of cups of coffee later, she seemed to have pulled herself together. Harry pulled out an envelope. 'Mrs Brandon, this is going to be like déjà vu, but I have with me something that I'd like you to look at.'

'More photos… Now what? Haven't the press done enough damage?'

'Mrs Brandon, these aren't photos. We found this amongst the effects of Giles Cranberry.'

'Giles Cranberry? But I hardly know the man.'

'Mrs Brandon,' Harry continued patiently, 'that isn't strictly true, is it?'

He placed the envelope onto the table and sat back and waited.

Harry was rewarded with a look of astonishment as she gently took out the folded piece of paper. Another look darted across her face, something akin to terror.

'Are you all right, Mrs Brandon?' She was suddenly looking as if she was about to be sick. 'Mrs Brandon? Shall I get you some water?'

She waved him away. 'No, I'll be fine in a minute.'

Harry waited. He would have liked to have thought of himself as waiting patiently, but he was fizzing with curiosity.

She looked at him with sudden anger. 'This marriage certificate means nothing. Giles Cranberry and my mother were married for a short time, just to get her into the country legally. That's all.'

'So Cranberry was your father for a while?'

'I will never, ever call him my father.'

'Then why are you so upset, Mrs Brandon?'

'It's nothing. Just memories, that's all. I was very young, about nine when we came to Britain.'

The sound of a car drawing up outside seemed to galvanise Petra into action. She quickly applied some lipstick, fluffed up her hair, and went to the door.

She came back into the living room, a big smile on her face, closely followed by a tall man wearing sunglasses and a tailored suit. 'Inspector, meet my new chauffeur, Sean.'

Blimey, she doesn't hang about, thought Harry, as he shook hands.

He picked up the marriage certificate and made to go.

'Aren't you going to leave that with me?' Petra asked.

'Not yet, I'm afraid. It could be evidence.'

'Evidence?' she asked. 'Of what, Inspector? That my mother was married for a brief time to a complete bastard?'

'Why do you say that, Mrs Brandon?'

She shook her head. 'It doesn't matter.' She flashed a smile at Sean and turned back to Harry, the smile gone. 'If that's everything, Inspector.'

'That's all for now,' he said. 'Thanks for the coffee.'

He was tempted to visit Steve Butcher on his way back, but common sense prevailed; there was no point, at least not for the moment.

He wanted to think about things. Circumstantial evidence was certainly mounting against Charles Brandon, and the revelation about Petra's relationship with Giles Cranberry was adding fuel to the fire.

His phone rang. It was Mainwaring.

A few minutes later, he had more to think about. The superintendent had summoned him to a meeting the following day. She had sounded on edge.

After the long drive, he was grateful to get home. Alex gave him a hug and pulled back, studying his face.

'What are you doing?' he asked.

'I'm checking that there are no further Welsh injuries.'

He nudged her out of the way, laughing.

'I've made a lasagne for dinner. I hope you're hungry.'

'I am,' he said, realising how much he was enjoying being looked after. He kept flip-flopping over what he wanted a relationship to look like, and Alex seemed ideal.

He was the problem. When he looked back, nearly all his relationships had suffered because of work. His marriage, even. He'd enjoyed married life with Maria, but again, when work came calling, he'd always answered.

He and Maria had been about to go on holiday when he'd been called into work. It was an emergency situation, but it was the straw that broke the camel's back, as far as Maria was concerned. She'd still gone on the holiday, had a fling with a musician, and when she returned, they'd separated and subsequently divorced.

Since then, Harry's relationship history had been checkered. He had always put the job first and any woman that was in his life had got to a point where she had to make her own choice. And that choice was normally pastures new.

Harry now accepted it as part of life.

Alex was different, partly because she was in the job and understood the consequences. However, whilst Harry had a huge regard for her, perhaps even a love, he wondered whether he could sustain a proper long-term relationship.

The next morning, he was outside the Brandon mansion.

Charles Brandon answered the door dressed immaculately in a blue serge suit and striped tie.

'Thank you for seeing me at short notice,' Harry said.

'Did I have a choice?' Brandon asked.

He looked tired. The stress of current events was clearly taking its toll.

He led Harry through to the kitchen. 'Coffee, Inspector?'

'Thanks.'

Harry watched as Brandon fumbled around making the coffee. 'You must miss your staff.'

Brandon laughed. 'Does it show? I've only the gardener left, and he's even worse than I am in the kitchen. Anyway, what can I do for you?'

'Mr Brandon, I paid your wife another visit yesterday–'

'Good Lord, Inspector, you'll be carrying the Welsh flag next.'

'And I have further questions as a result. Mr Brandon, are you aware of the relationship between your wife and Giles Cranberry?'

Brandon stopped in his tracks and looked at Harry. 'How did you find out? Petra wouldn't have told you.'

'She didn't. Cranberry still had the certificate of the marriage between him and Petra's mother.'

Brandon placed the jug of coffee on the kitchen table and sat heavily on a chair, its leg making a scraping noise against the tiled floor.

'Well, in that case, I'm well and truly fucked.'

Harry sat opposite. 'Why's that?'

'It's going to come out, and it'll be yet another motive for me to have murdered Giles.'

'What's going to come out?'

'Petra hated Giles with a vengeance,' Brandon said. 'Her mother married Giles so she could have a British passport, and people today might assume that she was also marrying into money. The truth is that she had plenty of money. His newspaper was floundering and needed a cash injection.'

'In that case, they both got what they wanted,' Harry said.

'They did. However, Giles wasn't the shrewdest of businessmen, and the newspaper didn't recover as quickly as he would have liked. Petra's mother put even more money into the business, in fact nearly everything she had, and things eventually got better.'

'That doesn't answer why Petra seems to hate Giles. Also, she said that the marriage didn't last long,' Harry said.

Brandon stared into his coffee cup. 'That's correct,' he said. 'The marriage didn't last long because Petra's mum died of a heart attack. Petra blamed Giles saying that the stress of funding the business had killed her mum.'

Brandon poured more coffee into the cups. 'As I'm painfully sure you are aware, Inspector, this reveals yet another potential motive for me to have murdered Giles. But I can assure you, I didn't.'

'Wouldn't all this have affected your own relationship with Cranberry?'

'No. Giles and I went back a long way. However, it affected things with Petra. She didn't like it that we were still friends.'

'I'm sure.' Harry gazed out of the kitchen window. Relationships could be so complicated. He sometimes wondered if men and women were meant to co-exist.

'Can't live with them, can't live without them,' Brandon was saying, as if he'd read Harry's mind.

26

'I just wanted to have a quick get-together and see where we've got to,' Harry said, looking around the table in the War Room. 'Sandy, you were going to see Gavin Smart, Petra Brandon's companion in one of the photos.'

'That's right, guv. He says he barely remembers the occasion but is adamant nothing happened between them. They went for a boozy lunch at a hotel and flirted, and that was all. I don't believe him when he says nothing happened, but I suppose it doesn't matter either way.'

'How was his manner when you spoke to him?' Harry asked.

'I got the impression he was terrified of his wife finding out, nothing else. I've done a background check on him and there have been rumours about him associating with other women apart from his wife, but that's about it.'

'Does he remember the photo being taken?' Harry asked.

'I don't know, guv, but surely as an MP he gets photographed all the time.'

'If we can find out when the picture was taken, there

might be some external CCTV that could identify the photographer.'

'I'll get back onto it, guv,' Sandy said.

Harry opened a folder. 'Regarding the photo showing Petra Brandon and Nigel Kendall, I think everyone in this room is now an expert on that relationship, thanks to our beloved press.'

There were nods and grins around the table.

'However,' Harry continued, 'I'm going to have another push at him to see if there's anything else.'

He turned a page in the folder.

'There is some news,' he said. 'The fingerprints we lifted from the cottage, where the shoot-out took place, have been analysed and a report has come back.'

A cheer went around the table.

'Does that mean we now know the identity of the assassin?' Dawn asked.

'No,' Harry said. 'Someone obviously knows, but we are not privy to that information. I'm afraid it's classified. It's not just above my paygrade, it's above the chief superintendent's as well.'

'Seriously, guv?' Carl Copeland looked put out. 'How does that work? A person shoots someone, we have the fingerprints that can lead to their conviction, and we are not allowed to use them?'

Harry nodded. 'In a nutshell, yes.'

What Harry didn't tell them was that he'd already had the fingerprint report for a few days, and had been so frustrated with its contents, he'd contacted a very senior officer to vent his frustration.

To damage his personal career advancement possibilities further, he had also mentioned it to his local MP, who he knew had the ear of the Home Secretary.

Harry had been summoned to a meeting with his superintendent. Liz Mainwaring hadn't told him what it concerned, but he had a feeling he had overstepped the mark by contacting the senior officer and the MP. He suspected she might not be happy. He looked at his watch; he didn't have long to wait to find out.

'Now then,' he continued, opening the final folder, 'we come to Charles Brandon. The apparent evidence is mounting up against him.'

'Apparent, guv?' Dawn asked.

'Yes, Dawn. Apparent. We've rarely had a crime where there is so much circumstantial evidence but nothing concrete.'

'Doesn't mean he's not guilty,' remarked Copeland.

'You're right. It doesn't.' Harry stood up and dragged the flip chart into the middle of the room. He scribbled "Charles Brandon" at the top of the sheet, and then paused, looking around at the team. 'Two men shot. Cranberry fatally. Brandon was there.'

As he spoke, Harry wrote on the chart.

'Brandon was being blackmailed over his wife's photographs. We found the body of one of his employees just outside his grounds, barely hidden. His wife's chauffeur attacked me, stole the photos, and sold them for publication. And now the latest – a positive link between Petra Brandon and Giles Cranberry. Petra's mum married Cranberry in order for her to stay in England, and whilst they were married, she put all of her money into his business. A short time after, she died from a heart attack causing Petra to harvest a grudge against Cranberry, which again brings Charles Brandon into the frame.'

'Perhaps Petra Brandon is framing her husband,' Sandy said. 'She could have organised the hit on Cranberry, and we know how she likes her men. If her husband gets a custodial sentence, she'd have his money, the property...'

'But assuming that both shots were organised by the same person, why would she have Finch killed?' Harry said. 'That makes little sense. She and Finch are friends. More to the point, why kill Brigitte? She was only working as a maid for the Brandons.'

'And why blackmail her own husband with pictures that implicate her and her friends?' Dawn said.

'In that case, it's all going around in circles,' Copeland said. 'Petra Brandon already has the freedom to see other men and has access to money, and as far as everything else you just said is concerned, you could offer exactly the same argument as defence for Charles Brandon, our chief suspect.'

Harry looked at Copeland. 'You've got a good point there, son.'

∼

Superintendent Elizabeth Mainwaring didn't look her normal self, Harry thought, as he was invited to take a seat. She was fiddling with her glasses and looking embarrassed. Next to her stood a tall man with lank hair. He was regarding Harry in the way a cat would inspect a mouse.

'Harry, thank you for popping across. I know you're busy,' Mainwaring said, wearing a thin smile.

Her formal tone set an alarm bell ringing. He'd been expecting a dressing down for not adhering to the chain of command and going directly to the top. He awaited his fate.

'Harry, this is John Hayward. As you know, my promotion to superintendent created a vacancy that hasn't been filled yet. John has been brought down from the North to step into that role. Naturally, that means DCI Hayward will be your line manager.'

Harry's heart sank, but he maintained an outward calm. He stood and shook hands with the DCI, noting that the man's hand was limp and clammy. Harry disliked him immediately. 'Pleased to meet you, sir,' he said politely. 'Welcome to the team.'

'I would suggest,' Mainwaring continued, 'that you brief DCI Hayward and bring him up to date with the investigation so far.'

Hayward leaned forward. 'I understand from Superintendent Mainwaring that there's a fresh development as far as Charles Brandon is concerned. Am I right in saying that there is now a powerful motive connecting the Brandons to the murder of Giles Cranberry?'

Harry shot a dark glance toward Mainwaring. She didn't meet his look but kept her gaze steadfastly on Hayward.

'Yes, sir, sort of. All the evidence we have against Charles Brandon is circumstantial and–'

'Then why haven't we arrested Brandon on suspicion of murder? If we have the motive, then what's stopping us? He's definitely got the means and the opportunity. Perhaps the wife is involved as well?'

'With respect, sir, we can arrest them whenever we wish. But as both of the Brandons seem to be fully cooperating with us, I see no reason why that shouldn't continue.'

'Harry feels the Brandons are innocent, and his instincts are normally excellent.'

'What if he's wrong, ma'am?' Hayward said. 'We could all end up with egg on our faces. I think we should bring Charles Brandon in for further questioning, and make sure the media knows all about it. At least that way, we look efficient and proactive.'

'But then the Brandons will get legal representation,' Harry said, 'and any further volunteered information will dry up. We'll just get a load of "No comments" from the Brandons, and all their friends and colleagues will become more guarded, making the investigation harder.'

'Harry's got a point,' Mainwaring said. 'We don't want to kill the golden goose. Harry has nurtured a relationship with the Brandons that may help to unearth the truth. I can't see that upsetting them is going to be beneficial at this stage.'

Harry could see Hayward wasn't happy, and he didn't want to step on his toes on his first day. He gave Hayward a face-saving lifeline.

'How about a compromise, ma'am?' he said. 'If there's no movement forward in the investigation in the next seventy-two hours, we could do as the DCI suggested.'

'I think forty-eight hours should be enough,' Hayward said, looking at Harry coldly.

That's the last time I'll bail you out, thought Harry.

'We'll leave it at seventy-two hours. If we're no further forward, we'll get together and look at our options.' Mainwaring looked at her watch. 'I have another meeting. I'll leave you two to get acquainted.'

As the door closed, Hayward sat in Mainwaring's chair, leaned on her desk, and looked across at Harry. 'The super seems to think highly of you, but obviously not enough to offer you the DCI role.'

The comment came across as barbed and bitchy.

'That's fine,' Harry said. 'I will just have to trust her judgement.'

There was a pause while Hayward appeared to examine the back of his hand. 'Inspector,' he said finally, 'if I had been Superintendent Mainwaring, and you had contacted the divisional commander over my head, I would have moved heaven and earth to remove you from my team. God help you if you do anything like that now I'm here.'

'I didn't go over her head to usurp her,' said Harry. 'I just contacted someone who I thought would help our investigation by unlocking a closed door. There's a big difference.'

'And what did it achieve?' Hayward said. 'Did you find

your mystery man's identity? No. All that happened was that you pissed off a load of our hierarchy for nothing.'

'And don't forget, a local MP,' Harry said, aware that he wasn't helping himself.

'Exactly,' Hayward said. He stood up and placed his hands on the desk, facing Harry. 'I want you to understand that while I'm your DCI, nothing, I repeat *nothing*, happens that I haven't already agreed. I don't want you to contact any superiors without running it by me first. Do you understand?'

Harry could see flushes of red on Hayward's neck. 'I understand, sir.' He understood all right, but he didn't necessarily agree.

He stood up. 'Will that be all, sir?'

'No,' Hayward said. 'That will not be all. Some of your colleagues may think you're a hotshot, but looking through your records, I think your style of policing is outdated and needs adjusting.'

'As you've just intimated, opinions vary,' Harry said, wondering how a man like Hayward had managed to enter the force.

'I'm sure. However, as your direct boss, it's my opinion that matters. The position of DCI should have been yours, but instead, I've had to come down here from Birmingham. So, you can be sure that your unhappiness at me being here is only matched by my displeasure at having to be here.'

Harry hadn't caught it before, but there was a slight Midlands accent apparent in his thin, reedy voice.

There was another pause as Hayward gave him a challenging look. 'I hope I'm getting through to you.'

'You are,' Harry replied.

'I'm guv or boss, if you don't mind,' Hayward said.

A long time ago, Harry had asked his team to just call him Harry. Sometimes they did, but mostly he was still "guv" as far as they were concerned.

'Okay then, boss,' Harry said.

Hayward sat back in the chair and smiled at him. He looked triumphant. 'That'll be all.'

Harry walked back to the corridor towards his office sensing that he and the new DCI might be on a collision course.

Sandy passed him in the corridor. 'Are you aright, guv? You look pissed off.'

'Do I?' Harry forced a smile. 'No, all is good. Where are you off to?'

'The new DCI has summoned me. Exciting times, eh?'

A couple of minutes later, Sandy was poking his head through Harry's open door.

'That was quick. Everything okay?' Harry asked.

Sandy was red-faced. 'He just wanted me to organise some tea for him. He could have just phoned an order through to the canteen, but he had to flex his muscles. I think he's a knob.'

'Now, now,' Harry admonished with a half-smile. 'Keep it professional, please.'

'Sorry. I meant to say, I think he's a knob, guv.'

27

Nick Marshall sat in the back seat of a black cab, his eyes closed, oblivious to the chaos of a busy rush hour in London.

The journey from Malaga had been uneventful, and he'd fortunately managed to contact one of his colleagues, Mike Jones, who gave him the welcome news that Rachel and Chelsea had arrived safely and were being looked after. He further assured Marshall that they would remove the tracker from the pendant.

His eyes opened as the taxi came to a sudden stop.

'Hope you're not in a rush, sir,' the cabby said. 'There's a blockage ahead, and it's a one-way street.'

'That's okay,' Marshall said. 'I'll walk the rest of the way.'

Old habits die hard, and Marshall found himself walking through a shop and then straight out again, keeping an eye out for a tail. He repeated this a few times and then doublebacked onto himself. By the time he reached Market Square, he was as confident as he could be that he wasn't being followed.

Walking up the steps to the front door of the townhouse,

he took a casual precautionary look around. He grasped the casing of the doorbell and gently pulled it. It swung open to reveal a numerical keyboard.

He tapped in his personal code. The door, which was constructed of high-density steel, swung open, allowing Marshall to enter.

This was a project that he and Mike had put together as a safeguard.

As the door shut behind him with a soft thud, Marshall walked into a hallway, where he was greeted by the sight of a short, stocky man with close-cropped hair and a big, bushy beard. He grinned at Marshall, revealing a couple of missing teeth.

'Christ, Nick, you've lost weight and you look a state.'

'Good to see you too, Mike. Where are the girls?'

'Don't worry, they are upstairs safe.'

Despite his friend's assurances, Marshall ran up the stairs. Chelsea was lying on her stomach, wearing headphones, watching a music show on TV. Rachel was leafing through a magazine.

She leapt up when she saw Marshall and threw her arms around his neck. 'You're safe,' she said. 'I was worried about you.'

Chelsea disentangled herself from the headphones and got up from the floor, and to Marshall's amazement, also gave him a hug.

'I'm sorry, Nick,' she said. 'I was furious and wished you hadn't entered our lives, because then Uncle Thomas would still be around.'

'What changed?' Marshall asked.

'I now know it wasn't your fault. You didn't mean for bad things to happen, and we know you're trying to put things right. Also, Mike has filled us in with some of your past exploits.'

'Has he now?' Marshall said, looking at his friend, who had just entered the room.

'I only told them a little,' Mike said, looking sheepish.

After a couple of hours, Marshall felt himself relaxing properly for the first time in days. This was a place in which he felt secure.

Marshall was pleased that Rachel and Chelsea were also safe. An immense burden of guilt had been hanging over him. He had inadvertently dragged these women into his mess. Of course, he would make it up to them. But first, there was work to do.

Mike had concocted a plan, which frankly, Marshall didn't expect to work because it was too simplistic.

Mike and some of his team had placed the tracker from Marshall's pendant into an empty apartment once lived in by Marshall, hoping that Vance and his men, with no other means of tracing Marshall or the women, would still be monitoring the tracking signal.

They had made the apartment look as though Marshall was still living there. They placed food in the cupboard, old clothes in the wardrobe, and had even put used crockery into the sink. The apartment had been rigged with covert cameras and microphones, so they could see and hear what was going on remotely.

It was on the top floor of a three-storey block, and in addition, they had rented a ground-floor apartment in the same building. Sitting in that apartment wearing headphones was one of Mike's operatives, who was monitoring the cameras on his laptop. Back at the townhouse, Marshall and Mike could also view the cameras and communicate back to the operative.

There was nothing to do now but wait. They didn't know where Vance was located, or if he would come at all, but it was worth a shot.

'How did you come to know each other?' Rachel asked Marshall, whilst Mike rustled up dinner.

'We were head-hunted and then recruited to a special covert unit by the British government. We've worked together for years. Mike also heads up the cleaning department.'

'Cleaning department?'

'In our business, you can't leave loose ends or evidence lying around. Sometimes you need a professional to clear away after you.'

'You mean dead bodies?'

Marshall looked at her. He'd lied enough to her. 'Yes, that's exactly what I mean.'

'Wow,' Rachel said. 'If I hadn't seen you in action in Spain, I'd have thought that all this would be bullshit. How do you notify the cleaners when there is an issue?'

'You pick up the phone and order a takeaway,' Marshall said, a smile forming on his face.

'What?'

'Dinner is served, such as it is.' Mike was back in the room with an apron around his waist.

Dinner was cheese on toast smeared with mustard and sprinkled with black pepper.

'Is this what you girls have been living on whilst you've been here?' Marshall asked.

'No,' Rachel said, 'Mike's been cooking some great stuff. Last night we had–'

A noise suddenly came from the monitors. Everyone quickly gathered around. The operatives face had appeared on the screen, urgently signalling for their attention.

'There's a car drawing up,' he said.

Mike pressed some keys and the screen changed. They could now view the same external image as the operative.

They watched as a man got out of the passenger side of the car, and then reached in for a briefcase. He waved as the car drove off.

'I'm so sorry,' the operative said. 'False alarm,'

'No problem,' Mike replied, flicking a button. 'Can we get back to our supper now?'

The face on the screen smiled. 'Of course. Bon appetite. Wait! Hold on a sec...hold on... There's another car coming. In fact, there's two...'

The screen changed again. Two dark coloured vehicles drew up and stopped.

'Their number plates are obscured,' the operative said. 'I think this might be it...'

'It looks like you were right. Good call,' Marshall said.

'Let's wait and see,' Mike said.

The headlamps of the cars switched off, and then there was nothing. It was almost as though they were waiting for a remote command. Then, simultaneously, a man from each car jumped out and ran into the shadows towards the entrance of the building.

'Two people on their way,' called Mike, himself now wearing a headset and chin mic.

'Got it,' the operative acknowledged.

On the screen, they could see the door to the apartment open, and the two men appeared. They were now wearing black balaclavas and carrying what appeared to be submachine guns.

They moved through the apartment quickly, clearly intent on finding their target.

As the men went from room to room, the image on the screen changed accordingly. They watched the men kick open the door to the bedroom and hold their weapons as if expecting to be attacked. They moved towards the wardrobes and yanked the doors open, standing back, their guns at the ready.

'Call the boss,' one of them said.

The other man lifted the bottom half of his balaclava and spoke into a radio mic. 'There's no-one here. What do you want us to do?' He listened to the voice on the other end and nodded. 'Okay, will do.'

Then he turned to his associate.

'Come on, let's go.'

They left the apartment, and the cameras tracked them as they left the building and sped off in their cars.

'Well, that was a waste of time,' Chelsea remarked.

'What happened to the operative in the downstairs flat?' Rachel asked, pointing to a segment of the screen. 'He seemed to disappear when the two men entered Marshall's apartment.'

Mike held up a hand as if to say "patience."

The operative reappeared on the screen. He held up two fingers followed by a thumbs up.

'Excellent, well done!' Mike said, looking pleased.

'Will someone please tell me what's going on?' Chelsea asked in a slightly stroppy voice.

'Of course,' Mike said, stroking his beard and smiling. 'The plan worked.'

'But nothing happened,' Chelsea said.

'Oh yes, it did. The two men were clearly sent by Vance to find and kill Marshall. Unable to accomplish their mission, they should be on their way back to Vance, or at least somewhere linked to Vance. Now we will be able to find them.'

'How?' Chelsea asked, still sounding frustrated.

'Because when those two men went into Marshall's flat, our operative planted trackers on both of their cars.'

28

Harry wasn't having a great day. The idea of having to report his every move to Pickles grated on him. Even Mainwaring hadn't tried to micromanage him that closely in their early days.

He grinned to himself. *Pickles.* A slightly pissed-off Sandy had done some digging on the new DCI's background at Birmingham.

'You've got DCI Hayward?' his opposite number had asked him. 'Old Pickles? You poor bastards!'

Sandy had ensured that the nickname followed Hayward from Birmingham to Farrow Road by letting it slip to Frank, the desk sergeant and station gossip. Harry had learned about this when he'd called Sandy to his office to get an update about Gavin Smart.

'Hell hath no fury like a woman scorned, but you are actually worse,' Harry commented. 'Remind me not to get on the wrong side of you. He only asked you to get him a cup of tea. What if he'd asked you to do something that was really demeaning?'

Sandy gave an embarrassed laugh. 'Anyway, guv, I've got good news for you.'

'Good news is just what we need. Give it to me.'

'You asked me to see if I could find out what date Gavin Smart was at the hotel with Petra when the photo was taken?'

'I did. Any luck?'

'Yes. The hotel barman remembered Gavin Smart and Petra Brandon having drinks together, and could remember the date, because it was the day after his birthday and he had a hangover. Smart advised him to have a hair of the dog and bought him a large vodka.'

Harry grinned. 'I hope there's more.'

'There is, guv. There's a camera covering the carpark at the front of the hotel. The hotel security man trawled through the recordings and had a result. He only phoned me half an hour ago. He's on a day off. Says he thinks the person who took the photograph of Gavin Smart and Petra Brandon is a woman.'

'What woman? Who?' Harry asked.

'I don't know, guv. He didn't recognise her. But he's going to email me later with the video file when he gets back on shift.'

'God give me strength,' Harry said. 'This is excellent work, Sandy, but it's like pulling teeth. When does he get back on shift?'

'Tomorrow morning, guv.'

Harry forced an impatient smile. 'Tomorrow morning it is then.'

A while later, Harry was sitting in The Moon. The pub was big and impersonal, just what he needed. He wanted to think. There seemed to be two key areas of his life – work and personal. Although the two sometimes merged. Both seemed under threat. For the first time in his career, Harry had to ask himself if he was good enough. Someone he regarded as an idiot was now his direct boss. He'd had his fair share of run-ins with his superiors before, but at least he had a modicum of respect for their authority. He could tell that John Hayward might be a problem.

Then there was Alex. Sweet, adorable, funny Alex. He knew he didn't deserve her.

Harry sensed Alex wasn't particularly happy. He wasn't surprised, as she had little to do whilst he was working. She had enjoyed the light undercover work at the Brandons' mansion, but now each day, it appeared she was just marking time. He didn't know what to do or say to her. He enjoyed having her around. But was that just a one-sided convenience?

He finished his pint and weighed up his options. Leave now and drive home, or have another drink and take public transport.

After a large whisky, he left The Moon, feeling better than when he'd went in. Alcohol was great for putting things into perspective, he decided.

Perhaps it was instinct, but as he passed Euston Square, he had a feeling he was being followed. An icy awareness replaced the warm glow of the whisky.

It was difficult to be certain because there was a stream of commuters heading in the same direction as him, clearly intent on getting to the Euston main line station and catching their trains on time.

He slowed his pace down, stopped at a newsstand, and picked up a magazine. Something in his mind nudged him to the fact he was acting like a stereotypical hero from an old black and white movie.

As he glanced through the magazine, he gave a disinterested look behind him. But there was just a sea of faces marching determinedly along the pavement, like soldiers on a mission.

Then he became conscious of a presence next to him. It was a man of medium build, with a shaved head, wearing a dark T-shirt and jeans. The man also picked up a magazine.

He turned to Harry and said in a low voice, 'Mr Black, you'd be terrible at espionage. I don't see you as a reader of Woman's Weekly, and I have followed you since you entered the pub earlier.'

'What do you want?' Harry asked, putting the magazine down quickly.

'A word. I'll meet you in the Crown and Anchor by the station in ten minutes. It's very much in your interest to make sure you're there.'

Then he was gone, blending in with the throng of commuters.

The Crown and Anchor was next to Euston Station and was a hive of activity. The benches outside were crammed with commuters enjoying a drink on their way home.

As Harry entered, he saw football being shown on a large screen, eagerly watched by customers. Harry found the man sitting on an upholstered bench by the window at the quieter end of the pub.

He sat down opposite. 'I'll give you two minutes to say whatever it is you're going to say, then I'm going,' he said. 'It's been a busy day and I'm tired.'

A sudden cheer made the man stand up and look towards the screen. 'Arsenal have scored,' he said. 'Wonders will never cease. Can I get you a drink? You look out of place without one. Another whisky perhaps?'

Harry shook his head. 'I'll just have to look out of place. Could you get to the point, please?'

The man sat down again. 'I'm from a well-known covert governmental department.' He paused and gave a half-smile. 'I know. It's a contradiction in terms.'

Harry looked at him, noting that there was a couple of

days' stubble on his face which matched the amount of hair on his head. His T-shirt looked old and frayed.

'You really look the part,' Harry said, with a degree of sarcasm.

The man caught the inference, and gave some back. 'We tend not to wear trench coats and trilby hats these days. Especially in a pub like this.'

Harry looked around. The man's shaven head look was replicated by many of the men watching the football. He subconsciously rubbed his own head. He was almost one of them.

'I don't expect you to believe who I am straight away,' continued the man, 'and I don't carry proof, in case I'm compromised in any way.'

'So how do I know you're not feeding me a load of old guff?' Harry asked.

The man took a sip of his drink and placed the glass carefully on its mat. He looked squarely at Harry. 'You are Detective Inspector Harry Black, based at Farrow Road. Your boss is newly appointed superintendent Elizabeth Mainwaring. However, as of today, you have a new line manager, John Hayward, who has taken over as DCI at Farrow Road temporarily. Would you like me to go into your personal details?'

Harry nodded, impressed. 'Absolutely. Tell me all about myself.'

'You have been married just the once, to a girl of Spanish origin called Maria, and have one son between you. You have a friend called Alex who is from Scotland and is currently staying at your flat. Shall I tell you your address, along with the name of the landlord of your local pub? By the way, I'm sorry about the death of your mother.'

'You're good,' Harry said slowly. 'You're very good. There was only one incorrect detail, but everything else is bang on.

I'm satisfied that you are telling the truth. Either that or there are microphones all over my flat and place of work.'

There was that half-smile again. 'Rule nothing out,' the man said.

Harry felt shocked and hoped the man was toying with him. The idea of someone listening to his daily routines was a bit much.

'You don't have to worry,' the man said. 'Can I now get to the point?'

'I wish you would,' Harry said.

'First, I need your assurance that this conversation never took place. You cannot repeat anything about this meeting to anyone.'

Harry nodded. 'Agreed.'

The man shook his head. 'No. I mean to *anyone*. I need you to understand that this is not a bit of harmless gossip to be shared in the vague hope that it won't be passed on. This is serious stuff that could harm other people's lives.'

There was another cheer from the other side of the pub. Harry could see people jumping up and down in front of the big screen.

It gave some reality to a surreal situation.

He turned back to the man. 'If you've done so much homework on me, you'll know that when I'm told something in confidence, I take it to the grave.'

'Fair enough.' The man stood up and peered at the screen. 'Liverpool have equalised.' He sat down again. 'You recently made some requests for information, and a Google search which alerted our monitoring station.'

'I'm sorry?' Harry asked, completely bewildered.

'All online searches are monitored for certain keywords. For example, if someone taps the word "bomb" into a computer, it will send a red flag to the authorities that the person concerned needs to be investigated urgently. As a result, we get to stop some terrorists in their tracks.'

'I understand that,' Harry said, 'but what's that got to do with me? In the course of my job, I search on the internet daily.'

'That's the point. We keep a close eye on what police are trawling the internet for, so that we can be completely up to date with any ongoing investigations. As a result, we can either be of help, and assist the investigation, or pull strings and close down the enquiry, particularly if it is going to lead to some sort of political embarrassment.'

'Ah, political embarrassment. There it is. I think I can see where this is going,' Harry said. 'You want me to stop looking into Charles Brandon.'

'No. If we wanted that to happen, we'd have advised the Home Secretary, the instruction would have been sent down the chain of command, and the enquiry would have been closed down. "Not in the public interest" is the phrase most commonly used. No, this is nothing to do with Brandon.'

The man paused to take a sip of his drink.

'You made a formal request for fingerprint identification, and then you made a fuss when the results came back. It's called classified information for a good reason, Harry. Would you mind taking off your jacket?'

'What?'

'Take off your jacket and place it on the chair next to you, as if you're getting too warm. Now, please.'

Harry did as he was told and watched him go through his pockets. He pulled out Harry's phone and gave it a cursory examination. He seemed satisfied and returned it to the jacket pocket.

'What's that all about?' Harry asked.

'Just ensuring nothing's being recorded,' the man said calmly.

'For goodness sake,' Harry exclaimed. 'Do you really think I'd...'

The man held a hand up, as if shushing a child. 'As I was saying, the fingerprints were classified for a reason. They belong to one of our operatives.'

'Hold on,' said Harry. 'Are you're telling me that the man who assassinated Giles Cranberry was working for you?'

The man nodded. 'Yes, but we didn't sanction the killing of Cranberry. This man gets his direct instructions from his handler, who is usually contacted by us. We get our instructions from a governmental department.'

Harry wished he'd accepted a drink. 'No wonder we seem to struggle in this investigation. But why would someone in government want Cranberry killed?'

'That's the million-dollar question,' the man said. 'When we pass on a target for elimination, we can normally see a good and obvious reason. It's usually someone who needs to be dealt with for the greater good, someone who might be plotting to cause harm or death. A terrorist, for example.'

'But our investigations into Giles Cranberry have so far revealed him to be harmless. I suppose you're going to tell me something different,' Harry said.

'No, I'm not. We found the same thing, and that's why we need your help.'

'My help?' Harry asked.

'Yes. We believe that someone in government has overstepped their authority and ordered Cranberry to be assassinated for their own reasons. It's difficult to investigate from our end because the governmental department who oversees our division might themselves be untrustworthy. Now you can understand why I made sure I wasn't being recorded by you.'

'Let me get this straight,' Harry said, not believing this

was actually happening. 'You want me to investigate this on your behalf?'

'Not necessarily,' the man said. 'Just be aware. Because of your investigation of Charles Brandon, you can contact any minister or governmental representative without arousing suspicion. We can help you by passing on any information that might help your overall investigation.'

'Christ,' Harry said. 'No pressure, then.'

'Why were you searching for Gerard Tournier?'

Harry sighed. 'An ex-con told me he'd heard some rumours about Tournier illegally selling guns. That's all. I knew it was probably rubbish, but I felt duty bound to check it out.'

'It might not be rubbish,' the man said. 'We think there may be a connection between Tournier and the same governmental department that authorised the killing of Giles Cranberry.'

'You can't be serious,' Harry said. 'Please tell me this is some sort of wind-up.'

'No wind-up, I assure you. This puts you in the perfect position. If Tournier is part of an official police investigation, that would make it more difficult for the government to sweep it under the carpet.'

'And what do I say to my boss? He's already marked my card,' Harry said.

'You can't say anything. This would have to be an unofficial enquiry, which would turn official when enough evidence had been found.'

Harry sat back in his chair. He didn't know what to say. Was he out of his depth? He hoped not. 'What's the connection between Tournier and this hitman of yours?'

'Okay. Let's call the hitman "Kilroy" for the sake of his security. The connection with Kilroy is a man called Eddy Vance. Vance was Kilroy's boss at one time and would have good reason to want to cause harm to Kilroy, because Kilroy helped to uncover a lucrative scam that Vance had going when he worked on behalf of the government.'

'And the connection between Vance and Tournier?'

'We believe that Tournier and Vance are working together, using their connections to export arms illegally from the UK. Once over the border, it's pretty easy to get the arms to their destinations.'

The man looked at his watch.

'I think I've given you enough of a headache for one day. I have to attend a meeting.'

'Before you go...' Harry said. 'What is your name? Or what should I call you?'

'I'm known as Smithy.'

'Okay, Smithy, one of the personal details you had about me was incorrect.'

'I would doubt that very much.'

'When you were telling me how much you knew about me, you mentioned I was once married, which was correct. You then said that I had a son. I don't.'

Smithy smiled and stood up to go. 'Whatever you say, Inspector, whatever you say.'

29

The encounter with the man had floored Harry. Surreal no longer described the day. Unreal was more accurate.

When he had arrived home, he'd sensed a coolness from Alex that he couldn't deal with, so had gone back out again. He walked slowly along the canal towpath, trying to make sense of everything. His head felt like an explosion of activity, with questions about how he should handle events from here on.

Could he have a son? There was doubt, but the man had been bang-on about everything else.

It was certainly possible. However, when he and Maria had split, there had been no indication. In fact, she'd taken up with another man almost immediately.

He attempted to push it from his mind. There was too much else to deal with, but the thought bubbled away in his consciousness.

He'd have liked to share this development with Alex, but something was off beam, and now wasn't the time. He couldn't share any of the latest developments with his team.

The assassin was one of the good guys; someone in government was the bad guy. Harry would have liked to have bounced all this additional information off someone else.

He sat on a bench and stared at the canal, watching the ducks on the water in the fading evening light.

The man's words kept swirling around him like a fog. 'You have one son between you.'

There has to be a mistake, Harry thought. Nevertheless, the thought of him perhaps having a son excited and intrigued him.

It was now dark, and the ducks had gone to bed.

When he returned to the flat, he was tempted to tell Alex that he might be a father, but he realised he would then have to spill the beans on his meeting with the governmental agent.

Instead, he had said nothing, which might have made matters worse.

She had looked at him somewhat coldly and told him there was a salad in the fridge. She went to bed, firmly shutting the door behind her. Harry had eaten his dinner, and then poured himself a very large single malt before falling asleep where he was, still fully clothed on the settee.

When he woke up, there was a note propped up against the whisky bottle.

"Gone to visit friends. Alex." No kiss. *Here we go again*, he thought, as he showered and changed.

He'd received a message summoning him to a meeting with the new DCI. When he arrived, he saw that someone had put a sticky-note on Hayward's door on which was crudely written, "Pickles inside, leave ajar." He scrunched it up and went in.

'Morning, sir, what can I do for you?'

'I just wanted to know where we are in this investigation.'

'Er, no change from yesterday. I last spoke to you when I

was on my way home. I have just this minute arrived back in. What makes you think that there are any further developments, boss?'

'Just wondering, Harry. Just wondering.' Hayward looked at him. 'You haven't forgotten my instructions to keep me fully informed, have you?'

A strange thing to ask, Harry thought. Could Hayward somehow have become aware of yesterday's clandestine meeting with the government agent? He shrugged off the thought.

'No, boss. I will update you as soon as there are further developments.'

'Thank you. That's all.'

Harry left the office, wondering whether Hayward had all his marbles. He went through to the canteen, where he knew some of his officers would be. There was a roar of laughter from a group of them. It quickly subsided when they saw Harry.

'All right, guv?' Copeland asked. 'You don't look happy.'

Harry put his hand in his pocket and pulled out the sticky-note he had pulled off Hayward's door. 'See this?' he said. 'Some immature idiot has thought it would be funny to stick this on the DCI's door.' He looked at the officers in turn. 'I'm sure it couldn't be any of you, and if you knew who it was, then you'd probably want to disassociate yourselves from someone who has probably left kindergarten prematurely.'

There was a silence behind him as Harry walked out of the canteen and back to his office.

He'd no sooner sat down when Sandy appeared. He was holding a folder, and there was a mixture of surprise and excitement on his face.

'What is it?' Harry asked.

'The hotel security man emailed me with the video file showing the identity of the woman who took the photo of

Gavin Smart. Guv, she might have taken the other photos as well. Guess what, guv. It's someone we know!'

'Who is it?'

Sandy opened the folder and took out a print of a screenshot. 'There you go, guv. Feast your eyes on that.'

Harry looked at it with disbelief. In front of him was a very clear image of Brigitte Walsh.

30

They'd moved quickly. Marshall had felt it was only a matter of time before Vance cottoned on to the ruse that had enabled the trackers to be attached to the vehicles. They'd caught up with the two cars before following behind at a respectful distance.

The men sat in silence, watching the twin sets of red tail-lights in front of them. They hoped the cars would lead them to Vance and were expecting his dwelling to be somewhere deep in the countryside, somewhere where there were no neighbours, no prying eyes. Instead, the cars in front entered a village and turned into a cul-de-sac.

'You've got to be joking,' Mike said. 'This can't be Vance's hide-out.'

'Hide out?' Marshall laughed. 'You've been watching too much television.'

Marshall drove past the cul-de-sac before parking discreetly two streets away.

It looked as if it was a well-to-do area, with large, red brick, executive-style houses nesting side by side. That it was a cul-de-sac made people entering the road easily noticed, which wasn't great as far as Marshall and Mike were concerned.

Marshall noticed various "Neighbourhood Watch" signs and realised that having a "hide-out" here may not be as daft as he'd originally thought.

'There's got to be a way around the back,' he said, bringing up a map of the area on his phone. The screen showed a promising expanse of green behind the houses.

'That's our way in,' Mike said.

'Our way in? No, Mike. You're staying in the car behind the wheel. If I get compromised, you can alert the others. If we both get caught, then we're scuppered. Apart from that, we don't know for certain Vance is even at the property.'

When they drove to the area behind the house, what had looked like an expanse of green on Marshall's phone was actually a mass of building rubble surrounded by wire fences.

'Are we sure this is the wisest move?' Mike asked his friend.

'No, but it's a move,' Marshall said. He stuffed his gun into the back of his belt, and then he was gone.

It was a warm, still night. Marshall knew that the slightest sound could attract attention. He cut through the wire fencing and ran to the rear of the property. He then fought his way through the bushes and trees that seemed to line the expanse of rear garden. After getting severely attacked by a particularly thorny bush, he was able to view the rear of the house.

Getting to Vance's villa in Spain had possibly been easier than this, he thought to himself.

He put a night-scope to his eyes. The property seemed unguarded at the back, and there was no sign of any dogs.

What would be the point of having a guard? Marshall reasoned. To guard what?

Moving closer to the house, he paused every so often to listen while keeping an eye out for any security cameras. He came to large patio area with a veranda and a set of wicker chairs with cushions. It looked to all the world as if it was an ordinary domestic dwelling. Marshall was wondering if he was entering the wrong house when he heard a burst of male laughter.

He crept along the patio and stopped outside patio doors, which were slightly ajar.

Carefully, he pushed the door wider so he could peer in. Four men were sitting around a table, and two men were standing. The two were dressed in the same attire as those who'd broken into Marshall's old apartment.

At the head of the table was Eddie Vance. He didn't look happy. 'I told you to make sure that he was inside the flat before you went in. What part of that didn't you understand?'

'I'm sorry Eddie, I–'

'It's Mr Vance to you, unless I'm pleased with you.'

'I'm sorry, Mr Vance. I think we must have misunderstood.'

'Did you leave any signs of entry?'

'The front door perhaps...'

'Perhaps?' Vance stood up and paced the room. Marshall could see the anger on his face. 'You're both idiots.'

One man looked up. 'It's only one man.'

Vance looked as though he was going to burst a blood vessel. 'That one man, as you call him, would have you both knotted together inside five seconds.'

That's probably the nicest thing he's ever said about me, thought Marshall, from his vantage point.

'Did anyone follow you?' Vance was asking.

The two men glanced at each other. 'No, definitely not, Mr Vance,' one of them said.

'Are you one hundred percent sure?'

'Absolutely, Mr Vance.'

Vance looked unconvinced. He turned to one of the other men. 'Get out front and keep an eye out.'

Marshall was suddenly grateful they'd used the road behind the house. It was unlikely that anyone would check the back. Only a nutcase would come in that way. He smiled to himself, looking at the scratch marks on his arms.

One man got up from the table and came towards the French windows. Marshall could see he was armed, the shoulder holster visible. He subconsciously felt for his own pistol and found it had gone. *Shit.* It was probably lying near the thorny bush.

Marshall left his position and dived into the shrubbery, mentally kicking himself for his stupidity. Although this was supposed to be a reconnaissance, not a raid, there was still a heavy risk involved. His weapon may have been needed.

The man pushed open the patio doors and stood in the shadows, lighting a cigarette. A second man followed him, holding a brandy glass. He sat on one of the wicker chairs and put his feet up on the chair opposite.

'It's going to be tight,' he said, taking a sip from his glass and setting it down.

'It certainly is,' the man with the cigarette agreed. 'Vance is expecting too much too quickly.'

Vance came through the curtains, holding something in his hand. 'What's this about expecting too much too quickly?'

The man with his feet up, started to backtrack. 'Mr Vance, we were just thinking that perhaps this is all happening too fast and–'

'Stop worrying.'

As he spoke, Vance threw something through the air, which landed on the seated man's lap. It was a grenade.

He leapt up. 'Shit!'

Vance laughed. 'It's not live, calm down.'

'Calm down? Fuck me!' The man was visibly shocked. 'Where did you get that from?'

'It's just a dud. I might have some fun with it on the next shipment. The captain will crap himself.'

From his new position amongst the bushes, Marshall's ears pricked up. A shipment? It had to be arms. That was Vance's raison d'être.

Marshall thought quickly. Things had changed.

He had been tempted to simply take Vance out of the game. But now, gunless, he couldn't do that. Going in unarmed would be suicidal.

Marshall frowned at the memory of Vance leaving his girlfriend to die at the villa in Spain. It said everything about the man. When he'd worked for the agency, stopping arms smugglers had been one of Marshall's priorities. He'd never thought that one day he'd be almost relishing the idea of killing his ex-boss.

From his position in the shrubbery, Marshall shifted his body to alleviate the pressure caused by crouching.

He needed more information, but how?

Vance and his men were still talking, but now it was just light-hearted banter.

The men who had been to Marshall's flat earlier came out onto the patio. 'Can I get you a drink, Mr Vance?' one of them asked.

'You creep,' said the man with the cigarette.

'No, you mustn't say that,' Vance said. 'Pouring drinks is all they are good for.' He turned to the man. 'Jack Daniels with plenty of ice. In fact, drinks all round.'

'Are we celebrating something, Mr Vance?'

'We would have been, if these two hadn't fucked up. I'm not happy that Marshall is alive. He has cost me.'

Vance looked into the distance with a deep frown. 'He'll keep for now,' he said, going back into the house.

Everyone followed him in, leaving the door ajar.

Thank God for that, thought Marshall from his cramped position.

He ran back over to the patio and listened.

'You'll do as I tell you.' Vance was saying. 'You can't be trusted. I want you both to stay here in case there is a change of plans.' Marshall could hear ice cubes against glass as Vance downed his drink.

'Right, let's go,' he was saying, and then Marshall heard the front door closing, followed by the throaty roar of a large vehicle starting up. Shame it wasn't one of the cars with the trackers attached, Marshall thought.

He peered through the curtains. There were just the two men left.

He was tempted to go in by himself and batter them senseless until he had some further information. However, a plan had formed.

Running back up the garden, he navigated his way back through the shrubbery. Marshall came to the thorny bush and rooted around until he he'd found his gun.

When he got back to their vehicle, Mike was dozing with the seat down.

'Come on, sleeping beauty,' Marshall said. 'We've work to do.'

∼

THE TWO MEN in the house were worried. They knew that they had screwed up and were eager to make amends to their boss. For the moment, all they could do was wait. One of them poured Jack Daniels into a couple of glasses. He froze as he heard a vehicle pull up outside.

There was a sharp rapping on the door. 'Hurry!' a voice was shouting urgently.

'Who is it?' he shouted.

'Message from Mr Vance. He's going to need you after all. Come quickly!'

He opened the door to be confronted by a short, bearded man with missing teeth. He was pointing a gun. 'Get back inside,' he said.

Vance's man backed into the house with his hands up. His colleague started to run towards the patio doors but stopped abruptly when a tall figure pushed his way through the curtains. He also had a gun.

'That same bush has attacked me three times tonight,' Marshall said. 'Why don't you people employ a gardener?'

31

Back at the town house, the two men sat side-by-side, trussed up. They looked worried, with good reason. Before leaving Vance's house, Marshall had carved a message into the table – "Fuck you, Vance." There was no reason Vance wouldn't believe the message came from his two men, especially with two glasses of Jack Daniels next to a half-empty bottle.

Apart from being tied up, the men were being treated well. They had been fed sandwiches and beer and were starting to relax.

'They are just hired thugs,' Marshall said. 'We're more likely to get something from them if we start with the friendly approach.'

The two men were sitting on chairs that were placed on plastic sheeting.

'Is that in case they piss themselves with all the beer they're drinking?' Chelsea asked.

Marshall didn't reply, just smiled. He pulled over a chair and sat facing the two men, who looked at him suspiciously.

'What are you going to do with us now?'

'We are going to have a chat. Before we start, is there anything I can get you?'

'Vodka,' one of them said. They both laughed.

'I wouldn't mind a rum,' said the other, and they laughed again.

'Have we any vodka and rum?' he asked Mike.

'I've got everything,' Mike said, and went off.

The two men looked at each other. They seemed confused by the way they were being treated.

'What are your names?' Marshall asked.

'I'm Mickey, and this is Donald,' one said with a smirk.

Marshall noted the one referred to as Donald was the more nervous of the two.

'Pleased to meet you, Mickey and Donald,' Marshall said. 'I'm the big bad wolf. We've been nice to you, up to now, so you're going to tell us everything you know about the shipment. Ah, here come your drinks.'

Mike tipped the liquid from the respective glasses into their mouths. They gulped it down greedily.

'Is there anything else that you need?' Marshall asked.

'Yeah, a couple of women,' Mickey said. He grinned at Chelsea. 'You'll do, babe.'

Marshall smiled coldly. 'No women. I'm waiting for you to tell me about the shipment.'

Mickey smirked at his friend. 'We're delivering a shipment of cashew nuts to some monkeys in Indonesia.'

Marshall nodded. 'That's funny. Okay, I'll try once more, then I'll stop being nice. Tell me about the shipment.'

Mickey grinned. 'Okay, I'll tell you. We're actually exporting condoms–'

'That was your last chance.' Marshall nodded at Mike, who yanked Donald up from his seat and dragged him into an adjoining room.

The grin left Mickey's face. 'Now what?

'Now, Mickey, you are going to tell me everything about Vance and the arms deal.'

'You can fuck yourself. I know nothing.'

Although the words were brave, Marshall could tell that he was worried. He went through to the adjoining room and looked at Donald, who was looking petrified.

'I will deal with you in a minute.' Marshall left him to stew and went back to Mickey. 'Okay, time to talk.'

'I told you, I know nothing.'

'Of course, you do, Mickey. Vance likes to talk about things. I know him well.'

'You'll get nothing out of me.'

'All right. It's time for you to find out what the plastic sheeting is for.' Marshall fetched a long, serrated-edged knife. He paused in front of Micky for a few seconds, twisting the blade so that it glinted under the light.

Then he stood behind him and pressed the point of the knife into the back of his neck with just enough pressure so that a rivulet of blood ran down the blade.

As Mickey screamed out in anticipation of being stabbed, Marshall shoved a cloth into his mouth which turned his scream into a gurgling, choking sound.

Marshall went to the other room and waved the bloodied knife in front of Donald, who was now white-faced with terror. 'As you can hear, your friend is being punished, and hasn't got long.' The noise from next door was getting worse. 'I don't know how much longer he'll cling on to life,' Marshall said, examining the blade. 'I might just finish him off. It's your turn now. Unless you have something for me?'

'All right, all right,' Donald said, panic across his face.

The bluff had worked a treat. Once Donald started to talk, it was as if he couldn't stop.

'That was clever,' remarked Rachel later that evening. 'I

thought that the plastic sheet was to contain the blood and any severed limbs.'

'That's what those two were supposed to think.'

'You wouldn't have...'

'Don't be daft. I'm not a barbarian. But sometimes it's effective to appear like one.'

'I suppose,' Rachel said. 'What happens now?'

'I have a sort of plan, but I need to think it through,' Marshall said thoughtfully.

Mike had locked the two men in the cellar and hidden a microphone in case they came out with any further information. But the two didn't seem to be talking to each other. That Donald had spilt the beans so easily had clearly angered Mickey.

'What happens when Vance discovers that these two have disappeared?'

'He'll probably assume they've done a runner,' Marshall said. 'I wouldn't imagine that Vance is the easiest person in the world to work for, so I'm sure it won't be the first time someone has disappeared from his employ.'

'What's our next step?' Mike asked.

Marshall looked at his watch. 'Given what we now know, we have to act quickly.'

'What do you want me to do?'

'I want you to stay here and keep everybody safe.'

'What? You're doing this on your own?' Mike asked.

'Definitely. If something goes wrong, you must take everything we know to the highest level.'

32

Vance wasn't usually present when the shipments went out. He would keep away, leaving the risk to his lieutenants. However, this was the biggest transaction he had ever undertaken, and he had decided it would do no harm for his men to see him firmly in charge.

His business partner would also be there, although he would be strictly hands off, and would wear clothes that would conceal his identity.

The first shipment was tomorrow evening. The thought of the amount of money that would soon pour into his bank account had put Vance into a good mood.

He had further reason to feel cheerful. The latest woman in his life, Shareen, was even more stunning than the last, in his opinion. She was tall with blonde, streaked hair, and wore skirts that accentuated her long, shapely legs.

They had met at a select nightclub in the West End. Vance couldn't remember who had chatted to who first, but he'd been smitten with her from the first moment. That Shareen didn't seem interested in his power or money made her even more interesting.

She didn't seem to be swayed by his charm either, but eventually he'd persuaded her to have dinner with him, during which he'd pulled out all the stops. They'd enjoyed cocktails before dining at Le Gavroche restaurant in Mayfair. Conversationally, she didn't seem to be blessed with a vast intellect, but she laughed at his jokes and made him feel good.

On that first date, she'd allowed him to drop her off at her home, but that was it. No kiss, no sex, no nothing. He'd liked that. It was rare. It had been the same on subsequent dates, although she was now allowing a kiss on the cheek.

The fact that he couldn't get her into bed was more than made up for by the envious looks of other men when they were out together. He could see them sneak lustful glances at her, which turned to jealous glares when they realised that the older man with the weather-beaten face and receding, red hair was actually with her.

He knew that he'd eventually win her round and get her into his bed. But for the moment, he was happy to play the long game.

His business partner, Gerard Tournier, had invited him and his new lady to dinner at his home, after which he and Tournier would have a separate meeting to discuss the mechanics of the shipment, leaving Shareen and Tournier's wife Celia to chat. He was looking forward to showing Shareen off to Tournier, who he knew would approve.

He had met Gerard Tournier in the early days, when Tournier had been the junior minister responsible for overseeing the purchase of arms on behalf of the French government. He had since been promoted to the position of French defence minister, although he lived much of the time on the outskirts of London with his English wife.

When he arrived at Shareen's house in his Maserati Grancabrio Sport, she was standing under her porch, wearing a low-cut, shimmering dress, over which was a fur-style coat.

'You needn't have waited outside,' he said. 'I'd have knocked.'

'You're so kind,' she said, receiving his kiss on her cheek. She smelt and looked wonderful, he thought. Tonight was going to go well.

The Tourniers lived in a large, grey stone house, surrounded by neat lawns and well-stocked floral borders.

Tournier's eyes lit up as Vance introduced Shareen. 'Enchanté,' he said in his French accent, holding her hand and looking deep into her eyes. Shareen giggled nervously.

His wife stepped forward. 'I'm Celia. Pleased to meet you,' she said. Celia was a heavyset woman with ruddy cheeks and smiling eyes, the central parting in her long, dark hair revealing an early onslaught of grey.

Gerard Tournier looked like the stereotypical accountant, sporting a three-piece suit and wearing thin-rimmed, round spectacles. When Shareen told him she was from Essex, he seemed delighted. 'Even in France, we have heard of the Essex girl,' he said with a knowing look.

'What have you heard?' she asked innocently.

Tournier just tapped the side of his nose. 'Ah, I cannot say more. My wife is present.'

Whatever you've heard isn't true, thought Vance. *It's taking me bloody ages to get her into bed.*

Shareen was reminiscing about something that had happened in a nightclub in Romford when she was a teenager.

Vance listened to her speak, his eyes tracing the curves of her body. *Shame about the common, almost whiny voice, and her lack of brains*, he thought. Still, he'd eventually get to shag her a few times, and then see where that took them.

After dinner, the men retired to Tournier's study with a

bottle of brandy for their meeting. Celia and Shareen sat in the conservatory.

A couple of hours later, the men came out of the study looking the worse for wear. The brandy bottle was now only half full. This was besides the many glasses of wine that they'd consumed over dinner.

'How was your meeting?' Celia enquired, as the two men slumped into chairs.

'What's it to you?' Tournier laughed. 'If I told you all about it, you'd switch off after two minutes, anyway.'

'True,' Celia said. She looked over at Vance, who was attempting to get back out of the chair. He looked like a tortoise trying to right itself. 'Why don't you both stay the night?' she asked. 'We've plenty of room.'

'That's a great idea,' Vance said enthusiastically, the prospect of sharing a bed with Shareen exciting his mind.

'I'm sorry, but I can't,' Shareen said. 'I've got dogs and a cat at home waiting to be fed.'

'I don't know how you're going to get home then,' Vance said. 'I can't drive. I'm well over the limit.'

'That's all right,' Shareen said. 'I'm insured to drive almost anything. If you like, I could drive your car, drop you off at your house, and then bring it back tomorrow morning bright and early.'

Vance looked at her, his drunken mind trying to work out how best to get her into bed. Perhaps she might come into his house when she dropped him off. And then who knows?

He stood up, swaying slightly, and downed the rest of his brandy.

They said their goodbyes and hugged their hosts, Tournier's hand lightly caressing Shareen's bottom as they did so.

The next morning, Vance was awoken by the sound of his

car beeping outside. He stumbled out of bed and pulled on his trousers.

Shareen was dressed in a light summer frock, looking fresh and radiant.

'How's your head?' she asked.

The hangover had really set in. Vance tried to recall the previous evening. He remembered the meeting with Tournier, and drinking the brandy, but everything seemed foggy after that.

'I'm fine,' he said. 'How about some breakfast?'

'I can't,' she said. 'I've a cab waiting outside. What are you doing this evening? I could come over and we could get to know each other better, if you know what I mean?'

Christ, she was thicker than he thought. Of course, he knew what she meant, but this evening?

He looked at her. 'The reason we were at the Tourniers was to go through the fine detail of a business transaction–'

'Yes, I know,' she said. 'That's how you got pissed on brandy.'

He frowned at the interruption. 'Well, the shipment is tonight. So I'm busy.' He had a sudden thought. 'Tell you what, you could come along and keep me company. Afterwards I'll treat you to a nice dinner, and then you could come back here and we might have a snuggle.'

In Vance's mind, she would see him as boss of his empire. She would be impressed and realise how powerful he was.

She smiled at him. 'All right then. I'll organise someone to look after my dogs overnight.'

I'm finally going to have my way with her, he thought. *Today's going to be a good day.*

33

They worked under the backdrop of the white cliffs. A winding, narrow road from the top of the cliffs to the docks below was the only way traffic could get in and out, making it a perfectly secure and safe place for what they had to do.

Two security men stood at the top and bottom of the road vetting everyone coming in and out of the docks. Vance didn't believe in taking chances, particularly with a transaction of this nature. Even the harbour master had been paid off.

Vance watched as the last of the heavy cases were being loaded onto the boat.

What looked like a standard pleasure boat had been converted to accommodate the cargo. The living area, below deck, had a removable wall, behind which the cases were being stacked. On completion, the wall would be reinstated, making the cases invisible.

'That's it. All done. They are all loaded,' the van driver said.

'You'll get paid in the usual way,' Vance said. 'You can piss off home once the cases have been checked.'

'It'll be fine,' the driver said, a resentful look on his face. 'We've done this loads of times without your supervision.'

'What's in the cases?' Shareen asked.

'Nothing for you to worry your pretty head about,' Vance replied.

He watched Gerard Tournier talking to the captain, while his men stood around, relaxing after the heavy lifting. They were all wearing baseball caps. Vance found it amusing that Tournier was also wearing a baseball cap and sunglasses to conceal his identity. It didn't really match his suit and tie.

Tournier wandered over. 'The captain's nearly ready to leave. His crew are just carrying out a sample check.'

'You'd think they'd trust us by now,' Vance said.

'You'd think,' agreed Tournier, pulling out a pack of cigarettes. He lit one and offered the pack to Vance, who shook his head. 'No French shit for me. They're disgusting.'

Tournier shook his head and put the pack away. 'Better than your tasteless Bensons.'

The captain approached them. 'I think we'll soon be ready to go. You received the transfer, okay?'

Vance snorted with laughter. 'Of course. We wouldn't be here otherwise.'

There was a shout from one of the crew. 'Captain, there are two cases missing.'

Everyone froze.

The captain ran over and counted the shipment. 'He's right. What's going on? What's happened to the rest of my shipment?'

Tournier spat the cigarette from his mouth. 'Where's the driver?'

'I'm here,' said the driver, looking baffled. 'There can't be a problem. I personally counted every box.'

'And when did you last do these checks?' Vance said.

'Last night, when we loaded them into the van.'

'And you didn't think to check them again today?' Vance almost spat. 'Where was the van last night?'

'Outside my house.'

'Are you serious?' Vance was nearly having an apoplectic fit. 'You left hundreds of thousands worth of stuff outside your fucking house?'

'It's always been okay before.'

'Who else knew that they were there?'

'No-one, I swear.' The driver was shaking with fear.

Vance grabbed hold of the driver's collar. 'You must have told someone, you piece of shit.'

Tournier started to laugh at Vance. 'It's everyone's fault, except yours. Why don't you accuse everyone? Perhaps the harbour master was in on it. Maybe even the French President. We've done this many times. You decide to involve yourself and, suddenly, we have a problem.'

'Are you saying this is down to me?' Vance asked.

'I know this man,' Tournier said, pointing to the driver. 'In fact, I know everyone here. We've all worked together many times.' His face changed. 'The only person we don't really know is your girlfriend, as lovely as she is. We only met her last night.'

'Don't be stupid, Gerard. Are you saying that Shareen is responsible for the missing cases? You are smoking too much French shit. Maybe other stuff too.'

'Have you thought she might be a, what is it called... a mole?'

'You think she's spying on us? Gerard, listen... She's a simple Essex girl, for Christ's sake.'

'I'm not simple,' Shareen said. 'We're not all the same, you know.' She giggled nervously.

Tournier ignored her. 'All I'm saying is that we don't know her. Exactly how long have *you* known her?'

Vance paused. Was it possible that she was involved

somehow? He thought back to when they'd first met. He gave her a look. 'It's true that I only met you a few days ago, and somehow you're in my life.'

'So what?' she said. 'You've been making all the running, and it was you who invited me here.'

'Yes,' he said. 'That is how it would appear. But you could be an undercover police officer.'

'That's a change of tone,' Tournier said. 'A minute ago, you were saying she was simple.'

'I know, but let's just make sure, shall we?' Vance said.

He grabbed at the neck of Shareen's dress; it ripped down her back, exposing her white bra strap.

'What the bleedin' hell are you doing?' she shouted. 'That's a brand new dress.'

'I'm making sure you're not wired or something.'

'Wired? What do you mean, wired? Have you gone bloody mad?' she said.

'Let me see what's under that dress,' he said, grabbing at her again.

Suddenly, he was knocked off his feet by a punch that seemed to have come from nowhere. He fell back onto the dusty ground amidst laughter from the men who were standing around.

Shareen rubbed her hand. 'My brothers taught me to fight. Bleedin' touch me again and you'll know all about it.'

Vance was red-faced with anger and embarrassment. He moved towards her, more slowly and warily this time. 'So, you want to play, do you?'

He feinted to the right and then to the left, and caught her with a vicious jab to her stomach. She doubled over. He hit her again. This time, with a hard punch that crunched into her cheek. She sprawled onto the ground and lay still.

Tournier clapped slowly. 'Well done, Vance,' he said. 'You've actually reached a new low in your life. You used all your strength to beat up an innocent girl. Was she a threat to your manhood?'

'You were the one who said she might be involved,' Vance said.

'I just said that we didn't actually know her. You didn't need to attack her like that. What if she goes to the police?'

'Fuck her,' Vance said. 'I want to know where these missing cases are.' He pointed to the driver. 'You, come here now.'

The driver walked to Vance, looking terrified. Vance took out a gun from the holster inside his jacket and pointed it at him. 'Tell me again. How did two cases of guns and ammunition disappear from a locked van?'

'I don't know, Mr Vance. I definitely counted them and–'

'I'm going to ask you again,' Vance said, aiming the gun between the man's eyes. 'Where's my shipment? You have three seconds to answer. Three... two...'

'Hold it,' a voice said in Vance's ear as cold metal was pressed against his head. 'I've got your missing shipment. Now drop the gun or you lose your head.'

Vance threw the pistol to the ground.

'The rest of you,' the voice continued, 'throw your guns down.'

There was a clatter as the pistols fell from their hands. Vance was pushed to one side as the man took off his baseball cap. It was Nick Marshall.

'How the fuck...' Vance said.

'I've been here a while,' Marshall said. 'One baseball cap pulled over the eyes looks like another, don't you think? The owner of this one is trussed up next to the boxes I took from the van.'

'But why did you take the boxes?' Tournier asked.

'Confusion and division,' Marshall said. 'I needed to know who was who.'

'In that case,' Tournier said, 'you'll know who I am and that I have diplomatic immunity.'

'That goes out of the window if you're arrested and charged by the police,' Marshall said. 'Certainly for this sort of crime.'

'Possibly,' Tournier said, 'but do you see any police officers? In fact, do we see anyone else at all? It strikes me that you are on your own, and there are six of us. You can't shoot all of us.'

Gerard Tournier reached into his inside pocket and pulled out a gun. 'For example, you didn't expect me to be armed, did you?'

Marshall again grabbed hold of Vance, this time holding him like a shield. He pointed his gun at Vance's ear. 'Drop it, Tournier, or your friend will have a headache.'

Tournier laughed. 'You're confusing me with someone who gives a shit.'

He pointed the gun and fired two shots into Vance's chest.

∼

THE FORCE of the shot swept them both over. Marshall felt a pain in his chest as they fell to the ground, and he thought the bullets may have gone through Vance's body and pierced his own, but then realised it was just the buckle of Vance's shoulder holster.

They lay in a heap. Marshall prised Vance's dead weight off his body and got to his feet.

Two of Vance's men had their weapons trained on him, their intentions clear.

Tournier had jumped on the boat, which was now pulling away from the dock. 'I've heard so much about you, Marshall. I would have loved to have had a conversation with you, but I'm afraid you are a very loose end.'

He gestured to the two gunmen.

'You can kill him now.'

Marshall could sense the fingers on both triggers tighten and braced himself.

No shot came.

Both the men were looking in disbelief past Marshall's shoulder. He turned to see Shareen holding a small pistol, which she'd presumably had hidden under her skirt.

'National Crime Agency,' she said. 'The name is Una Crow. Drop your guns now.'

The Essex accent was gone. Her voice had been loud, clear, and commanding.

The two men looked at each other and then fired in unison. She fired back, hitting one of the men. Marshall leapt to Vance's body, grabbed the gun from his shoulder holster, and shot dead the other man.

He ran towards where Crow was sitting on the ground. She was looking down at the blood that was spreading rapidly across the material of her dress.

She struggled to her feet, one hand pressing her stomach. 'It's just a flesh wound,' she said. 'Get after Tournier. I'll look after this lot.'

She waved her gun at the few men who were left standing around. They looked anxious and clearly didn't want to take any further part in the proceedings.

The boat had moved away from the dock. Marshall ran towards it, but he knew he wouldn't make it. He could see Tournier at the wheel, took aim, and then realised that if he shot Tournier, no-one would be steering the boat, and innocent people on other boats could be injured. He lowered his gun, trying to think of an alternative.

Suddenly, another vessel appeared. At first Marshall thought it was just another leisure boat, similar to the many others that were idling near the dock. But as the boat drew nearer, it became apparent that it was aiming straight for Tournier's vessel. He watched as it skimmed alongside and saw a man leap onto the deck of Tournier's boat. He nearly fell straight off again but steadied himself by grabbing hold of the steering wheel.

His action caused the boat to lurch, sending both men tumbling across the deck. Tournier was up first. Marshall tried to shout a warning as he produced a gun and fired it at the man.

The boat's rocky action made the shot go wide, and before Tournier could aim again, the man had kicked the gun from Tournier's grasp and into the water.

The boat was now going around in circles of its own volition.

Nick Marshall could only watch as Tournier picked up a wrench and hurled himself at the newcomer. The man ducked and thudded a fist into Tournier's stomach. As Tournier clutched his midriff, the man unhooked a fire extinguisher from its mounting and hit the Frenchman on the side of his head.

Tournier fell back into the boat, out of sight.

The man clearly wasn't sure how to handle a boat, but after some shouts of encouragement and advice, it eventually nudged against the dock, where Marshall grabbed a rope and secured the vessel.

The man leapt down and suddenly sat sharply on the ground. He looked a pale green colour. 'I haven't got good sea legs,' he explained.

He looked up at Una Crow, whose tattered dress was covered in blood. She still had her gun trained on the men.

'That looks nasty. Are you okay?'

'I'm fine,' she said. 'I think it's just a flesh wound.'

She turned towards the stranger, still keeping her gun trained on the men. 'You were amazing,' she said.

'I agree,' Marshall said. 'That was a brave thing to do. But who are you?'

The man stood up and patted himself down. He thrust out a hand. 'I'm DI Harry Black,' he said. 'I don't suppose either of you happens to know a bloke called Smithy?'

34

Her eyes flickered as they adjusted to the light. They had fed tubes into her body to keep her system intact, and bandages covered her midriff. She twisted her head towards the figure that was dozing on a chair.

'If you're going to keep a protective eye on me, you could at least stay awake.'

Marshall stood up, stretched, and moved towards the bed. 'How are you feeling?'

She smiled. 'I'm alive. I must admit that when he shot me in the stomach, I thought I would never see my cat, dogs, or family again.'

'In that order?'

She laughed and then winced.

'Thank you for saving my life,' Marshall said.

'You saved mine,' she replied.

'How?'

'I could only pretend to be unconscious for a certain amount of time,' she said. 'Thankfully, you popped up from nowhere. How did that happen?'

'We'd captured two of Vance's men, who gave us the details of the shipment. I didn't arrive with a particular plan and saw one man having a crafty smoke. I noticed he was wearing the same baseball cap as the others, so I knocked him cold and borrowed it.'

'But why were you involved at all?' Una asked.

'Let's just say I had a vested interest in getting Vance out of the game.' Marshall said. 'What about you?'

'As you now know, I work for the National Crime Agency, and we've been tracking Gerard Tournier for some time. We needed to get proof of his involvement, and when we discovered Vance was a business partner, it gave us an idea of how I could infiltrate the network and get the information we needed.'

She paused while a nurse came into the room and checked the readings on the apparatus the tubes were linked to. The nurse nodded, as if satisfied, and left the room again.

'Go on,' Marshall encouraged.

'I made sure that Vance made a play for me, and I made sure I responded in such a way to arouse his interest. Then Tournier and his wife invited us for dinner, giving me a chance to hide my phone in his office, which recorded their conversation. Vance was drunk, so after driving him home in his own car, I met up with the director of the NCA and handed him the information. In the morning, I went back to Vance, who, to my surprise, invited me to the actual transaction. Perhaps he wanted to show off. Anyway, my appearance with Vance at the docks nearly unseated everything. My colleagues who were waiting nearby were uncertain what action to take, so did nothing until they'd heard from the director.'

'Risky stuff.' Marshall nodded. 'You did very well.'

'Thanks,' Una said. 'So did you.' She coughed. 'Would you pass me some water, please?'

Marshall obliged, holding the plastic beaker to her lips. She wasn't looking well. 'I think I'll leave you in peace for a while,' he said.

'No, don't go,' she said, almost sharply. 'I'm better than I look.'

'For your sake, I hope so,' he said with a slight grin.

'Cheeky,' she said. 'I'm enjoying the company. Please sit down and pour yourself a drink. I can only offer water and orange juice. I wish there was a bar.'

'Amen to that,' said a different voice. They looked round to see Harry holding a paper bag. 'I hope I'm not intruding,' he said, 'but we didn't get time to chat earlier, and I'm still in the dark as much as I was before I met you both. I come with fruit and chocolates.'

'Have a seat,' Marshall said, pulling across a plastic chair. 'Come and join Una Crow's fan club. I think we've probably got a lot to ask each other.'

∼

As far as Harry was concerned, it had all started with a phone call from Smithy.

Harry had just got off to sleep and was less than impressed.

'What was the point of all the secret agent stuff at Euston,' he'd asked grumpily, 'if you're just going to phone my mobile, especially at this time of the morning?'

Smithy ignored his question. 'You've got a golden opportunity to arrest Gerard Tournier and his entourage. However, you're going to have to act quickly.'

'How quickly?' Harry had asked.

'I'd be putting clothes on now, if I was you.'

Smithy had given him details, the time and location.

'Why can't you just arrest them yourselves?' Harry asked.

'Our department doesn't operate in an official capacity,' Smithy said. 'Yes, we could arrest the minions, but Tournier would walk free, declaring diplomatic immunity. No-one would know any different – the police, the press, anyone. However, if a serving British police officer witnesses the scene and then makes a formal arrest, then it's a completely different story. Tournier would have difficulty wriggling out of that, because then it would be a formal official enquiry, conducted in the public sector.'

'I see,' said Harry, forcing himself awake. 'So how many people are involved in this?'

'According to our agent, just Tournier and a man called Vance, who used to work on behalf of the government. Listen, there isn't much time. Our agent might be in danger.'

'How will I know which is your agent?'

'She's playing the part of Vance's girlfriend. That's all you need to know for now.'

'Can I bring some officers with me?' Harry asked.

'Absolutely not. If you do this through official channels and it goes wrong, it could become an international incident.'

'Let's get this straight. There's just me and this agent against an unknown quantity of bad guys?'

'Not quite. We'll be keeping an eye out from afar, and we will step in if there are any major problems.'

'It sounds a bit flimsy to me.'

'If we want this to work properly, then it's the only way. Take it or leave it,' he said. 'We can do this without you. However, with you, we will get a guaranteed result, and you'll get what you need.'

'All right,' Harry said. 'Let's get on with it.'

Harry had driven to the meeting point, feeling very much on his own. Normally he could involve his team, who had worked closely with him before in difficult situations. He only had Smithy's word that there was going to be some sort of back-up. To be honest, he only had Smithy's word about everything.

The sat-nav eventually took him to the top of a track, where the electronic voice informed him he'd reached his destination.

Smithy had said the transaction would happen at the docks, but the sat-nav must have had a seizure and brought him to the wrong place. Ahead of him was a jetty on which was a lone fisherman. Moored to the jetty were a couple of expensive looking private boats.

'Excuse me,' he said to the angler. 'Do you know where Moorlands Dock is?'

The fisherman grunted and pointed somewhere out at sea.

'No,' Harry persisted, 'it's a dock.'

'Young man, can I be of assistance?'

Harry looked round to see the occupant of a small cruiser. She was a stoutish lady of senior years, but her eyes were bright and intelligent.

'Did I hear you say Moorlands Dock?' She pointed across the water. 'You need to be over there. Let me show you.'

She disappeared into her cabin and re-emerged with a pair of binoculars. Harry squinted through the eyepieces and saw boats congregated around a dock. There was a larger boat being loaded with wooden cases by people wearing baseball caps. It looked perfectly normal at first, but then he saw someone brandish a gun.

Shit. It was happening, and he wasn't even close to the action.

'I need to get over there,' he said. 'What's the quickest I can get there by road?'

'About ten minutes,' the lady replied.

'More like half-an-hour,' the fisherman interrupted. 'Don't forget the roadworks in the town centre.'

Harry had blown it. *Shit, shit, and double-shit.*

'Is there a problem, young man?' the lady asked.

'Yes,' Harry replied. 'I'm a police officer and I need to get near to what's going on over there.' He pointed across the bay.

'That's easy,' the lady said excitedly. 'Jump on board and I'll get you over there.'

'Well, I...' Harry didn't like to admit that he wasn't the best person to be riding the waves.

The engine of the cruiser had revved up. 'Come along, Mr Policeman,' the lady shouted over the noise. 'Hurry!'

Unwillingly, Harry scrambled onto the cruiser and held on as the vessel seemed to take off.

'Can you get me closer to that port?' Harry shouted, pointing ahead.

'Is that where the baddies are? Oh, how wonderful,' she said. 'How exciting!'

As they drew nearer, he watched the situation unfurl and was approaching the port as Tournier tried to make his escape.

'That boat there!' Harry shouted to the lady. 'I need to get on it.'

What are you thinking? his inner self was asking. *Are you nuts?*

'How thrilling!' she said again. The excitement levels must have really ramped up for her over the next few minutes. Harry later thought the lady would keep dinner parties entertained with this story for the rest of her days.

She handled the craft expertly and did well to get it next to Tournier's boat without crashing into it. Harry looked at the gap between the two boats. 'Can you get any nearer?' he shouted at the lady.

'Not without crashing,' she shouted back. 'Go on, you can do it. Just hurry up and get on with it!'

Harry stared at the white, foamy water separating the boats, took a deep breath, and jumped.

As he landed on Tournier's boat, the impetus carried him forward. He grabbed at the steering wheel to stop himself falling over the other side. He would ideally have loved to have stayed there to regain his composure, but there wasn't time. Tournier was already on the attack.

After the ensuing tussle that resulted in Harry knocking Tournier unconscious with the fire extinguisher, Harry had formally arrested him. Men in dark suits and lanyards had appeared from nowhere, and taken Tournier away, but there had been no sign of Smithy.

Una Crow had been carted off in an ambulance. She had bravely held on, despite being seriously wounded. She was accompanied by the man he now knew to be Nick Marshall.

After visiting them at the hospital, he had come away feeling surreal. These were people who ran towards danger regularly, while everyone else ran from it. These were people who worked in the shadows, who got things done behind the scenes, and received no official thanks.

They had seemed friendly enough, but there had been no loose conversation, just polite chat. However, having witnessed the activity at the docks, he knew that these were extraordinary people.

As he drove away from the hospital, Harry suddenly felt a bit flat.

Yes, Tournier had been captured, but he'd done it without his colleagues, and without the goodwill of his superiors.

That made a difference.

He'd probably get a bollocking tomorrow, or maybe even lose his job, if Hayward had anything to do with it. Today's events hadn't helped his main investigation one iota, so he had no excuse.

He drew up outside his flat and stopped the engine. The

place was in darkness, but he could see the curtains were still open. Harry remembered Alex's note saying that she'd gone to visit friends. Christ, that seemed like a lifetime ago.

He didn't want to go inside, and he definitely didn't want to go to bed.

He thumbed a number. 'Sandy, you on your own?'

'Guv, where've you been? Pickles has been on the warpath.'

'Sod Pickles. Have you got any booze?'

35

The next day, Harry was summoned to Hayward's office. It was the one formerly used by Superintendent Mainwaring. It felt strange seeing him in her old chair.

'Where were you yesterday?' Hayward asked, his eyes burning like a fire pit.

'Everything is in the arrest report, boss.'

'Everything is *not* in the arrest report. Are you taking the piss out of me?'

'Boss?'

Hayward held up the report. 'Less than half a page, essentially saying that you witnessed Gerard Tournier shooting someone called Vance, and that you arrested him.'

'That's pretty much it.'

Hayward looked as though he was going to explode. 'Do you understand how much trouble you're in?' he said. 'The top brass has been asking for the details surrounding the arrest of Gerard Tournier, and guess what? We didn't know what to tell them – we're not even sure where he is! I made it clear that I wanted to know everything that you were up to, and now you've deliberately gone against me.'

Hayward leaned across his desk. 'Superintendent Mainwaring wants to know the full picture, as do I.' He leaned back and folded his arms. 'I'm waiting, Inspector.'

Harry's problem was that now it was over, he didn't know how much of the truth he could reveal. He'd been hoping that Smithy would smooth things with his bosses. He tried to pacify the irate DCI by giving the bare bones.

'Sir, the information concerning Gerard Tournier came from an informant. The identity of that informant may or may not be disclosed in due course. As a result of the information given, I was able to witness Tournier, and others, in the act of smuggling arms onboard a vessel. I also witnessed Tournier shoot and kill someone called Edward Vance. I entered his boat whilst he was escaping and used reasonable force to restrain him. I then arrested him.'

'That's almost exactly what your report says,' Hayward said. 'That's not good enough. Why did you do this on your own? Why didn't you call for back-up when you witnessed the shooting?'

This was going to get more difficult, Harry decided. Every statement he made would beg another question. Una Crow had told him that the operation was ongoing, and that Smithy would be in touch, but not to give any details out until then.

'Normally I would have called for back-up, sir, but this was a unique situation. There wasn't time. I had to act quickly.'

'None of this alters the fact that I explicitly told you to keep me in the loop, Inspector.'

'I'm sorry, sir, but these were awkward circumstances.'

'I don't give a damn. We can't have our officers going rogue, Inspector. You're probably going to face a disciplinary hearing. In the meantime, I'm going to make sure you–'

His words were cut off by the office door opening and the arrival of Mainwaring. She was followed by a man in a smart, grey suit and tie. He was wearing spectacles, but Harry recognised him immediately and felt immediate relief.

'This is Derek Smitherington,' Mainwaring said. 'Derek is the head of the National Crime Agency.'

'Hello again, Harry,' Smithy said. 'I hope you're not in too much strife. I would have got here sooner, but as you can appreciate, there was a lot to wade through.'

He placed his case on the desk and turned to Hayward.

'Superintendent Mainwaring has kindly given me permission to quickly debrief DI Black. Do you mind if we use your office?'

Hayward got up from his seat, looking annoyed. 'No problem.'

'We'll leave you both to it,' Mainwaring said. 'Come on, John.'

When the door had closed, Smitherington sat back in the seat, took off his spectacles, and rubbed his eyes. 'If I'm tired,' he said, 'you must be bloody exhausted after what you've been through.'

'What do I call you?' Harry asked. 'Smitherington or Smithy?'

'You can call me what you like, after what you've done for us,' he said with a grin. 'I prefer Smithy. Even my wife calls me Smithy. Now, let's get to it.'

Half an hour later, he sat back in his seat.

'Thank you so much, Harry,' he said. 'Everyone's reports match perfectly. The picture is complete.'

'What happens now?' Harry asked.

'Tournier will have to face the consequence of his actions in a court of law. It will dominate the headlines on both sides of the English Channel, but there won't be much detail. The public don't tend to care what happens in other countries anyway, particularly with politicians.' Smithy stood up. 'You did an outstanding job, Harry, the sort of job my own team would be proud of. If you ever want a change of career...'

'No, thanks,' Harry said fervently. 'I'm still feeling seasick. However, there is something you could do for me.'

'Name it,' Smithy said.

'As you know, I'm investigating the death of Giles Cranberry. I realise you can't tell me who the hitman was, but if Cranberry wasn't a threat to the nation's security, then someone in government has ordered the hit for other reasons.'

'And you want me to try and find out who it was,' Smithy said. 'It won't be easy because there are several levels between whoever ordered the hit and the person carrying it out. However, I'll see what I can do.'

When Smithy had gone, Harry wandered back to his office and stared into the distance.

He couldn't see Brandon arranging Cranberry's murder but had to concede that circumstantial evidence had piled up against him.

Then there was Brigitte. She had snapped at least one of the damning photos of Petra and her illicit lovers. Why?

Harry had been shocked. How involved had Brigitte been? Had she been the blackmailer who had engineered everything and then been found out? Was she then murdered by Brandon who would have had the motive, means, and opportunity?

Again, all roads kept leading to Charles Brandon.

36

She sat in her snug sitting room, the clicking of the knitting needles competing with the drumming of the rain as it splashed against the lattice windows of the cottage.

Nick Marshall stood in the shadows of the hallway, watching the woman with the white hair and glasses work on the woolly creation, marvelling at the technique, and the patience.

The rain stopped, as did the needles.

'Is there someone there?' she called out.

There wasn't a trace of fear in her voice.

Marshall stepped out into the sitting room. The woman looked up at him calmly.

'How did you find me?' she asked. 'Never mind, it's not important. What do you want?'

'I need some information,' Marshall said.

'That's not allowed,' she replied. 'You know the rules.'

'Yes, but you're going to have to make an exception in this case. I need to know who originally commissioned the shootings of Cranberry and Finch. It's appearing that someone in government has gone rogue and innocent people are being targeted.'

Minutes later, Marshall was exiting the cottage, leaving his handler to knit in peace.

37

Harry saw DCI John Hayward's number come up on his phone, and was tempted not to answer it, but he automatically thumbed the green button.

'Yes, boss.'

'Today changes nothing, Harry. I don't care if you were working with the National Crime Agency, you should still have reported directly to me.'

'As I said, I was in a difficult situation–'

'*You* were in a difficult situation? How difficult do you think *my* situation is when I don't know where my own officers are or what they are up to? What do I tell the superintendent when she asks me how things are going, and I don't bloody well know? You answer me that!'

Harry had a degree of sympathy for Hayward's point and tried a conciliatory approach. 'Perhaps our relationship got off on the wrong foot. Why don't we have a drink together and start afresh?'

'There's no reason to do that,' Hayward said, dashing any hopes for some sort of reconciliation. 'The police force is all about discipline. The superintendent gives me an order, I carry it out. I give you an order, you carry it out. Is that clear?'

'Very clear, boss,' Harry said.

'I want you to arrest Charles Brandon tomorrow morning, first thing.'

'Sorry? I thought Superintendent Mainwaring had given me seventy-two hours before arresting Brandon.'

'I couldn't give two fucks. The newspapers are going bonkers and there are rumblings from upstairs.'

'Is the superintendent aware of this?'

'It doesn't matter. I'm giving you a direct order. This is a high-profile matter and we need to be seen to be proactive.'

'Yes, sir.'

Harry returned to his flat to find Alex had returned from visiting her friends but had packed the rest of her things and gone. There was an envelope placed on his coffee table. He read the contents with a sense of inevitability. His eyes drawn to the phrase, "Perhaps we are not ready for each other yet."

He placed the letter back on the table and sat down heavily on the sofa, pulling the tie from his neck and opening the collar of his shirt. He wasn't sure if he'd done something wrong, but something was clearly amiss. He sat, staring at the wall as if it held all the answers.

Harry realised that, while he would miss Alex, he couldn't blame her for bailing out. Perhaps she'd come to terms with the fact that their relationship came with consequences.

His phone suddenly pinged. He grabbed it, half-hoping it was her.

'Fancy a drink?'

Harry stared at the anonymous text.

'Who is this?' he texted back.

'I'll meet you at the Red Lion in fifteen minutes. Don't be late.'

As Harry pulled into the carpark, the pub garden was full

of people enjoying themselves. He felt a momentary pang as he thought of Alex. This could have been them relaxing in the early evening sunshine, away from the stresses of work.

He shook himself free of the thought. He was what he was. His private life was always secondary to The Job. He walked into the pub, and saw him straightaway, sat in a corner, nursing an orange juice. Harry admired the fact that he could make himself so nondescript.

'Hello, Smithy,' he said.

'It's a nicer boozer than the one in Euston,' Smithy said. 'Sorry to drag you over here, but I have news for you.'

'You could have saved yourself a load of time and texted me your news,' Harry said.

'There are reasons why we work the way we do,' Smithy said. 'Grab yourself a drink.'

A couple of minutes later, Harry was sitting, looking expectantly at Smithy. 'Well?'

Smithy looked around casually. No-one was within earshot. 'I have just received information that will help you.'

Harry sat forward. 'Go on.'

Smithy's voice dropped to an almost inaudible level. 'It turns out that it was the same person that commissioned the shootings of both Finch and Cranberry.'

Harry frowned. 'Is he absolutely sure?'

'His information came from a highly reliable source.'

'I don't suppose he put forward a name?'

'He did.'

When Smithy gave him the name, Harry nodded. 'All right, thank you very much. Was there anything else?'

'Yes. My source asked me to wish you good luck.'

Smithy downed the remainder of his drink and got up.

'We owe you a debt of gratitude, Harry. If you ever need anything else...'

'Could you wait for a minute?' Harry said.

Smithy sat back down.

Harry took a long draught of his beer. He felt nervous and vulnerable. He placed the near-empty glass on a beer mat and cleared his throat. 'When we met previously, you mentioned I had a son. How certain are you?'

'I apologise for that,' Smithy said softly. 'We couldn't know at that time that you were unaware of the fact. In answer to your question, we are reasonably certain.'

'Reasonably certain? That's not much to go on. Do you know of a whereabouts, a location of where I might find him?'

'I've no other details.'

'Is he definitely mine?'

Smithy shrugged. 'I guess the next steps are up to you.'

After he'd gone, Harry sat staring into space. There seemed to have been a lot to think about lately. He wished Alex was still around; he wanted to share his thoughts with someone.

A son. He might have a son.

He toasted an imaginary drinking companion and finished his pint.

The next morning, he was up early and had a quick breakfast. He was in his car when the phone rang.

It was Hayward. 'I'm making sure that Brandon will be brought in today.'

'I'm on my way to make an arrest right now,' Harry said.

'Excellent,' said Hayward. 'Now we're getting somewhere.'

Thirty minutes later, Harry was knocking on a door. It opened to reveal a face that looked as though the occupant had been sleeping out on the streets. Worry lines were etched in his features, a beard had sprouted, and the hair was unkempt. He looked as though he hadn't washed for a few days.

'What do you want?' he asked.

'Nigel Kendall,' Harry said, 'I'm arresting you for the murder of Giles Cranberry and the attempted murder of Peter Finch. You do not have to say anything, but anything you do say–'

Kendall's mouth fell open. 'What?'

Harry pushed Kendall back through the front door. 'I am going to have to arrest you,' he said. 'But on what charge now depends upon you.'

Harry looked around the bedsit. It was a mess. Dirty dishes and pans were piled up beside the sink. The bed was unmade; the pillows were filthy.

'I'm on sick-leave,' Kendall said. 'I've got stress. You've no right to treat me like this. You're like a harbinger of doom. After the last time I saw you, I lost everything – my home, my boyfriend, and my self-respect. Now you're arresting me. I haven't killed anyone, I swear.'

'Not directly,' Harry said. 'But it was you that ordered the murder of Cranberry. It was as if you pulled the trigger yourself.'

'This is ridiculous!' Kendall said. 'None of this makes sense. Why would I order the murder of Giles Cranberry? And why Peter Finch?'

'Exactly,' Harry said. 'Why indeed? The only reason I'm not hoisting you back to the station right now is because I don't believe it was your idea. I think someone put pressure on you to authorise the assassination of Finch and Cranberry.'

'I'm refusing to even talk about this stupid accusation.'

'Very well,' Harry said. 'You're leaving me no alternative. I will have to arrest you, but you may end up taking the flack for the murder and will get sent away for many years. You may even get implicated in the murder of Brigitte Walsh. Mr Kendall, if you're being blackmailed, now is the time to come clean.'

Nigel Kendall looked at Harry. It was as if he was calculating something in his head.

'All right,' he said. Kendall sat heavily on a chair, put his head in his hands, and sobbed. 'I suppose it doesn't matter anymore,' he said. 'My life has gone to pieces. I'll tell you everything.'

A couple of hours later, Kendall was in a cell at Farrow Road station and Harry was sitting in front of the DCI.

'You did *what*?' Hayward thundered. 'You deliberately misled me. You told me you were on your way to arrest Brandon, which were your explicit instructions.'

'With respect, sir, I told you I was on my way to make an arrest. I didn't say who.'

Harry watched Hayward's face seem to go through different shades of crimson. He then put his hands on his desk. 'All right,' he said in a voice that almost choked. 'Tell me why you've arrested Nigel Kendall. This had better be good, or I swear–'

'I think I've had enough from you,' Harry said sharply.

'What?' Haywards asked, looking startled.

'Since your arrival, you've treated me with less respect than you would an animal. This will stop now, or I will take action. Are we clear?'

Hayward looked shaken, but Harry carried on calmly.

'The reason Kendall is downstairs is that he was instrumental in the death of Giles Cranberry. He used his position as permanent secretary to authorise the killings. However, he doesn't have a motive as such. He was coerced into ordering the sanctions by someone who had a deep hold over him.'

'Who?'

'A friend of his, who was blackmailing him over something that seems innocuous now but would have been a big deal at the time.'

'I see,' Hayward said.

Harry doubted if he did actually "see." Hayward was still looking slightly shocked.

Harry pressed home the advantage. 'So, I have kept you in the loop, as you instructed, and now, I'm going to make the big arrest.'

38

It was a Halloween that no-one would forget.

The House of Commons was buzzing ahead of Prime Minister's Questions. Normally, the seats would fill up just before the arrival of the Prime Minister, but today, all the MPs had commandeered their places well ahead of question time.

There were two distinct moods in the Commons. One side of the house sensed that their leader was on the ropes and were quiet and despondent, whereas the Tories were jubilantly awaiting the arrival of the Labour Party leader with anticipation.

The word was that the time had come for Charles Brandon to step down, and today was possibly the day.

A jeer erupted from the Tory benches as the Labour leader arrived, and then a massive cheer as the Prime Minister took his seat.

Peter Finch, from his position on the Tory benches, didn't wave his order paper around and shout like his colleagues. He sat, arms folded, looking at his friend on the opposite benches, who kept his head down, studying his notes.

If the house was expecting a dramatic resignation by the leader of the opposition early into the proceedings, they would have been disappointed. It seemed to be business as usual.

Unusually, a vote was due to take place just after the question period. This was an emergency vote concerning child welfare. The Prime Minister had dithered over it and had been lambasted by the press. As a result, to appear efficient, he had brought the vote forward.

The obligatory statements were made, and everyone waited for the outcome.

'All those in favour, say aye!' roared the Speaker of the House.

'Aye!' came the chorus.

'All those not in favour, say no!'

'No!' came another chorus.

The Speaker stood up. 'Division! Clear the lobby!'

A bell rang and, as per parliamentary procedure, the MPs made their way to the main doors where they had the obligatory eight minutes to choose a lobby according to their vote.

Brandon and Finch, joined by Gavin Smart and a few other colleagues, were walking towards the lobbies, deep in conversation about the vote, when their path was blocked by a man in a black Crombie. A couple of police officers stood behind him.

'Inspector Black, what is the meaning of this?' Brandon demanded. 'Couldn't you have waited until after the proceedings before bothering me with yet more questions?'

Harry ignored him and faced the man next to him. 'Peter Finch, I am arresting you for the murders of Giles Cranberry and Brigitte Walsh. Anything you...'

'Come off it, Inspector,' Brandon said. 'That's even more ridiculous than me being accused. What could possibly be Peter's motive?'

'The usual stuff,' Harry said. 'Money, greed, and power. Now, if you'll excuse me...'

Suddenly, a flood of MPs, unaware of the situation, barged through the middle of the group, separating Finch from the officers. He took the opportunity to make a break for it and ran at full pelt down the hallway towards Central Lobby, his leather-soled shoes slipping and slithering along the ornate, tiled floor.

Harry and his colleagues broke free from the throng and took off after him.

The figures in the historic paintings that lined the corridor seemed to look down with disdain at the melee before them, as the officers ran through the members corridor into the Central Lobby.

A crowd of tourists had entered the lobby, together with children wearing Halloween costumes. They watched the proceedings with interest, their camera phones held high.

Finch grabbed hold of a large woman wearing earphones, who was oblivious to the events unfolding. He held her tightly, his hand vice-like around her throat. She flailed her arms, struggling to breathe.

'Stay back,' he shouted at the officers, who did as they were told.

He dragged her along the floor, passing the statue of David Lloyd George.

Sandy Sanders, who was hiding behind the monument, leapt out and hurled himself at Finch. Finch let go of the woman and head-butted Sanders, before vaulting the oak-paneled desk and seizing the receptionist.

Although senior in years, she was having none of it and ferociously jabbed at Finch's face with her pen. Finch snatched the pen and twisted her wrist, bending it backwards. She screamed in pain. He pushed the point of the pen hard against her neck. 'One step closer, and you'll be responsible for her death,' he said to the approaching officers.

Finch sounded icy-calm, and very much in control.

He's showing not an ounce of emotion, thought Harry. *That makes him very dangerous.*

The receptionist was now quietly trembling with fear, as Finch pulled her backwards through the thick, wooden door behind the desk, and closed it. There were sounds of a large object being dragged behind the frame, and then there was silence.

'Where does this door lead to?' Harry shouted in frustration.

There were shrugs and shakes of the head.

'All right,' he said to his officers, 'we haven't got time to waste. We'll have to push through. There's enough of us. Come on.'

They put their shoulders to the door and heaved. Inch by inch, the door opened, revealing that a filing cabinet was the cause of the blockage.

Harry squeezed through the gap, closely followed by the other officers.

He found himself in a storage area. He looked around quickly before pushing open another door marked "supplies."

There was a toilet door, from which he could hear a whimpering sound.

Harry rapped on the door. 'Who is in there?'

There was the faintest sound of a sob.

Harry didn't hesitate, he kicked the door down to reveal the receptionist sitting on the toilet seat. She was shivering with fear.

She pointed at the window behind her. 'He went out there,' she said, tears making their way down her cheeks.

'Do you know where it leads to?' he asked.

The receptionist shook her head.

Harry squeezed through the window head-first and landed in a heap on the other side. Sanders was next, followed by a couple of uniformed officers. Harry didn't wait for them. He was already running along a covered area adjacent to the Parliament building, which he assumed was normally used for deliveries.

Turning a corner, he saw an armed police officer in front of him guarding a huge door.

'Has anyone gone out this way?' asked Harry.

'Only one of the MPs.'

'Which one?'

'Peter Finch. Why?'

'Didn't control radio you to tell you we're in the process of chasing him?' Harry asked, exasperated.

The officer laughed. 'We don't get any communication down here. The walls are too thick and there's wire fencing. It's a waste of time even wearing a radio.'

'If you happen to see him again,' Harry said, 'he's wanted for murder.'

The officer's face paled. 'I'm sorry, sir.'

'Just get this door open,' Harry said tersely.

The door opened out onto the embankment. The autumn sunshine was dazzling. Harry put his hand over his eyes. To his left was Westminster Bridge. Cruisers and riverboats hosted sight-seeing tours along the Thames.

There was no sign of Peter Finch. It seemed inconceivable that he could be that far ahead.

Harry ran onto the bridge. Passing underneath was a Halloween celebration party boat. He looked down as a mass of drunken revellers looked up. They were wearing costumes.

'Jump!' they roared. 'Come and join the party!'

I've done enough of jumping onto boats, he thought tersely.

He returned to the Embankment, where Sandy Sanders

was speaking into a mouthpiece connected to a radio. He looked up as Harry approached. 'No sign of Finch yet, guv. I've just spoken to the control room monitoring the local CCTV to see if they can get a visual on him.'

There was a sound from the radio, and Sanders was speaking again, holding in his earpiece with his fingers.

He looked at Harry. 'That was efficient. They have someone permanently monitoring the embankment for terrorist reasons. Finch was seen running along here and then out of range of the cameras.'

'And where after that?' Harry almost shouted in frustration

SANDERS LISTENED to new information coming from his earpiece. 'Guv, control have checked the CCTV surrounding these premises. They're saying someone matching Finch's description boarded a boat a few minutes ago. They're getting further details now.'

Harry waited impatiently.

Suddenly the radio burst into life again. Sandy listened and then turned to Harry. 'That's now confirmed. CCTV shows Finch boarding The Golden Hind Leg. It's a Halloween booze cruise.'

'Get control to contact the boat and patch me through. I want to talk to them.'

A minute later and Harry was speaking to the skipper.

'A man who is helping us with our enquiries boarded your boat a few minutes ago. We think he got on at Westminster Pier.'

'I'll take your word for it,' the skipper said. 'I tend not to notice or care who gets on or off the boat, providing they have a ticket.'

'We'll need to get an officer onto your boat who can identify the person we're after.'

'That's going to be difficult. I can only stop the boat at designated pick-up points.'

'And where's your next designated stop?'

'St Katherine's Dock near Tower bridge. However, there are major works going on, so I can't even stop there today.'

'Can you at least slow the boat enough for someone to jump on?' Harry asked.

'Yes, I suppose so,' the skipper replied.

Sandy looked at Harry. 'Seriously? Please tell me you're not thinking of...'

'I know,' Harry said. 'All of a sudden, I seem to be the go-to expert when it comes to boarding boats.'

'You only need to find out if Finch is on board, guv,' Sandy said. 'If he is, we can then legitimately pull over the boat and take him away. You don't have to take him yourself.'

Harry had a nasty feeling it wasn't going to be that simple.

As the skipper had warned, there was a huge facelift taking place in the area around St Katherine's Docks. Scaffolding was erected everywhere, even under Tower bridge.

Harry was perched on a length of wood in between two scaffolding poles. He saw the boat approaching and positioned himself for the jump.

The Golden Hind Leg was nothing like the famous boat captained by Sir Francis Drake, although it did have a short token mast that would just fit when going under bridges.

As the skipper had promised, the boat slowed right down, and Harry braced himself. He could already hear the sounds of music and revelry coming from inside the cabin. As the boat passed under him, he realised the drop down would be further than he thought, but he was committed.

He only had the one chance.

He landed badly, thanks to a sudden swell in the water,

and sprawled onto the deck, gashing his head on the anchor-wind mechanism.

Then Harry sat up and took stock. He had a grazed ankle and there was blood running down his face. Pulling a tissue from his pocket, he dabbed at his head. Then, back on his feet, he looked around. The boat was now back in the middle of the river and had resumed its normal speed.

He could hear music coming from the deck below. He knew that's where Finch must have headed.

Harry made his way to the door leading to the lower deck, and as he pushed it open, a group of witches and vampires came flooding out.

One of them looked at Harry. 'Blimey, mate, love your make-up. But who are you supposed to be?'

Harry wiped his face, making it look worse.

'There's someone who just came on board,' Harry said. 'He's easily recognisable because he isn't wearing a costume and doesn't have a mask.

'He now looks like the Joker out of Batman,' one of the vampires said.

'What do you mean?' Harry asked.

'Nancy painted him,' came the reply.

'Who is Nancy?' Harry asked, growing ever more frustrated. He wiped more blood from his face.

'Me,' said a witch. 'When he got on board, he looked boring, so I put a big smile on him with my lipstick.'

'And he let you?' Harry asked incredulously.

'Oh yes,' the witch smiled. 'In fact he encouraged me.'

'Did you see where he went next?' Harry asked her.

'Yes I saw him go into the driver's cabin.' She looked closely at Harry's face. 'That looks like real blood. That's clever. How do you do that?'

Harry went down the steps to the deck below and was hit with a mixture of body heat and noise. He pushed his way through the melee and came to a wood-panelled lobby that had doors marked with gold script.

Passing the ornate signs for the toilets, he came to an entrance marked, "Private. Captain."

He peered into a small, round window edged with brass that separated the wheelhouse from the rest of the boat. Vaguely, he could see the backs of two figures at the wheel, but it was impossible to see who they were.

He rubbed at the grime on the glass, smearing it with his blood. Now he now couldn't see anything.

Harry went into the toilet to get some tissue, and caught sight of himself in the mirror.

He looked unrecognisable. His face, shirt, and tie were covered in blood. It gave him an idea. He took off his tie and put it around his head, and with the help of a penknife, tore his shirt into shreds.

Back into the lobby, he pushed open the skipper's door.

'It's zombie time,' he called out, staggering into the wheelhouse and clutching onto the side as if he was drunk.

The skipper turned quickly. 'Customers are not allowed in here!'

There were two people in the wheelhouse. The skipper was wearing a cap with "The Golden Hind Leg" embroidered on the front. The other was a man complete with the impromptu make up, just as the witch had described. Red lipstick was dramatically overdone around his mouth, making him look as if he had an enormous, permanent grin.

Despite the make-up, Harry easily recognised Peter Finch.

'Good afternoon,' Harry said, swaying. 'Where's the lavatory?'

He could see the skipper was looking terrified. 'It's the next door along.'

Harry lurched out of the wheelhouse and dived back into the toilet, pulling out his radio.

'The bird is in the tree, the bird is in the tree.'

'What, Finch is on board, guv?' Sanders' voice answered.

Harry sighed. Sanders had obviously never watched a war film.

'Yes, confirmed,' he said.

His job was done. All he to do now was wait for his colleagues to divert the boat and make the arrest.

He started to relax.

Then he had a thought. Sandy would be contacting the skipper to organise the diversion, not knowing that Finch was standing next to him. He grabbed the radio again and called Sandy, but there was no reply.

He rushed towards the wheelhouse, hoping to repeat his drunken performance, but he was too late. As he pushed the door open, he could hear Sanders' voice over the airwaves giving the skipper instructions on where to bring the boat in. Finch had what looked like a chef's knife against the skipper's throat.

'I thought you looked familiar, Inspector,' Finch said. 'You're obviously on your own. Why don't you have a seat? I'm sure you realise that any false move will result in this man's death.'

The skipper had signed off from his conversation with Sanders, and was holding the wheel, staring fixedly ahead, his body trembling.

'I want you to turn the boat around, so that we are going back the way we came,' Finch said.

The skipper nodded and started to turn the wheel.

'Out of interest, how did you know it was me that was behind everything, Inspector?' Finch asked, keeping the knife by the skipper's throat. His voice sounded polite and composed.

'I had a lot of luck,' Harry said.

Finch smiled. 'You must have. Why couldn't you have just arrested Charles Brandon like you were supposed to? I gave you more than enough evidence.'

'I'm just a bit stubborn, I suppose,' Harry said. 'Anyway, I thought the two of you were friends?'

'We were. But I have to protect my interests,' Finch replied. 'And that comes first.'

Not only was Finch's voice calm, but his demeanor was as if he was at a garden party talking about pruning.

Harry's mind was racing, but there was nothing he could do, for the moment.

The boat made its return along the Thames, and eventually, he could see the scaffolding under Tower Bridge and St Katherine's Dock. Even the marina had limited access.

I hope all these repairs are worth the mayhem being caused, Harry thought to himself.

'Start moving the boat under there,' Finch said, pointing to a scaffold structure that was clinging to the underside of Tower Bridge.

'But it's too low for the boat!' the skipper said.

'Just do it.'

Harry could see Finch's escape plan immediately.

On the water, in front of one of the towers of the bridge was a temporary works platform, on which was a series of ladders the top of which led onto the bridge. If Finch managed to get up to the bridge, he would be able to mingle with the crowd, and the hunt might have to start all over again.

Suddenly, the door to the wheelhouse burst open, and three witches appeared.

'We've all noticed that you've turned the boat around,' one of them said in a shrill voice. 'You've cut our trip short you cheapskate.'

Above, there was a loud crack as the scaffolding overhead snapped the wooden mast in two, bringing the boat to a juddering halt. The force of the impact hurled the witches across the wheelhouse and cannoned them into the men.

By the time Harry had surfaced from the tangle of arms and legs, Finch had disappeared.

Harry ran up to the next deck and looked around wildly. Then he saw him.

Finch had reached the works platform and started to climb up the sheer ladder.

Most of the wooden mast of the boat was still intact. The top had sheared off leaving a jagged shard of wood sticking up from the deck.

The top of the mast was lying by Harry's feet. He picked it up and charged after Finch. As he reached the bottom of the ladder, Finch was halfway up, but Harry could see he was slowing. The chase had taken its toll on him.

Harry stuffed the mast-top into his belt and climbed the ladder, reminding himself to keep looking up. He didn't like heights, and the ladder was completely vertical.

But he found himself gaining on Finch, who had just reached the next platform, where another ladder would take him to the top. Harry didn't know what Finch's game plan was, but knew he had to stop him.

Harry climbed the final few rungs and reached out to haul himself onto the platform. As he pulled himself over, he was suddenly conscious of a figure standing over him.

Harry felt a searing hot pain as Finch plunged the chef's knife into his shoulder.

Finch yanked the knife back out, ready to stab again, but Harry pulled out the top of the wooden mast from his belt and jabbed it hard between Finch's legs. Finch staggered back, allowing Harry to scramble onto the platform and face his attacker.

Finch was clutching his groin, his pain obvious. He had dropped the chef's knife onto the platform. Harry was gratified to see that, for once, Finch's face had lost its calmness.

His shoulder felt as though it was burning; he knew he was bleeding heavily under his clothes but did his best to keep his face impassive.

'Why don't you give yourself up?' he said.

Finch looked at him. 'Why would I?'

Scooping up the knife, he launched himself at Harry, stabbing close to Harry's face, who blocked the attack with his good arm. Blood from his shoulder wound was dripping onto the wood. Finch was shaping up for another attack, breathing heavily, perspiration pouring down his face.

'That's the trouble with you MPs,' Harry said, trying to sound light-hearted. 'You're out of shape.'

Despite his manner, Harry was concerned. Between the gash on his head sustained earlier and his shoulder wound, he was losing a lot of blood. Now it felt as though it was pouring out. He had to stop Finch quickly. He had cuffs with him. All he had to do was get Finch face-down onto the floor.

Finch lunged at Harry again, the knife cutting the air. Harry ducked down and hit Finch's knees with the piece of wooden mast. Finch stumbled and fell forward, the momentum propelling him towards the edge of the platform. He tried to right himself, but his slippery, leather-soled shoes skidded on the blood, and he went over.

Harry expected to hear a splash and looked down from the platform, about to radio his colleagues. But there was complete silence.

Finch was impaled on the broken mast of the boat.

His horrified face, with its huge lipstick grin, was looking sightlessly towards the sky.

Harry stared down from the platform, knowing the awful vision would be etched on his mind for a long time to come.

He radioed Sanders, then made his way up the remaining steps, welcoming the sound of sirens in the distance.

As he stepped onto the bridge, crowds were looking down in horror at the site down below.

'That's incredible,' one woman was saying. 'That Halloween dummy looks so realistic.'

'Yes, it's amazing what they can do these days,' replied her friend.

Despite himself, Harry smiled.

He made his way along the pavement, leaving bloody footprints behind him. He suddenly felt unwell and approached a group of tourists. They backed away in horror.

'It's all right,' he said. 'I'm a police officer.'

Then he fainted.

39

They sat on a terrace that overlooked the Grand Union Canal. The pub was busy with early evening trade. As a result, the only table large enough to accommodate everyone was outside under the external heaters.

'Didn't you invite Pickles to our celebration?' Carl Copeland asked with a mischievous look.

'Do you mean DI Hayward?' Harry said. 'I did, but he was too busy.'

Harry heard a muted comment, followed by a burst of laughter, but ignored it. It appeared that Hayward hadn't endeared himself to the other officers, either.

His shoulder had been stitched, and as a result, he was wearing a sling. A huge plaster sat just above his right eye. Still, he felt surprisingly cheerful.

He picked up his glass with his free hand. 'Cheers, everyone.'

'When do we get the full story?' Dawn asked. 'It feels like you've been a bit secretive on this one, guv.'

'I wasn't being secretive,' Harry said. 'At first, I genuinely didn't have a clue. As you all know, everything seemed to point towards Charles Brandon. In fact, there was so much circumstantial evidence, it was harder *not* to arrest him.'

'Yes, even Cranberry's own newspaper was asking why Brandon was walking around,' Sandy said.

'I'd had a random tip-off about an alleged corrupt French politician that seemed unrelated to the Cranberry shooting at the time,' Harry said. 'However, when I did an online search for Gerard Tournier, it automatically alerted the secret service. Then when I got stroppy about the assassin's fingerprints found at the cottage, and upset a few officials, it caused the NCA to really take an interest in what I was up to. So much so, they contacted me.'

'The secret service contacted you?' Copeland asked almost disbelievingly.

Harry nodded. 'There was no-one more surprised than me, I can tell you. Anyway, it worked out that we could scratch each other's backs. They didn't want to go through all the politics and procedures of an official investigation because Gerard Tournier would have been tipped off, declared immunity, and disappeared into the French system, everything washed away under cover of British and French politics. That's how I found myself arresting Gerard Tournier. The NCA wanted someone they could trust to make a simple arrest for what was an obvious crime. And because it was official, it couldn't be swept under the carpet.'

'Wow, that's incredible,' Dawn said, having a gulp of wine.

'It was a bit surreal,' Harry admitted. 'The NCA were pleased with the result and gave me privileged information that then led to the arrest of Peter Finch.'

'What privileged information?' Carl Copeland asked.

Harry smiled at Copeland's blunt question. 'As I understand it, the person hired to eliminate Cranberry contacted his handler, who gave him the information required.'

Harry paused, seeing Copeland's blank look.

'The handler is the person who receives tasks from government agencies, and then finds and commissions the best person for the job.'

'I'm surprised the handler told the assassin who the client was,' Sandy said.

'Usually, it wouldn't happen,' Harry said. 'Normally, there is a wall of secrecy between the agency and the handler, and the handler and the assassin. But in this case, because events were so close to home, the handler obviously thought the information should be passed on.'

Harry paused to see if anyone else had any questions or comments, but everyone was just staring at him in rapt attention.

'It turned out that the same person commissioned both shootings, and that person was Nigel Kendall, who was the permanent secretary and therefore had responsibility for that department. I went to see Kendall and discovered that he was doing whatever Finch told him to do. Finch was blackmailing him, and therefore had control over his actions.'

'You make it sound simple,' Dawn said. 'But why did Finch arrange Cranberry's murder? Why was Brigitte Walsh killed?'

'So many questions!' Harry said, laughing. 'Finch was pulling the strings as far as the illegal arms trading was concerned. He was the main man. It started a few years ago when a government agency was set up to monitor illegal arms trafficking. But it was discovered that instead, the agency was illegally selling information about the destination of the arms to outside sources.'

'Then countries like Iran would know what was being sold to their enemies, for example,' Sandy said.

'Exactly,' Harry said. 'When the scam was discovered, the boss of the agency, a guy called Eddie Vance, got booted out.

But, to save the government's embarrassment, he was never brought to justice. So then he moved to Spain and carried on as before, but this time well under the radar.'

'Incredible,' Dawn said. 'What a total injustice.'

Harry nodded. 'Precisely. Giles Cranberry took it upon himself and used his newspaper to investigate, and it started causing some discomfort in governmental circles. Finch realised it was only a matter of time before the paper trail would lead to him. So he took drastic action and set up a scenario which would make Charles Brandon look like the culprit. Finch didn't care who took the rap as long as the fingers of blame didn't point at him. That's why he arranged the double shooting. It got rid of Cranberry, who was becoming a very real threat, and it helped to eliminate himself from any form of suspicion.'

'To be fair, the plan worked,' Sanders said. 'But why have two separate hitmen? One assassin could have done both jobs.'

'Good question,' conceded Harry. 'Finch didn't pass his reasoning to Kendall so we will never know for sure. But my understanding is that when a professional assassin is hired to take someone out, it's normally from long distance, to protect the identity of the shooter. A shot from long distance requires huge concentration. By the time a second shot is lined up, there is a possibility that the subject, alerted by the first shot, will have disappeared from the scene. I believe, in this case, because the shot to wound Finch had to be so accurate, a second hitman was the ideal solution. It also had the effect of muddying the waters as far as the investigation was concerned.'

There was another pause as the group appeared to mull this over.

Dawn spoke next. 'So how was Finch blackmailing Kendall?'

'Finch and Kendall used to attend secret gambling meetings together, and they got close,' Harry said. 'Kendall confided to Finch that he was seeing Petra Brandon in secret. Finch then arranged for photos to be taken that he could use to blackmail Kendall. He threatened to send the photos to the press unless Kendall did what he said. Kendall had no money because of his gambling and didn't want to lose his boyfriend and his home, so he complied and gave the instruction for the shootings to take place. However, two lads in Wales stole the copies of those photos when they mugged me and sold them to the press anyway.'

'Therefore Finch's hold over Kendall was broken? He was kicked out of his home anyway and therefore saw no reason not to confess,' Copeland said.

'Correct. All he had was his job, and it was on the cards that he would lose that in the future when someone did an audit and discovered the truth.'

'And now, I suppose, he will lose everything, including his freedom,' Dawn said.

'I would expect so,' Harry said. 'Although there will be mitigating factors in his defence. That's for the CPS to decide.'

'One more thing,' Copeland said. 'What was Brigitte Walsh's involvement? Why was she killed?'

Harry shifted his arm uncomfortably. The pain in his shoulder was suddenly feeling worse as the effect of the pain killers wore off.

'Are you okay, guv?' Dawn asked.

Harry nodded. 'According to Kendall, Finch befriended Brigitte during his visits to Brandon's house, and they started a relationship. He persuaded her to take publicity shots of him and Petra, claiming that it would enhance his profile. He said it didn't matter because Petra was going to leave Charles, anyway. He also got her to take the photo of Petra with Gavin Smart because, had Finch taken it, he might have been recognised. Then Brigitte found the photos in Charles Brandon's office desk, together with the ransom note. Perhaps it was then that she realised that the man she idolised might be up to no good. But she didn't know what to do next. It must have been difficult for her. I got to know her a bit and she was a decent woman. She probably didn't want him to get into trouble but still wanted to do the right thing.'

'She obviously had no idea what a monster Finch was,' Sanders said.

'When I visited the Brandons' house, I think it gave her the idea of contacting me,' Harry said. 'I don't think we'll ever know the truth about her death. Perhaps she confronted Finch with what she knew, and he killed her to silence her. Or he just killed her to implicate Brandon further.'

'That's got to be some kind of a monster who can do all that and still sleep at night,' Dawn said.

'And yet,' Harry said, 'when I interviewed him at the hospital, he was friendly and charming. The lady with the tea trolley was smitten.'

'She had a lucky escape,' said Dawn.

'Absolutely,' Harry said. 'Finch was the ultimate puppet master. He had everyone dancing to his tune. Including us.' He looked at his empty glass. 'I think we should all have another.'

'Aren't you on painkillers, guv?' Dawn asked.

'I'll take them tomorrow,' Harry said. 'Right now, we celebrate.'

∼

HE LOOKED down at the grave and the fresh flowers that adorned the newly laid headstone. Curious to see who they were from, Harry bent down and read the note that was attached. It was from Alex.

"I'm sorry I never got to meet you, and only knew you through your son. You must have been so proud of him. I really hope that one day, when the time is right for both of us, I can be part of his future. Rest in peace, Alex. xx."

He smiled. Alex was a clever woman, that was for sure. She'd intimated that she was still in his life, without telling him directly.

Harry thought of his sister Helen's open invitation to visit her and her family in New Zealand. The idea was starting to have some appeal.

But first, there was the small matter of trying to find his son.

40

The warm breeze ruffled Chelsea's hair as she walked up from the beach. From across the road, she could see her mother chatting to the locals outside their bar, a tray in one hand. A Spanish guitarist entertained the customers.

Nick had been as good as his word – better. The workmen had just finished the outside patio bar area. The new tables and umbrellas outside the bar looked inviting, and trade was increasing every day.

The sadness of Uncle Thomas's death hadn't diminished. He had been a rock that they could cling to in times of trouble. Nick had said that he'd always be there for them. But he wasn't going to be physically with them each day, working behind the bar and cooking their favourite pasta dish when they felt low. As Thomas had done.

Her mum had told her that Nick had been offered a job, something to do with putting together a special department to combat corruption. Having seen Nick in action, Chelsea knew he'd be brilliant.

Nick had commissioned a local artist to do a painting of

Uncle Thomas, taken from a recent photo. The portrait hung over the refurbished bar with the slogan "Keep strong, be brave" etched into the frame.

The guitarist started to play flamenco style.

She smiled as her mum shrieked with laughter at the antics of one of the regulars. He'd put a coat over his head and stuck his hands out of the front, like the horns of a bull. His friend was waving a red scarf and posturing like a matador. Chelsea watched her mum join in the fun and wave her arms, clicking her fingers like a flamenco dancer.

Then a man she hadn't seen before got up from one of the tables and joined in. He gyrated around her mum, getting close. He grabbed hold of her, trapping her arms under his own, and forced her to dance with him. Leaning in, he tried to kiss her, but her mum ducked her head out of the way.

As Chelsea ran towards them, there was a howl of agony from the man. His face had suddenly changed from drunken leeriness to one of terror.

With her arms pinned to her side, her mum had reached down and had grabbed his testicles. She was twisting them hard through his trousers. He'd relinquished his hold on her, and was trying to get away, but she maintained a vice-like grip.

As Chelsea reached them, she heard her mother say, 'And if I see you around here again, I'll cut them off and feed them to you. Do you understand?'

The man nodded vehemently.

'Everything all right, Mum?' Chelsea asked, as the man limped away clutching his groin.

'Everything is fine, darling. I think we've had to deal with much bigger fish than this in recent times. Don't you?'

NOTE FROM THE AUTHOR

~

I sincerely hope you enjoyed this novel.
Authors are dependent on what people say about their books, so I would be so grateful if you could spare a minute to leave a review.
Thank you, Gordon.

~

HARRY BLACK THRILLERS

Harry will return in:-
The Twisted Sinner

Further information about this and much more, can be found on:
https://gordonwarden.com

ABOUT THE AUTHOR

Gordon was born in Edinburgh, Scotland but has spent much of his life in London and the South-East.

These days, he lives in Brittany, France, where, apart from writing, he is renovating a farmhouse and enjoying the beautiful beaches and scenery.

ALSO BY GORDON WARDEN

The Cheat Killers.

Women's husbands are being murdered in an unusual fashion. In addition, clues are deliberately being left at the scene. Why? Does the killer want to be discovered, or are they just taunting the police?

Harry must find out quickly, but in the process he has to contend with a new boss, and gets embroiled in a situation where he nearly loses his life.

In addition, an attractive new colleague appears on the scene. Will Harry be able to resist her advances?

Just like a rollercoaster, this novel starts off slowly and then picks up pace, twisting and turning at speed. You'll find yourself clinging on for dear life!

The Cheat Killers. Out now.

∽

The Cheat Killers is the first of the Harry Black series

Printed in Great Britain
by Amazon